SORCERY IN SAN FRANCISCO

SORCERY IN SAN FRANCISCO
CASE FILES OF AN URBAN DRUID™ BOOK 2

AUBURN TEMPEST
MICHAEL ANDERLE

This book is a work of fiction. All of the characters, organizations, and events portrayed in this novel are either products of the author's imagination or are used fictitiously. Sometimes both.

Copyright © 2022 LMBPN Publishing
Cover by Fantasy Book Design
Cover copyright © LMBPN Publishing
A Michael Anderle Production

LMBPN Publishing supports the right to free expression and the value of copyright. The purpose of copyright is to encourage writers and artists to produce the creative works that enrich our culture.

The distribution of this book without permission is a theft of the author's intellectual property. If you would like permission to use material from the book (other than for review purposes), please contact support@lmbpn.com. Thank you for your support of the author's rights.

LMBPN Publishing
PMB 196, 2540 South Maryland Pkwy
Las Vegas, NV 89109

Version 1.00, August 2022
eBook ISBN: 979-8-88541-175-2
Print ISBN: 979-8-88541-811-9

THE SORCERY IN SAN FRANCISCO TEAM

Thanks to our JIT Team:

Diane L. Smith
Dorothy Lloyd
Christopher Gilliard
Dave Hicks
Jim Caplan
Deb Mader
Micky Cocker
Jeff Goode
John Ashmore
Paul Westman

Editor
SkyFyre Editing Team

THE USUAL SUSPECTS

Clan Cumhaill
   Aiden – the oldest of Fi's brothers, druid tank, Toronto police officer, married to Kinu, and father of Jackson, Meg, Ireland, and Carragh.
   Brendan – Fi's brother, second in the birth order, formerly deceased, given back to the family after the Culling and restricted to living on the mythical Celtic island, Emhain Abhlach with Emmet.
   Bodhmall – Fionn's paternal aunt who raised him and taught him how to be a druid.
   Calum – Fi's brother, third in the birth order, druid archer, Toronto police officer, and married to Kevin. Together they are foster parents to Bizzy, an otterkie shifter.
   Dillan – Fi's brother, fourth in the birth order, druid rogue, Toronto police officer, and in love with Evangeline, Angel of the Choir, formerly a reaper, and now a guardian angel.
   Dionysus – God of Wine and Fertility, Light Weaver, Hunter God, guardian of the mythical Celtic island Emhain Abhlach, and honorary Cumhaill.
   Emmet – Fi's brother, fifth in the birth order, druid buffer,

guardian and committed caretaker of the mythical Celtic island Emhain Abhlach.

Fiona –youngest of the six Cumhaill kids, chosen by Fionn to represent the Fianna Warriors in a new generation of urban druids, Hunter God, Celtic shaman, guardian of the mythical Celtic island Emhain Abhlach, bonded companion to Bruin and Dart.

Fionn, a.k.a. Finn MacCool – Hunter God, mythical warrior in Irish mythology, guardian of the mythical Celtic island Emhain Abhlach, ancestor of and mentor to Fi and her family.

Kevin – artist, high school sweetheart, and husband to Calum

Lara – Fi's grandmother, nature druid, and the Snow White of the Druid Order.

Liam – one of Fi's best friends, now her stepbrother, operator/bartender for Shenanigans

Lugh – Fi's grandfather, druid historian, Keeper of the Shrine, and Elder of the Druid Order

Niall – Fi's father, retired Toronto police officer, married to Shannon and living in Ireland with his parents

Nikon Tsambikos – ancient Greek immortal, Light Weaver, guardian of the mythical Celtic island Emhain Abhlach, and honorary Cumhaill.

Shannon – mother of Liam, became the pseudo mother to the Cumhaill kids after her husband and their mother died when they were young. Her husband Mark was Niall's partner and died in the line of duty.

Sloan Mackenzie – Fi's soulmate, druid healer, Keeper of the Toronto Shrine, and guardian of the mythical Celtic island, Emhain Abhlach.

Wallace Mackenzie – Sloan's father, master druid healer, Elder of the Druid Order, recently separated from Sloan's mother Janet Mackenzie.

Animal Companions

Aurora – Tad's red-tailed kite.
Bruinior the Brave (Bruin) a.k.a. Killer Clawbearer – Fiona's mythical battle bear and Bear of native myth and legend.
Daisy – Calum's epileptic skunk companion.
Dartamont (Dart) – Fiona's Western dragon, involved with Saxa, and oldest brother to twenty-two other dragons.
Dax – Lara's badger.
Doc Martin (Doc) – Emmet's pine martin followed him home from the Santa Claus Parade.
Nyrora (Rory) – Dillan's Koinonos Dragon. Dark purple with gold webbing for her wings, she bonds with him at rest, creating a living tattoo on his skin.

More Greeks

Andromeda Tsambikos – Nikon's younger sister, ancient Greek immortal, Light Weaver, guardian of the mythical Celtic island Emhain Abhlach, and legal counsel for SITFO.
Nikon Tsambikos Senior – Nikon's grandfather, ancient Greek immortal, Light Weaver, and guardian of the mythical Celtic island Emhain Abhlach.
Politimi Tsambikos – Nikon's younger sister and ancient Greek immortal.

The Moon Called

Anyx – lion shifter, Garnet's beta, and mate to Zuzanna
Garnet Grant – lion shifter, Alpha of the Toronto Moon Called, Grand Governor of the Lakeshore Guild of Empowered Ones, Fi's friend, mentor, and boss at SITFO, mated to Myra and father of adopted bear shifter Imari.
Myra – ash nymph, Fae Historian, mated to Garnet, owner/operator of Myra's Mystical Emporium, mother of adopted bear shifter Imari.
Thaos – lion shifter, one of Garnet's valued pack enforcers, third in the pack hierarchy.

Zuzanna – lion shifter, mate to Anyx, works with SITFO as a member of the Toronto Special Investigations Unit.

The Vampires
Benjamin – vampire, companion to Laurel.
Xavier – vampire, King of the Toronto Seethes.

The Nine Families of the Druid Order
Lugh and Lara Cumhaill – parents of Niall, grandparents of Aiden, Brendan, Calum, Dillan, Emmet, and Fiona.
James and Caitrona Dempsey – parents of Brian and Reagan.
Evan and Iris Doyle – parents of Ciara.
Connor and Kate Flannigan – parents of Erik.
Wallace Mackenzie – father of Sloan, ex-husband to Janet.
Tad McNiff – recently took his place as a Head of the Nine Families after his father, Riordan, gave himself over to Mingin in a quest for ultimate power.
Finley and Elaine O'Malley – parents of Lia.
Brian and Gwyneth Perry – parents of Jarrod, Darcy, and Davin.
Sean and Maude Scott – parents of Seamus.

Friends
Laurel – ghost, companion to Benjamin, Fi's high school friend
Merlin/Pan Dora/ Emrys – druid and wizard of legend, owner of Queens on Queen drag club and the attached soup kitchen, union bonded to the champagne-colored Western dragon, Empress Cazzienth.
Patty – Man o' Green, union bonded to Cyteira the Queen of Wyrms, a.k.a. the Wyrm Dragon Queen.
Suede Silverbirch – elven representative on Toronto's Lakeshore Guild of Empowered Ones.

Zxata – ash nymph, Myra's brother, nymph representative on Toronto's Lakeshore Guild of Empowered Ones.

More Hunter Gods

Ahren – Hunter God, shaman, navigates the astral plane as a golden eagle.

Samuel – Hunter God, shaman, navigates the astral plane as an ebony wolf.

Quon Shen – Hunter God, shaman, navigates the astral plane as a water dragon.

Team Trouble

Brody – wolf shifter/vampire hybrid, new member-in-training for Team Trouble

Dantanion Jann (Dan the djinn) – djinn, member of Team Trouble

Diesel Demarco – goliath, new member-in-training for Team Trouble

Jenna – siren, new member-in-training for Team Trouble

John Maxwell – Deputy Commissioner of the Royal Canadian Mounted Police, founder of SITFO the Special Investigations Task Force for Ontario

Iceland Dragons – Free Dragons of Tintagel

Bryvanay – black, majestic, and slightly smaller than Utiss.

Cazzienth Empress of the West (Cazzie) – glistening champagne-colored dragon with gold and burnt orange wings, and a strong tail that ends in a treacherous-looking ball-spike.

Saxa – a sunshine yellow dragon with dark, gold wings and a blunt snout of the same color.

Utiss – a massive purple dragon and the dominant male of the Free Dragons of Tintagel.

Ireland Dragons

Drakes – Chua.
Westerns – Abeloth, Cadmus, Chezzo, Dart, Esym, Kaida, Scarlett, Torrim.
Wyrms – Scarlett, +6 we haven't met.
Wyverns – 7 we haven't met.

Pronunciations
Adelphos – *adelfos* – Greek for "brother" or "my brother."
Cumhaill – *Cool* – Fiona and the family's last name (modern).
mac Cumhaill – *MacCool* – Fiona and the family's last name (traditional).
Mo chroi – *muh chree* – Irish for my heart/my love.
Slan! – *slawn* – health be with you.
Slainte mhath – *slawn cha va* – cheers, good health.

Irish Terms
Arragh – a guttural sound for when something bad happened.
Banjaxed – broken, ruined, completely obliterated.
Bogger – those who live in the boggy countryside.
Bollocks – a man's testicles.
Bollix – thrown into disorder, bungled, messed up.
Boyo – boy, lad.
Cock-crow – close enough that you can hear a cock crow.
Craic – gossip, fun, entertainment.
Culchie – those who live in the agricultural countryside.
Donkey's years – a long time.
Dosser – a layabout, lazy person.
Eejit – slightly less severe than idiot.
Fair whack away – far away.
Feck – an exclamation less severe than fuck.
Flute – a man's penis.
Gammie – injured, not working properly.
Hape – a heap.

Howeyah/Howaya/Howya – a greeting not necessarily requiring an answer.

Irish – traditional Irish language (commonly referred to as Irish Gaelic unless you're Irish).

Knackers – a man's testicles.

Mocker – a hex.

Och – used to express agreement or disagreement to something said.

Shite – less offensive than shit

Gobshite – fool, acting in unwanted behavior.

Wee – small.

CHAPTER ONE

My goals when I climb out of bed each morning aren't complicated—get through the next fifteen or sixteen hours without someone dying, trying to kill me or someone I love, or starting a cataclysmic event that alters our world.

Been there, done that. It's less fun than it sounds.

You'd think that if the world suddenly had a magical overload and people were getting powers, it would be awesome, right?

Not so much.

Since the fall of the veil between realms, people have been waking up with powers and visible fae traits they didn't have the night before.

Families are broken.

Businesses get boycotted.

Violence ensues.

That's where Team Trouble comes in. My band of merry men and I are the equalizers, the educators, the ones out there helping the world regain its footing despite the crazy times we live in.

Things will level off—I believe that.

The awakening of fae traits will slow, people will grow to understand different isn't equivalent to dangerous or evil, and

Merlin and Sloan will connect with the right minds and figure out how to get the veil back up or at least partly up.

I send a rush of manifesting energy into the world around me and hope Mother Nature or the Greek Fates or someone with clout is listening.

Closing my eyes, I breathe deep into my lungs.

Despite the chaos of the time, having access to magic is amazing. Since the fall of the veil, ambient energy is thick in the air around us. The sky is pink with the power of fae prana. It buzzes like static over our skin and smells like cherry Coke.

"Hello? Fiona?"

"Over here, Diesel." I lift the purple-winged bunny out of my lap and send Mopsy flying up to the branches above. Strangers frighten him, and he's kicking his fuzzy feet as he goes and flinging rabbit raisins through the air.

Thankfully, I'm out of raisin range.

After extricating myself from my woven basket chair, I shuffle along the little path we've worn in the moss to find Diesel staring up at the golden webs and the blinking lights of the tiny winnot faeries buzzing around above.

They are like a mash-up between Tinkerbell and a firefly. I doubt he has the fae sight to see them. He likely only sees their golden glow.

Diesel Demarco is a seven-foot-four, broad-shouldered, muscle-framed guy who had an awakening a few months ago. No big surprise…he discovered he has goliath genes. The triggering of his fae genes doesn't offer him powers per se, but he is super big and strong, and his skin is as tough as if he's wearing armor.

He's also one of three newbie additions to Team Trouble's warrior squad.

Sweeping my hand from side to side, I gesture at my sacred grove. "Welcome to my druid sanctuary, my source of renewed strength, and my all-around favorite place to zone out. Did you have any trouble finding us?"

"No. Not at all. I parked in the driveway next door. Are you sure they won't mind?"

"Nope. They are us." I lead him out of the grove and into the backyard. "That's my childhood home where my oldest brother lives with his wife and four kidlets. This is my home with Sloan, and my brother Dillan lives with us. That's where my brother Calum lives with his husband Kevin and their foster daughter, Bizzy. It's all one big happy family around here."

"That's nice. You're fortunate."

"True story. So, are you ready for your first mission in the wild and woolly world of fae craziness?"

"I think so."

"Excellent. This is going to be fun." We strike off toward the back of my house and find Dillan standing in the grass, gazing up at the sky. "Whatcha doin'?"

"Whoever is magicking the cloud shapes this morning has a healthy imagination and a dirty mind."

I follow Dillan's pointed finger and burst out laughing, thankful I'm not drinking coffee, or I'd have a hazelnut blend coming out of my nose. "That's so rude."

The fae races have truly enjoyed their coming out and have exposed humans to many of their wild and wonderous ways.

When I say *exposed*, that's exactly what I mean.

Human hang-ups and inhibitions are not something the fae share or care about. I bet they're going out of their way to shock the non-magical societies just for shits and giggles.

Growing up, my brothers and I would often lay on a sunny hill and watch the white, puffy clouds drift overhead. We'd search for images or situations above.

There's no need to search now.

The clouds are fair game for fae amusement, and for the most part, they're usually very amusing.

Dillan tilts his head to one side to get a better angle and laughs. "I'm not sure whether that's even possible."

I tilt my head the same way as Dillan's to consider the logistics of the scene unfolding. "It is certainly ambitious, don't you think?"

Calum and Kevin exit the back of their house next door and stroll across the shared backyard.

"Hey, what are you guys—holy hell." Kevin covers Bizzy's eyes and frowns at the sky. "Is that a thing?"

Calum chuckles. "Not with the parts *we* have to work with."

Kevin laughs. "I'm taking the Bizz Monster over to play with the kids and will tell Kinu to keep the monkeys inside until this titillating tableau has blown past."

"Good call." Calum steps in beside me and tilts his head. "Wow, that's ambitious."

I chuckle. "Exactly. It doesn't look all that comfortable either."

The door opens behind us, and Sloan comes out to join the fun. "Och, Diesel, welcome. We're happy—wait. What are ye all doing standin' around out on the back lawn?"

I point at the animated clouds. "Checking out the pornographic peep show."

"Well, would ye look at that?" Sloan's eyebrows arch. "That's creative. I'll give them that."

"Right? It would kind of take the perfect storm to get everyone fitting like that."

Nikon snaps in, joins us in staring up at the sky, and chuckles. "I've done that. Good times."

That completely rips my attention from the abstract of the profane puffs above. "For reals?"

Calum grins. "You think you know a person."

Dillan snorts. "Greek, the man who puts the nimble in nimbostratus."

Nikon bows. "Really, I can't take the credit. That particular choreography of bodies was the brainchild of our beloved God of Fun and Fertility. All the best orgies begin and end with him."

"Oh, my beloved Dionysus," I return my attention to the cloud erotica. "Do you think this could be a message from him, somehow?"

"Don't you think him skywriting an actual message would be easier?" Calum asks.

"Maybe you're right. It would be a rather convoluted way for him to tell us he's watching over us and is okay."

Ever since Dionysus bartered himself to the Greek Fates in exchange for Sloan's life, I've been searching for any clue that he's okay. We've been to his loft here in Toronto, to his temple in Greece, and I even pushed past my dislike of Eros to ask if he might be able to find something out through the gods and goddesses of the pantheon.

Still nothing.

It's been two weeks and nothing.

"What about that move, Greek?" Dillan points at the sky. "Have you ever done that?"

"Yeah, baby. He has done that." Calum grins.

I hold my hands up over my eyes. "Okay, I'm done with this game. It was fun as an abstract, but when I start seeing my friends and brothers up there, that's too much. Besides, we have a guest. We're supposed to mentor him on how things run around here."

Kevin returns from dropping off Bizzy as I'm ranting and looks up. "Oh, Calum, remember that one? Greek, you're still my hero."

"Lalalalalala." With my hands over my ears, I head back inside.

Nikon laughs, following. "I'm telling you, Fi. That is Dionysus' doing. He's inspired."

Stopping, I turn back and tip my face to the sky. "Tarzan, if that *is* you...we love and miss you and can't wait for you to get home where you belong."

The guys follow me inside, chuckling, but thankfully, they say no more about their sexcapades.

"Are we ready to go?" I grab my weapons vest and Sloan's off the hook by the door, hoping to change the subject. "Maxwell told me to let him know when we're leaving so he can call ahead. He's worried that us snapping into a military encampment might make someone trigger happy."

"One sec." Nikon holds up a finger. "I've got a call coming in from Maxwell now." He taps his phone to accept the call and presses it to his ear. "Hey, Maxwell, we're just about to leave. What's up?"

I shake my head and meet Diesel's gaze. "Sorry."

Dillan laughs. "Don't be. You said you're supposed to be showing him how we roll, then yeah, this is us."

"It's fine," Diesel says. "It's wonderful, actually."

I hear the loneliness in his words but don't have time to suss out why before Nikon groans. "Sure. I'm on it. Send me the address."

There's only one thing Maxwell would ask Nikon to do that would elicit this kind of response.

"I take it he needs you to repair a portal rift?" I slide my vest over my head and secure the straps against my ribs. "Where are we headed?"

"Sudbury. There's a tear between realms up at Science North. Authorities are worried that something might come through and dislodge the Big Nickel."

I laugh. "Can you imagine?"

"What's the Big Nickel?" Sloan asks.

My jaw drops. "You don't know? What kind of historian are you? It's only the world's largest coin."

Dillan laughs. "It's in the name, Irish."

Sloan blinks. "Oh, it's *actually* a big nickel."

"You better believe it," Calum says. "Paris has the Eiffel Tower. New York has the Statue of Liberty. We've got a thirty-foot nickel erected on the side of a hill."

"That's how Canadians roll." Dillan nods.

"Or don't roll," I correct. "It's not round. It's a twelve-sided circle."

"A dodecagon," Sloan says.

My head cranks around, and I blink at him. "Why are you taking up gray matter knowing that?"

"So he can win at the Big Nickel convo, obvi," Dillan teases. "How long have you been holding out to dazzle us with that tidbit of elite brilliance, Irish?"

He rolls his eyes. "It's a basic mathematical shape."

Dillan snorts. "No, a basic math shape is a square, circle, or rectangle. A dodgy canyon is next-level."

"Only, I think it was a dude canon." I fall into the familiar wordplay.

"No. It was a dodge crayon," Calum adds.

Sloan shakes his head. "While yer all standin' here bein' eejits, yer giant nickel is likely bein' bowled over by a herd of centaurs comin' through a rift between realms. Shouldn't we get Nikon there to seal up the seam?"

"Excellent point, hotness...but it's the *Big* Nickel, not the *Giant* Nickel."

Dillan nods. "Right. Size matters."

"Can ye all shut yer gobs so we can go?"

I laugh and stick my hand into the center of our circle. "To Sudbury, Greek. We've got your back. Who's coming?"

"I'm out unless you need me," Calum says.

I shake my head. "No. You and Kev have plans. We'll be fine. Dillan? Are you coming?"

"Yeah, I've got an hour before I need to be anywhere. I'm in."

I nod at Nikon. "Okay, we're set."

Sudbury, Ontario, is four hours north of Toronto if the weather is good and the roads are clear. Or it's the snap of a moment if Nikon has a Google image of where he needs to be.

We materialize in the open countryside of the Sudbury outskirts, and a swirling energy vortex and the angry pink skies of a magical storm brewing greet us.

"You've got this, Greek." I pat his back and wince as the energy arcing off his skin shocks my palm like dozens of electrical barbs biting me. "Damn, dude. Not cool. I hate it when your skin gets like that."

He gives me a deadpan stare. "Oh, sorry. I love it when every cell in my body fires at once."

"Testy, but I'll forgive you. I know how cranky it makes you to piece the realms back together. Just remember what Patty taught you. Zip it up and don't get sucked in."

Nikon's head turns first to me, then to Dillan. "Would you mind, D?"

My brother wraps an arm across my back and tugs me away. "Let's give them space to work, baby girl. Irish, are you going to hold things together? It would be good if Nikon didn't do that spatial split thing again."

Yeah, I hated that.

Although him cycling through the colors of the spectrum was kind of cool.

"We've got this, Greek." Sloan positions himself behind Nikon and grips his shoulder. "I'm here to help with the stresses on yer system."

I decide if Nikon doesn't want my input, I might as well catch Diesel up on what's going on. "Nikon is an immortal with a strong connection to fae prana and commands spatial magic. He's been our secret weapon against these spontaneous rifts between realms."

"Sloan's healing affinity helps him through the physical

demands of interacting with the rift energy?" He watches the scene unfold.

"Yes."

Nikon plants his feet and raises his palms to face the swirling energy of the rift.

"Now he has to close the seam on this side and the other side at the same time," I whisper. "The hardest part is stretching his connection to close the seam on the fae realm side."

"What if things already came through? Should we check the area to make sure we're not sealing creatures on this side that should be on that side?"

"Well, yeah. That's a great point. Let's do that."

"Point to the new guy." Dillan pulls his hood up and looks around.

I close my eyes and reach out with my connection to nature. "Hold on." I point down the hill to our left. "We've got a stowaway. Good call, Diesel. Give us a moment, boys."

Dillan, Diesel, and I jog to the crest of the hill and scan the land below. If I wasn't looking for something specific, I would likely have missed it.

I know it's there, though, because when I reached out, I could sense the tension in the local furry friendlies and the presence of a creature that is very much "other" to this realm.

The overgrowth due to the prana surges has changed so much of the landscape that it's mind-boggling. Below lays a ragged brown and green field, stretching toward a line of trees with scattered thorn bushes and patches of both dead grass and large tufts of growth.

In November it might have seemed normal, but this is mid-May. Everything should be sprouting with new growth and sprigs with buds ready to bloom. With the overgrowth, it should be wild and green.

"What's that there?" I point at a creature lying flat in the brown grass. It's not immediately visible, but when you know you're looking for something, you can see it.

"What is it?"

"I don't know, but it's watching us." I know I'm right, and now that I'm focused on it, my shield is tingling hot. "Get ready, boys. My early warning system is starting to burn. This is not a cute and cuddly creature."

"Something's entering the rift," Nikon says, his voice strangled as he takes a few hurried steps backward. "Something big."

I glance back toward the vortex and see the insect head and pincers of the creature poking through the hole. Sticky goop is hanging from curved mandible spikes, and as it sees us, it clacks those black mandible spikes, flicking sticky strands at us.

"Don't let that hit you," I say, backing up. "I don't know what the hell that is but other than being gross, I get the distinct impression it's very not good."

"It's a female rake spider," Sloan says. "Yer right, *a ghra*, their venom is deadly."

"Yay, me."

"Fucking spiders." Dillan backs away. "Why did it have to be spiders?"

I look between the rift and the much smaller spider down the hill. "The good news is that I don't think angry parent spider can fit through the hole. The bad news is we have to get the wanderlust baby spider back up here and through the hole before we close it."

"When you say baby, you mean that six-foot, ten-legged hair monstrosity hiding in the dead grass with its fangs dripping venom?" Diesel asks.

I nod. "Yep, that's what I mean. Fun, eh?"

"You need to rethink your definition of fun."

Dillan lifts his knuckles toward Diesel and nods. "Preach."

The mother rake spider lets out a hideous screech, and the baby returns her call.

"Okay, we need to get this reunion happening so we can seal the rift. Nikon, you make sure that rift doesn't get any bigger and Mama Creepy demon spider can't get through. Hotness, if the three of us close in on the problem child, do you think you could *poof* in behind it and *poof* it up here so it can see its mama?"

"What about the venom?" Diesel asks.

"Agreed, there's a risk, but Sloan's fast. *Poof* in, touch the creepy critter, *poof* it to mama, *poof* out."

Sloan doesn't look keen to do it, but he nods. "It's a sound plan. Let me pop home to get my gloves."

Diesel blinks and looks at me. "Did he portal back to Toronto to get his gloves?"

Sloan *poofs* back, holding the gloves he uses in his apothecary when he's dealing with a particularly toxic potion or plant. He pulls the first one on, secures the cuff around his elbow, and does the other arm.

When he's ready, he nods. "Off ye go. When we see how the wee wretch takes to yer approach, I'll portal in and get it up here. Greek, be ready to get out of the way."

Nikon is standing as close to the portal rift as possible while still staying out of snap or drip range of the worried adult and its goopy pincers. "You don't have to tell me twice. As soon as Fi yells that you're coming, I'll be gone."

I check in with Dillan and Diesel and call my body armor. When the ink of the tree of life stretching over my skin is in place, I call Birga to my palm. "All righty, then, it looks like we're up. We've got this, boys."

CHAPTER TWO

Dillan, Diesel, and I make our way down the slope of the hill and toward the little rascal that escaped the fae realm by slipping through a rift. "Hey, little guy. Somebody big and scary is looking for you. Any chance you feel like going home without making a fuss?"

The rake spider adjusts its footing, its legs twitching and positioning as if it's going to pounce.

"Yeah no, don't do that." I stop and release Birga back to her resting place. "See, we're not here to hurt you. There's no need to get testy."

The adult spider screeches again, and the baby responds. I take a few more slow steps toward the ring of dead grass. From this close, I can see the little beast's venom on the ground where the grass is dead.

"Be fast, hotness. I've got a feeling the venom is even more toxic than we thought."

"Trust me, luv. I don't want to be in pincer range any longer than is necessary."

My shield is tingling and that tells me our little guy isn't as dug in as he seems. I slide my foot sideways and close the distance between Diesel and me. "Diesel, stay tight with me, please. Dillan, call *Impenetrable Sphere.*"

With my hands raised in front of me, I do the same. "*Impenetrable Sphere.*" My orb of protection surrounds Diesel and me while Dillan's surrounds him.

"What should I do or not do?" Diesel asks.

"Stay with me and if the spider launches, hold your ground. You're not going to freak out or anything, are you?"

"Not planning to. Do you think your invisible bubble will hold?"

"It was strong enough to hold up against half a dozen hopped-up dragons during a game of Dillan volleyball. I'm confident we'll be safe…at least short term."

"See if ye can get it to rear up, *a ghra*. Then its focus will stay locked on ye."

Dillan grumbles beside us. "Seriously, fuck you, Irish. You know I love you man, but fuck you."

I chuckle and take another step toward the rake. "Dillan hates spiders."

"One more step should do it, luv."

My shield heads up from a warm tingle to a burning hum. "Yep, get ready."

Focused on watching for the spider to rear up on its back legs to threaten me, I'm not ready for it to fly at me like a ten-legged demon going for my head.

Dillan screams shrilly.

I raise my palms, calling for strength from the air around us, and reinforcing my sphere. "Mackenzie, now or never, babe."

One moment I'm staring at the soft-bellied bits of a homicidal baby rake spider the size of a pony—with fangs, pincers, and long knobby legs—and the next it's gone. "He's coming, Greek!"

I check that the area is clear, then I drop the sphere and start running back up the hill. "Talk to me, guys. Is everyone okay?"

There's no response, and by the time I crest the hill, my heart is thumping and making a damned fine effort of busting out of my ribs.

The reason they didn't respond is evident immediately. The last of the spider invader's legs are passing through the rift right now.

Sloan has Nikon in a protective bubble, and Nikon has his hands up and is gritting his teeth, grimacing.

Magical energy is arcing out from the swirling chaos of colors that makes up the fabric of the rift.

"How you doing, Greek? Can you hold yourself together this time?"

"I think so…it's better each time."

"Because you rock, Tsambikos," Dillan says.

"I've got ye, Greek," Sloan says.

"Yeah, you do," I say, so thankful the spiders are gone, and no more ugly pincers are sticking through the hole and dripping venomous goo.

A blast of energy explodes from the rift, and I brace against the fizz and fury of the energy storm.

Nikon's expression says it all.

He hates this. It hurts, and if anyone else could do it, he'd tap out.

"You've got this, Greek. Tug that zipper."

Diesel looks at me, and I shrug. "Okay, that sounded lewd somehow, but that's not how I meant it. Our friend Patty taught him how to close portal openings. He said to envision it as a zipper needing to be closed."

"I'm buying you boys many rounds of beer the first chance we get," Dillan says. "Are you going to go lava lamp this time, do you think?"

"I don't think so. I think I'm done."

As the words leave his lips, the rift closes, and the chaos ends in a vacuum of silence and stillness.

"Yay you." I hurry over to get an arm around his hips. He

looks like he's about to list to the side and faceplant in front of the Big Nickel. "Once again, you're the man of the hour. Mischief managed."

Sloan *poofs* us home, and we sit Nikon down and pull out the chicken tetrazzini leftovers from last night. "There's nothing like carb-loading after a big workout," Dillan says. "We'll have you back to full strength in no time."

Nikon accepts the Gatorade and takes a long drink. "There's no way I'd turn down an offer for Sloan's cooking, but I'm not too far gone. There's a chance I may be getting the hang of things."

"I'm not surprised in the slightest." I set my phone down on the breakfast bar and pivot to open the fridge. The fresh parmesan is in the cheese bin, and the cheese grater is in the top drawer. "You're really leveling up."

"And it only took twelve centuries. Yay me."

I laugh and hand him the cheese.

Sloan comes upstairs from returning his gloves to the apothecary. "I spoke to Maxwell and reported yer Big Nickel safe. He's calling our military contact in San Francisco now, and we'll meet him in twenty minutes."

"Cool. Who's our contact?"

He pauses. "I'm not sure I want to tell ye that."

"What? Why?"

"Because yer gonna say something inappropriate."

"Me? Inappropriate? No, I won't."

"Och, ye will. Ye won't be able to help yerself."

"Try me." I straighten, sober, and speak in a dry, serious tone. "Sloan, darling. Who are we to meet in San Francisco?"

He rolls his eyes. "We're meetin' Colonel Mustard at half past eleven."

"Colonel Mustard?" I bite my lips together. "You're making that up to taunt me."

"No. I'm not. And I know ye well enough to hear all the things ye want to say. On second thought, say them because I'd rather ye get it out of yer system than make a foolish slip when we're standin' in front of the man."

"You're serious." Dillan's jaw drops. "You're meeting Colonel Mustard?"

"In the army camp," I say.

"With a candlestick," Nikon adds, forking in pasta.

We all laugh…except Sloan.

I wave away his censure. "It's an excellent name to have in the military."

Sloan scowls. "It's unfortunate. I bet the whole time he was coming up in the ranks he dreaded the point when he made colonel for that reason."

"No way. It's awesome."

"Yer ridiculous."

"I think you've got that backward, hotness." I turn toward the steps and start upstairs. "Give me two minutes to pee and grab my bag. Then I'll be ready."

I hear Dillan chuckle as I go. "You'll have to excuse my sister, Diesel. She thinks we need to know when she visits the bathroom."

"I can hear you, asshat."

"Tell me I'm wrong."

I ignore him…because he's not wrong

Five minutes later, Nikon has finished his tetrazzini, I've retrieved our go-bag, and we're gathering to leave. "Has everyone got everything?"

"All set." Diesel's backpack looks so tiny hanging on his

massive shoulder.

Sloan takes our bag and slings it over his shoulder.

Nikon checks in with us and holds out his hand. "Then let's rock and roll."

"You're not bringing a bag, Greek?"

He reaches around to his back pocket and holds up a package with a toothbrush. "I'll snap home and change when I need to. In the meantime, I'm covered."

"A man who packs light. I get it." I lean over the railing and call downstairs. "Manx, we're ready to roll, buddy."

I wait the beat it takes for Manx to race up the stairs and join us. "All set?"

"Aye. Lookin' forward to it."

"Then we're off. Wish us luck."

Calum hugs me and kisses my cheek. "Safe home, sista. Love you lots."

I release him and hug Kevin next while Calum knuckle bumps the others. After the past two years, with Brenny dying and me getting sucked into every vortex of magical mayhem imaginable, we try not to leave things unsaid. It may be a little sappy, but it's easier on our hearts. "We love you too. Hold down the fort. We'll be back as soon as we can."

Dillan nods. "Yeah, how long can it take to find a missing city, amirite? San Francisco is too big to lose in the couch cushions. It's there. I'm guessing the military noobs don't know enough about glamours to find it."

I hope it's as easy as that, but with our track record, I'm not holding my breath.

Nikon snaps us the twenty-six hundred miles from Toronto to San Francisco in a blink. Distance or power drain have never hindered his portaling ability like Sloan's do, but even still, since his recent leveling due to the fall of the veil, I'd swear it's even faster.

We take form at the coordinates Maxwell gave us, which is the Lime Point military outpost at the north end of the Golden Gate Bridge—or at least where the Golden Gate Bridge should be. The military forces have set up right on Highway 101 and are blocking traffic from falling off the end of the road and into the drink.

The moment we arrive, soldiers clutch their guns, giving us a serious stare down.

I hold up my SITFU badge and meet them with a smile. "Fiona Cumhaill, Fae Liaison of Toronto. We were asked to come to consult on your San Francisco issue. Colonel Mustard is expecting us."

When the soldier lifts his radio to announce us, Nikon chuckles under his breath. "Really? Your San Francisco issue?"

"Yes, really. Them losing track of San Francisco is an issue."

"This way, please. IDs out. No magic use inside the encampment."

We follow the instructions, and he takes us to a fold-up table under an open-air tent. A female soldier meets us with a nod and pats the top of a beige machine. "Pass your identification badges under the scanner. When you get a green light, you can wait next to the building."

Okeedoodle. I scan my badge, get my green light, and move out of the way.

The building she referred to is one of two long, modular trailers set with the doors facing one another and probably fifty feet between them. A metal roof acts as a canopy over both and creates a shaded courtyard in between.

When she's finished checking all the scans, the soldier gets up from her station and joins us. With her hand on the door to one of the trailers, she pegs us with a serious look. "There is to be no magic used in the building, near the colonel, or anywhere in the outpost. Understood?"

"Sir, yes sir," I say, falling back on the military movies I've watched.

I ignore the snickering behind me and step through the door when signaled to do so. The inside reminds me of every school portable I've ever been in. Our footfalls sound hollow on the floor, the furniture is spartan and utilitarian, and at the far end, there is a desk facing us with a man in uniform getting to his feet.

"Jesus H, I have underwear older than you four."

I'm used to this as the first response.

"I assure you, you don't, sir. Nikon is an immortal Greek born in the days of chitons and chariots, but I understand your reaction. I am Fiona Cumhaill." I step forward and offer him my hand.

He doesn't shake. Instead, he straightens and crosses his arms. "I'll tell you plain, little girl. This is a serious matter, and I don't think you have the chops to do anything but muddy the waters. I certainly didn't ask you to come, and I'm chafed raw that I have orders to give you access to our operation."

"I'm six months into these types of visits, Colonel. I assure you, this is nothing I haven't heard before. The point is, you *have* orders to give us access, so we'll agree to disagree and do our best to get the job done."

He meets my gaze and, if I'm reading him right, is surprised I didn't go boohooing out of the room. He purses his lips and looks past me to where Diesel, Nikon, and Sloan are standing. "And you boys take your orders from her?"

"She runs the show, but she doesn't order us," Sloan says. "We do what she asks because she's that talented."

Colonel Mustard considers that for a moment and returns his attention to me. "So, what have you been told?"

"Three days ago, San Francisco vanished. No bridge, no cable cars, no Alcatraz. At first, you kept it quiet hoping it would magically reappear, but it hasn't."

"It did, but only briefly."

"It did? When was that?"

"9:42 this morning."

"How long did it stay?"

"Less than fifteen minutes."

I'm not sure what that might mean, but it's new information to consider.

"When it's gone, is it truly missin' or simply not visible?" Sloan asks.

"We had ground troops scour the land where the city should've been. It wasn't there."

"Could it still be a glamour?" I ask. "Maybe like Emhain Abhlach when it disappeared."

Sloan shakes his head. "I don't think so. Emhain Abhlach disappeared when the Light Weavers concealed it from view. It was still physically there, but the magic was illusionary, and the wardin' kept people from findin' it. The city wasn't physically displaced."

"You've dealt with another city that disappeared?" Colonel Mustard asks.

I nod. "Back in December, but Sloan's right, it's not the same kind of magic. This is something different."

"We should walk the area and see if we can pick up anything magical," Nikon suggests. "Maybe your shield will kick in, and we'll get a read on something."

I consider that. "What if the city returns and we're standing there?"

"Two of us portal, Red. I'll take Diesel, and you can stick with Sloan. If we need to get out fast, Sloan and I will portal us back here."

"Yeah, okay, that sounds—"

A raucous noise outside ends our conversation and has us

turning toward the exit. The door swings open and a soldier leans in. "It's back, sir. Just now."

The colonel escorts us to the metal barricade where Highway 101 leaves land and spans the water on the Golden Gate Bridge. The iconic red suspension bridge is indeed back in place.

"All right boys, it lasted less than fifteen minutes the last time it was back. Let's not waste time. Greek, take us to either where the bridge reconnects with land or as far as you can make it before you sense something. If there's warding up or magic in play, I don't want to breach it until we have a chance to assess."

"So, yer thinkin' we'll walk in and take it slow?" Sloan asks.

"Yeah. I want to give my shield a chance to weigh in on whether or not it's safe to enter."

"What if we're in the city and it blinks out again?" Diesel asks.

"Then I suppose we'll get a better sense of what happens when the city disappears."

"I suppose so."

Before we do this, I turn back and meet the stern gaze of Colonel Mustard. "Is there anything else you need from us or need to tell us, Colonel?"

He purses his lips. "Can't think of a thing."

I take Nikon's hand and squeeze. "All righty then, San Francisco here we come."

CHAPTER THREE

Nikon snaps me, Sloan, Diesel, and Manx one mile to the other end of the Golden Gate Bridge and we take form right where the road crosses the threshold over land and water. Before we attempt to enter the city, I take a moment to assess.

Raising my palms, I reach out with my connection with nature and try to determine if there's anything I need to be concerned about. "*Detect Magic.*"

"Wow, can you feel that?" My fingers tingle wildly, and the magical energy grows stronger. It takes hold, vibrating up my hands, wrists, and arms. "Me no likey."

"It's rather disconcertin', isn't it?" Sloan says.

"Rather," Nikon agrees. "What about your shield, Red? Anything we should be aware of on that front?"

I close my eyes to focus, but honestly, my only discomfort comes from in front of me not behind. "Nope. All is quiet."

"I wonder what that means," Diesel says.

Nikon chuffs. "I'd bet my left nut that whatever is happening, this is one hundred percent a magic gone haywire event. Yet Fi's shield isn't concerned. Does that weird anyone else out?"

"Yeah, a bit," I admit. "But it's better than my shield burning and going crazy."

"I suppose."

"So, what's the plan?" Sloan checks his watch. "We're coming on six minutes. If it disappears again, do we want to be on the inside or the outside?"

I glance around to take a consensus. "Inside? That way, at least, we have a chance to source out the cause."

Everyone nods their agreement.

"Okay then, let's see what we can find out."

Stepping through the magical field isn't exactly painful but isn't pleasant either. It takes us walking a couple of yards to push through the barrier and shake off the feeling of being trapped in a wall of magic.

Once we're in, though, it abates.

"Okay, what now?" I glance around the rural lands and the city beyond that.

Sloan is lost in thought, staring back toward the highway behind us.

"Is there something wrong, hotness? Are you rethinking us going into the city?"

He has his hands extended in front of his body and is pushing against the invisible barrier. "I wanted to test the magical field goin' the other direction to see if it felt the same, but it seems it only offers a one-way passage."

"Are you sure?" I raise my palms and do the same. He's right. Whatever magical energy makes up the boundary field ensures it's an innie and not an outtie. "San Francisco is *Hotel California*. You can enter, but you can never leave."

"Great song," Diesel says.

"It's likely a great city, but never say never. I like Toronto, thanks."

Nikon sighs. "Well, we're here now. I bet once we figure out what's gone wrong and fix it, the city will resume two-way traffic."

I nod. "Agreed. If this is a 'magic gone haywire' event, we need to figure out the source of the magic, the original intention, what went wrong, and how to undo the damage done."

"Easy-peasy." Nikon waves it off. "With us on the job, we'll be home by dinner."

I glance at him sidelong and chuckle. "Yeah, sure. No problem."

We follow the highway south until it bends along the water and cars start to use it again. Yes, the army barricaded people from coming into the city, but within the city, things seem fairly normal.

"Do you think they know they've been blinking in and out of existence for the past three days?" I ask.

"We could ask them," Diesel suggests.

A car rushes past, and I shuffle farther off the shoulder. "Good idea. We need to get off this highway anyway. Let's go find people and see what we can learn."

"Where to?" Nikon asks.

"What do we know about San Francisco?" I ask. "Greek? Have you been here before?"

"Yeah. I may have wandered these streets for a time. Things have changed since then, I'm sure."

"Maybe or maybe not. I'm sure the fundamentals are the same. Do you have any old contacts we might be able to connect with?"

"None that would be happy to see me."

"Seriously? I have a hard time believing there is anyone who wouldn't want a drop-in from you. I lurve your face."

Nikon chuckles. "I lurve your face too, but believe it or not, that isn't a universal opinion, and I'd rather not go down that road if we don't have to."

My inner nosy girl wants to jump all over that. Are we talking about a jilted lover, a friendship gone wrong, an old enemy? So many questions.

Now is probably not the time, so instead of letting nosy Fi loose, I rein her in. "Where would there be lots of people in the old days of when you walked these streets, Greek?"

"Fisherman's Wharf, Chinatown, any of the museums, Oracle Park, Golden Gate Park. There are a dozen places we could go to find a crowd. Why? What are you thinking?"

"I think we should ask around and find out what people know."

Diesel flashes me a look. "Do you think random people on the street will know what's going on?"

"The only way to find out is to ask, amirite?" I pull my phone out of my pocket. "So, let's ask."

Nikon laughs and leans toward my phone. "Hey, Google, where in San Francisco should we look for the source of a giant magical fuck-up?"

I roll my eyes.

He shrugs. "You said we should ask."

I'm prepared for a monotone voice uttering, *"I can't find the source of a giant magical fuck-up"* but we get nothing. I check that my phone is on. It is but—"I've got no signal. You?"

The three of them pull out their phones, and it's no love all the way around.

"Is this a magical interference thing?" I ask.

Sloan nods. "Likely so. Either random chaotic interference is shortin' out the system, or designed interference is preventin' incomin' communications."

"You think it's intentional and someone is preventing communications?"

"Not exactly. What I meant was the magical spell that went haywire could've had a component of privacy or security to it, which the instability of the power influx has enhanced."

Oh, that's a bit better. "Since I went there, isn't it possible that someone intentionally hijacked the city and blocked outgoing travel and communications?"

"It's possible, but to what end?"

"I have no idea. It occurred to me that maybe this isn't a magical fuck-up and someone might be engineering the lockdown."

"I don't suppose we'll find that out until we learn what kind of spell is in play."

Diesel holds up a finger. "Speaking of blocking outgoing travel. I wonder if Nikon will be able to teleport out of here. You couldn't walk through, but can his magical portal take us through?"

Nikon holds up a finger but doesn't go anywhere. "That would be a negative. You were right, Red. We're living a *Hotel California* scenario."

I was afraid of that.

Manx lifts his nose to the breeze and sniffs. "I smell restaurants."

"Where there are restaurants, there are people. Good thinking, Manxy. Let's—"

The next moments are a blur of magical bombardment. My ears ring, and I drop to one knee and clench my eyes shut. My skin ignites hot with the prickles of what feels like a million fire ants. There's a shift in the world around us, and it feels like first our insides are being pulled through a great resistance. Then, like a slingshot released, we're jettisoned forward.

As quickly as it starts, it stops.

I shake my head, stand, and widen my stance to keep from ass-planting. "What the hell was that?"

Sloan looks as shaken as I feel. He points at the two moons high in the mauve sky above. "I'm no expert, *a ghra*, but I'd say we blinked."

Diesel curses under his breath. "That felt like more than a blink."

I brush my palms together to clean off the pebbles and dirt from the shoulder of the highway and pat Manx's fur. "Are you all right, puss?"

"I'll live, but I'd appreciate it if we didn't have to do that again."

I study our surroundings. "On the contrary, we need to blink at least once more to get home."

"Oh, aye, that's true too. Once more then."

Nikon laces his fingers and cracks his knuckles. "So, this is the fae realm, is it?"

"I guess so. Or a pocket that acts like it anyway." There's a glimmer of excitement in his eyes, and it piques my curiosity. "Why does that amuse you so much?"

Nikon meets my gaze and grins. "It's been a long time since I experienced anything new. When you live as an immortal long enough, you run out of new experiences. I've never been pulled into the fae realm before."

I chuckle. "Well, I'm happy you're happy. Enjoy it while it lasts. Our goal is to *not* be in the fae realm. Not even a pocket of it."

"Fair enough. So, what now?"

"Why are you looking at me?"

"Well, you are the only one here who has been to the fae realm. That makes you the expert."

The face Sloan makes resembles the reaction my brothers have when they swig back a glug of chunky milk. "She's hardly an expert. She tracked down a witch, pissed off a prince of the Unseelie Court, and got herself royally slain. It's a wonder she even lived through that field trip."

"I resemble that remark, but I say I'm the closest we have right now. The fact is I *did* survive, and I was able to save you, so it was totes worth it. That which doesn't kill you makes you stronger."

I'm not sure that's true when visiting the fae realm, but whatevs. "Let's get back to our restaurant plan. I suppose we don't have to ask people if they're aware the city is blinking, but I'd still like to regroup."

"A Drink and Think then?" Nikon asks.

"Yeah. I think definitely."

Nikon snaps us along the water to Fisherman's Wharf. We find a waterfront seafood spot and get a table. They aren't keen on having Manx inside, so we take a table on the patio and settle in.

"Something Sloan said earlier is sticking with me." I dip a hushpuppy into the creamy sauce and pop the ball of deep-fried cornmeal-based batter into my mouth. "You said you thought it might've been a spell that became unstable when the veil fell."

Sloan sips his Coke from a straw and swallows. "Do you disagree?"

"No. It's not that. I was wondering what the parameters of a spell like that would be. If this was the house of a witch or wizard that had warding on it blinking in and out, I could wrap my head around it."

"But it's bigger than that," Diesel says.

"Right. This is happening to an entire city."

Nikon cracks a lobster claw and dips the meat in melted butter. "So, what the fuck was warded before things went haywire. Is that the question?"

"Exactly. I think it would have to be something substantial."

Nikon holds up a claw. "Either that or the instability expanded things well beyond the original purpose."

"Right. So, how do we figure that out?" I ask.

Sloan wipes his fingers on his napkin and sets it back in his lap. "I suppose that's the big question."

We finish our lunch and learn we can't pay with debit or credit due to the "being sucked into a fae realm" problem and no connection to the payment programs.

Our server explains this to us with an incredible amount of calm and I'm astounded. How are these people continuing as if it's business as usual? Don't they realize how whacked it is that they're blinking in and out of existence in the human realm while they're getting ready for happy hour?

It's freaking *me* out, and I just got here.

Sloan picks up the tab with cash from his wallet. Luckily both he and Nikon carry cash because Diesel and I don't. Even better, they both had the foresight to convert some to US dollars in advance of our mission.

With our tummies full and our discombobulation settling, we walk along to Pier 39 and check out the sea lions. The pier juts out into the water toward Alcatraz. There is a wooden boardwalk and tourists and locals milling around everywhere.

I pull out my phone to Google info on Alcatraz and remember there are no Internet or cell signals.

Right. That sucks.

Sliding it back into my pocket, I go old-school. "Hotness, can I borrow some cash? I want to buy a book on San Francisco history and notable points of interest."

Sloan pulls his billfold and peels me off three fifties. I laugh and peg him with a look. "What kind of books have you been buying? I was thinking twenty bucks."

He chuckles. "Odds are, at some point over the next hours or days, we'll get separated."

I snort. "Yeah, more than likely."

"At which point, I don't want ye unable to take care of yerself. Yer not borrowin' the money. What is mine is ours to be shared without apology."

"I need me a sugar daddy," Diesel says. "Or, I guess, a rich cougar would be more my thing."

I chuckle and shuffle off with my allowance in hand.

Nikon follows me into one of the tourist shops, and we

peruse the selections. I don't want to lug around a heavy tome all day, so I stick to paperbacks I can easily tuck into my purse.

"What do you think about this one?" I hold it up for Nikon to see.

"Lonely Planet guides are good. Sure."

I grab that, a couple of chocolate bars, a bottle of water, and hand the girl one of my fifties. While we wait for my change, I bump shoulders with Nikon. "So, what's the skinny on the person you're not keen on reconnecting with? Who is this person who won't want to see your face? They must be awful. They obviously have no taste. You rock socks."

He inhales and sighs heavily. "Danika is a local witch. We had a good thing, and when it turned into a great thing, I blew her off and walked away."

"Why would you—oh, I get it. When you got to 'great thing territory' you worried Hecate would step in and end things…or rather, end *her*."

I see the truth in his eyes. "Over the centuries, I was pretty skilled at keeping people at a distance, but Dani got through my defenses somehow. I didn't realize it until she brought up forever and having a family."

My heart breaks for him. Hecate killed the one woman he dared to love after his breakup with the Goddess of Magic and Spells. She was pregnant with his child, so he lost both lives.

After that, he battened down the hatches and resigned himself to never loving anyone.

"I'm so sorry, sweetie." I wrap my arms around him and squeeze him tight.

He hugs me and steps back. "It was a long time ago. It is what it is, and I accept it was all my fault."

The clerk is waiting with my change.

I accept it, and we file out of the shop. Hugging his arm, I press my cheek against his shoulder as we stroll back down the pier. "Eyes forward, amirite?"

"Absolutely because almost everything in the rearview mirror sucks balls."

I squeeze his arm and release him. "That's fine. It's in the past, and you're immortal, so those were your warm-up years. Now you've regained control of things and are ready to burst into a supernova. What was it that Eros said to me? To launch an arrow forward, first, you must draw it backward."

Nikon chuckles and arches a brow. "Did you seriously just quote Eros? Wow, you really are making an effort not to hate him."

"I try not to hate anyone—because it's bad for my energy—but yeah, I recognize he's a friend of yours as well as Dionysus, and I think you have spectacular taste in friends."

He winks at me. "The absolute best."

The two of us find Sloan, Manx, and Diesel standing against a railing, watching the sea lions bask in the sun. Beyond the pier's edge, twenty or thirty floating docks bob independently in the water. The sea lions have drawn a crowd of about forty people who are fascinated with their antics and are taking pictures and hanging out.

Honestly, Manx and Diesel have drawn the attention of quite a few as well. I guess it's not every day people see a lynx trotting around town with a seven-foot-tall guy in black fatigues and a shirt barely holding itself together at the seams.

"How are things, boys? Did we miss anything?"

"Actually, ye did." Sloan eases back from the rail and makes room for me to stand. When I slide in, he steps in behind me and rests his chin on my shoulder. "Tell them what ye told us, sham."

Manx is standing on his back paws looking out over the rail and grinning. "Those sea lions aren't all regular sea lions. Quite a few of them are selkies. I can smell the difference."

"Selkies? Are you sure?"

"Och, if there's one type of shifter we get a lot of back home, it's selkies. I'm sure."

I set my elbows on the rail and take stock of the close to three hundred fin-footed animals sunbathing before us. "I suppose it's a great way to hide in plain sight. I can't tell the difference between any of them."

Sloan nods. "Agreed. They certainly fit in here."

"Well, good for them. Life would be lovely if I could bask in the sun with friends all day long."

"You can." Nikon chuckles. "All you have to do is say the word."

"She'd last a week at most," Sloan says. "Our time away after Montreal proved that."

He's not wrong. "I do have a taste for action and adventure. As much as I love living *la vida loca*, Sloan's right. I would get stir crazy after a while."

"Then we go somewhere big on watersports. Jet skiing is fun...or you could learn to surf."

"That I could get into." I think about that while I watch a tour boat shuttling people to an island across the water. "That's Alcatraz there, right?"

"That's it," Nikon says. "Do you want me to pop us over so you can do the touristy thing?"

"I'd love to, but I think we should get back to the problem at hand. Now that we've sorted our bearings, where do you think we should start our phasing city investigation?"

Diesel, Nikon, and I have got nothing.

The three of us end up staring at Sloan, waiting for him to impart his wisdom to us.

He arches a brow and chuckles. "I think checkin' in with the local guild would be good. Whether this is an established spell that went wrong with the influx of energy or a new spell someone tried with an increased reserve of power, we're still lookin' to speak to the magic makers of the community."

"Witches, wizards, and sorcerers, then, eh?"

Sloan nods. "And the local guild will know who in those

communities has the strength in power to cause a magical mess this massive."

"Okeedoodle, the San Francisco Guild it is."

Nikon snaps us to a lovely urban park with a pond and about a hundred people milling around. "Welcome to Golden Gate Park, home of de Young Museum, the California Academy of Sciences, the Japanese Tea Garden, the Conservatory of Flowers, and the branch office for the California Guild of Governors."

"Branch office?" I repeat.

"Yeah. The main office is in L.A., but there are a few branch offices up and down the coastline."

"It's a lovely area," Sloan says.

"Offering gardens, glades, and quiet lakes, Golden Gate Park is the emerald heart of San Francisco," I read from my tour book. "It says this thousand-acre park draws hikers, bikers, art lovers, and music fans."

Nikon arches a brow and chuckles. "Are you going to do that everywhere we go?"

"Maybe." I look at him and slide my handy-dandy tourist book back into my purse. "My book doesn't have anything about empowered headquarters, though, so this is all you, Greek."

"All right. It's been a minute since I've been here, but I'm sure we'll figure it out. Access is through a door in the historic greenhouse. Or, at least, it was a decade ago."

I glance at Sloan. "Did you hear that, hotness? Historic greenhouse."

He laughs. "Yer ridiculous. Just because it has the word historic doesn't mean it'll draw me in."

"Good one. I call bullshit for two hundred, Alex."

Nikon strikes off along the path, and we follow.

It is a lovely park.

We pass an arboretum, a music concourse, and then the Academy of Sciences building. A handball game is in full swing on the handball courts and some goofing around on the tennis courts.

"Wow, they're right." I flip through my book again. "A classic city park where everyone, from first-time visitors to go-every-weekend locals, finds something amazing to see or do."

"Seriously, Red. If I have to take that book away from you. I will—"

A bolt of energy comes in hard and fast from the right. It catches Nikon in the shoulder and throws him spinning in the air.

"We're under attack!"

CHAPTER FOUR

I call Birga to my hand and activate my armor at the same moment. Spinning toward the direction of the attack, I release Bruin. "Somebody is firing on us, Bear. The hit came from the trees by that brick outbuilding."

Bruin's presence bursts free as he dispatches to find whoever is attacking. Sloan is on the ground, tending to Nikon. Diesel and I block the line of sight.

I take a knee, and press my hand to the soft, manicured grass. "*Grasping Vine.*" I draw the creeping vine I sense in the wooded area where the strike came from. Strengthening it, I call it into action to seek our opponent.

Diesel snaps an iron picket off one of the low fences and grips it in his massive fist. "Have you got this?"

"Yep. Go do your thing."

Bruin roars and the sound of magic battle fire rings out. "Fi, we're good, luv. Off ye go."

A glance shows Sloan lifting Nikon to his feet. Awesomesauce. I don't need to be told twice. "You're with me, puss. See if you can get close enough to join the fun."

Manx and I run forward, over a couple of rolling mounds of grass, and join the battle in progress.

Bruin is facing off against an elven wizard, a purple-haired witch, and a beast of a guy with blue skin. Manx banks right and follows the hill line before cresting it to join Bruin.

Diesel goes in hard, swinging for the fences.

I return Birga to my forearm and drop to one knee a second time. *"Erupting Earth."*

Focusing my intention on their feet, I send shockwaves of instability to the ground beneath them.

"Fissure Fault." As the ground crumbles and a crevasse opens beneath their feet, they counter.

The blue beast is facing off with Bruin. Manx and Diesel are keeping the elf busy, and the witch is lending them support and focusing on me. They're good, and it's obvious they have fought together for a while.

Three fiery balls of magical energy come at me like hardball pitches. I rise to my feet, call Birga back, grip, and rip.

Having five older brothers, I'm no slouch at hitting a pitch. Especially pitches aimed at my head. I send the first one straight back at the elf and knock the other two balls of energy out of play.

The surprise on his face is amazeballs.

"Danika? What the fuck?" Nikon has rejoined the action and is glaring at our attackers.

"You know them?" the elf asks.

"Bruin and Manx, hold." I hold up my hand and pause our retaliation.

Nikon is furious. He's glaring at the purple-haired witch and storming into the mix. "Are you seriously so pissed at me you're willing to get your people killed?"

The witch barks a laugh. "We wouldn't be the ones getting killed."

The blue guy gives her a WTF look and widens his eyes. "You're not the one fighting a fucking grizzly."

We've gathered a crowd of terrified onlookers, and I decide to de-escalate things.

"Thanks, Bear. You rock, buddy." I pat my chest, and he dematerializes and ghosts back to me.

That piques their interest, but if they have questions, they don't let on.

Nikon rolls his shoulder as he leads the charge toward the three. "Shit, Dani. Endangering my friends and yours was petty and beneath you."

If Nikon hadn't told me they were once in love, there is no way I would've guessed it. The witch pegs him with such an icy gaze that I'm sure everyone across the city feels the arctic chill.

She sneers, "Believe it or not; this isn't about you getting what you deserve. We responded to the illegal use of portal magic within the city. You're in the wrong here, not me. I didn't recognize you. Since when do you cut your hair and go without guyliner?"

Nikon cut his hair short and chic as one of the major wins of freeing himself from Hecate's hold. For the past thousand years, every time he tried to alter his appearance, he reverted to looking the way he did when he was a teenager and her lover.

Wearing goth makeup was the only way he could express his personality for centuries.

"After a millennium, I was due for a makeover."

The elven wizard straightens. "The problem remains that you used unauthorized portal magic. We have to take you in."

Nikon rolls his eyes. "We were coming in when you attacked us."

"If you were coming in, why are you here?"

He looks genuinely confused. "The last time I was here, your base was in Golden Gate Park."

The elf shakes his head. "We moved locations about ten years ago. We're in the Legion of Honor now."

I throw up my palms. "Then we were off base, but that doesn't give you the right to attack. We're in a public park. Don't you have safety protocols in place that discourage battling among the non-magicals?"

"Who are you, exactly?" Danika pegs me with a stink-eyed scowl.

"We're the response team to the fact that San Francisco is blinking between realms."

Danika chuckles. "Nikon is part of the response team? Wow, you must be desperate."

I hold up a finger. "Maybe back up the hostility so we can go to your branch office headquarters. This city is majorly screwed, and we're here to help."

"Well, it would help if know-nothing wannabes weren't portaling all over the city while we're trying to stabilize things."

I chuckle. "By all over town, you mean twice? We portaled to Fisherman's Wharf and here."

"We're well aware, Red," she says. "We've been tracking you since you came through the field."

I blink. "Then why not introduce yourself and find out why we're here?"

"Why would the lions care if a few beetles crawled into their compound?"

"Seriously?" My mouth falls open and power sparks from my fingertips. "You don't know us, chickypoo. I get that you and the Greek have a soured history but getting into a pissing match with the cavalry is stupid. You're wasting our time and you endangered your team. Get over yourself."

She's about to respond when the elf grabs her upper arm and tugs her back. "How about we start again? I am Val Ryn, that is Trent, and you seem to know Danika. We're the forward scouts for the San Francisco branch of the Empowered Ones."

I accept his introductions and think starting again sounds like a great idea. "I am Fiona Cumhaill. This is Diesel, Sloan, his companion Manx, and Nikon Tsambikos. I'm the Fae Liaison for Toronto, and we're part of a consulting team that goes out when the world is going haywire because of the fall of the veil."

"Well, you could've saved yourself the trip," Danika says. "We don't need your help. We've got things under control."

I laugh. "You think so? This city isn't even in the human realm now, and you have no outgoing communications. How is that under control?"

"We're handling it."

Her bravado is more anger than reality, and I shrug and look at the other two of her party. "How about you take us in and maybe we can talk to someone who doesn't have her head shoved up her ass."

My shield flares a split second before she launches. When her palm thrusts out toward my chest, a blast of magic releases. My armor absorbs the hit, and I grab her arm, knock her off-balance, and slam her to the ground.

I release the power that's been building in my cells, and she bucks and kicks against the ground as if it's magically electrocuting her.

Which, in essence, it is.

"Enough, Red." Nikon grips me around the waist and lifts me off his old flame. He carries me a couple of feet away and sets me on my feet. "Believe it or not, we're all on the same side."

"*I* get that, but I don't think your old girlfriend sees it that way. If she needs a lesson in manners, I'm happy to school her."

Nikon cups my cheek and turns my gaze to meet his. "Let's get this job done and go home, shall we? I want to get gone."

Danika chuffs. "That's right. Getting gone is what you're best at, isn't it, Nik?"

Nikon is facing me when her comment hits and I see the hurt and regret he carries within him.

I pat his shoulder and give him as much love and support as I can with a smile. "Yeah, let's getter done. I've had enough of the hospitality of the Golden City."

With the kerfuffle over, the San Francisco welcoming committee escorts us to another location. The funniest part about that is that the wizard elf intends to portal us back, but he doesn't have the juice to move all of us at once, so Nikon ends up getting us where we need to go.

At least, *I* think it's funny.

Can they accuse us of illegal transport when they don't have the goods to get the job done?

I think not.

"The Legion of Honor is an impressive Neoclassical building in an amazing setting in Lincoln Park. It sits at the heart of a gorgeous green space with a golf course and coastal woodlands. The building was a gift from the socialite, philanthropist, and patron of the arts, Alma de Bretteville Spreckels. Because of her love for all things Parisian, the museum's design is a replica of the Palais de la Légion d'Honneur in Paris." When I finish reading from my book, I glance at the others.

Nikon rolls his eyes, but he's finding my tour guide routine funny.

I made him smile. Mission accomplished.

I tuck the travel book back into my purse and get back to the problems at hand. Sloan is genuinely interested and soaks up all information.

He's a sponge like that.

"Yer wee book is correct. It is quite an impressive buildin'."

"And recognized as one of San Fran's most exquisite museums," Nikon adds.

Danika throws us a disgruntled look over her shoulder but whatevs.

I'm sorry you didn't get to avoid this personal torture, Greek. I direct my thoughts at him.

Me too. Honestly, it's probably karma biting me in the ass. She deserved better than she got from me, and I was too ashamed to admit the problem and too afraid for her safety that she'd try to do something about it.

I wonder what she'd think if she knew the patron goddess of magic and witchcraft was a jelly bitch that refused to take her claws out of you.

I suppose we'll never know.

What do you mean? You're not going to clear the air with her? The witch bitch curse is broken. You can let her in on things now.

To what end? What we had was a long time ago, Fi. We've both moved on. What good will it do to open old wounds?

I chuckle. *Obviously, those wounds have festered and need to be irrigated.*

He shakes his head. *No. What's done is done.*

I step in beside him and hug his arm. *Dude, it doesn't matter if it was the Fates or karma or the Ostara bunny that brought you here. The fact is you're here, and she's here, and the two of you have fences to mend. Pull up your big boy pants and make the girl stop hating you.*

You're such a softy. He leans sideways and kisses my temple. *I hate that you're right.*

I chuckle and pat his arm before stepping away.

The vicious glare Danika flashes my way is impressive. Usually, it takes people more than one conversation to dislike me that strongly. Either she is that pissed we came to help or where there's smoke there's fire.

Is Danika still fanning the flames of passion for our Greek? This might get interesting.

We climb the stone ramp leading up to the front of the building. It's a symmetrical layout with arches and pillars and an open courtyard beyond a colonnade.

"This looks more Greek than Parisian if you ask me," I say.

"There are definite Greek influences in the design," Nikon says.

"It reminds me of when you took me to the temples."

"It would. There is Greek influence in a lot of this architecture."

We top the stairs leading to the courtyard and head to the back right corner. I watch Danika as she moves through the space with her team. Yes, she's angry about Nikon being back here, but despite that, my instincts tell me there's more going on.

I see why Nikon loved her…or almost loved her. She's a strong woman yet has delicate features. Her hair is dark violet at the top of her head and lightens with a dramatic ombre to a pretty mauve color brushing her shoulders. She's confident and is killing it in skinny jeans and knee-high leather boots with silver buckles. She's also running an empowered team, so she must be competent and know how to lead.

I see the draw.

I sense the glamour as we step through the magical resistance. It feels much like the one Garnet has on the archway of his Toronto home. There's a brief moment of friction. Then, as if a bubble has burst, we pass through, and the museum fades away.

The home base of the San Francisco branch is cool. The opposite of our business office at the Batcave, their space is futuristic and sleek.

"This is swanky." Sloan looks around.

I chuckle. "If you want the bridge of the starship *Enterprise*, I'm sure Dionysus will oblige. Nikon will give us another floor of the Acropolis, won't you, Greek?"

He arches a brow and chuckles. "Why the hell not? You've already got five floors. Why stop now? You realize your landlord is a pushover for anything you ask, right?"

I hold up a finger. "Technically, you've given us four floors. Dionysus' loft doesn't count. He magicked that on top of our building. That was an aftermarket add-on."

"Semantics, but fine. I'll give you that."

The blue beast guy, Trent, nods as we pass a floor-to-ceiling weapons rack and breaks off. "Have a good one. I'm grabbing something to eat. Fighting your bear took it out of me. Tell me he's as wiped as I am."

I chuckle. "Sorry. He's a mythical battle bear. He gains prana by fighting. He was only warming up."

He holds up his hands. "Then I'm glad you turned out to be friendlies because that bear packs a wallop."

I pat my sternum. "Yeah, he's pretty awesome."

We fan out in what I can only describe as a high-tech war room. A round table in the center of the room has LED maps lit up on the surface and small holograms standing perpendicular that detail topography and buildings.

There are stand-up console stations positioned in five equally spaced locations around the perimeter, and where we have a small wall of monitors, they have no monitors, but the wall is one big screen.

Yowzers. Talk about war room envy.

"Juniper Ravello, these people are the cause of the unsanctioned portaling." Danika swings a dismissive hand toward us. "They *say* they came to help with the spatial displacement."

I don't appreciate the way she draws that out.

Angry or not, Nikon's ex is not a good hostess.

She's flat-out rude.

"We didn't just *say* we came to help," I correct. "We *did* come here to help. Back in the human world the military is at a loss and called us in."

The woman Danika gestured to is tall, gaunt, and fae. With her wide globe eyes and the iridescent sheen to her skin, I'd guess she's a high fae or maybe from some ancient race I don't know about.

There are so many things about the fae realm I still don't know about.

There's no way she was part of society looking like this. Either she has a gift to glamour, or she's a new appointment since the fae cat got out of the bag.

Juniper gives me a visual once-over as well. It seems she's happier with what she sees than Danika was. "You're the Toronto druid, aren't you? The one who descends from Finn MacCool?"

"That's right. I'm Fiona."

"I have a healthy respect for your ancestor. Finn did many great things for and within the fae realm as a shaman."

"He's a wonderful man. I've cherished every moment I've had the pleasure of interacting with him."

She doesn't have eyebrows, but if she did, they would be raised. "You've interacted with him?"

"Yes. Multiple times. I'm a shaman as he was, so we've maneuvered the astral plane together. As well, he's drawn me back in time three or four times when he's needed to impart wisdom of some sort."

"You are fortunate, indeed. Not everyone has an ancestor with enough power to visit his heirs."

"He comes from rare stock."

"Did his guidance play a part in you discovering the coming of the Time of the Colliding Realms? It was you who rallied the troops, was it not?"

"It was a team discovery, but yes, that's right."

"Well, I for one, thank you. If we hadn't had the forewarning of what was to come, the chaos and destruction we encountered would've been much worse."

"I'm glad our discoveries helped."

"Now you've come to help with our city's spatial displacement?"

"Pull together and rise above." I quote the mantra of the people since the veil fell.

"Absolutely. Well, we are pleased to have you. Sadly, the power flux from your two portals was ill-timed. It set us back on stabilizing the energy field that's gotten out of our control, but we'll compensate."

"We're sorry about that. We weren't aware you were on a magical portal lockdown."

"No. You couldn't have known."

"Since we're talking about our arrival and being unaware. Having your response team identify themselves before engaging fire and attacking us would've been appreciated. Since when have empowered officers had the authorization to shoot first?"

Juniper glances toward her team, and her expression tightens. "They haven't."

Danika pegs me with a glare that promises retaliation. "I deemed them a threat and acted accordingly."

Juniper waves that away. "My apologies. That was an unfortunate first contact, yet here we are, all on the same page. Welcome to the Golden City. Come, let me show you what we know."

CHAPTER FIVE

Juniper gestures toward the war table in the center of the room and Sloan, Nikon, Diesel, Val Ryn, Danika, and I gather around. Before us is a city map that extends out to the water and islands beyond.

I identify Fisherman's Wharf, find Alcatraz, the Golden Gate Bridge, and I think I've got a decent sense of what I'm looking at.

There is a blue line in the water encircling Alcatraz and an orange line that encompasses the entire city.

"What are the two colored boundaries?" I ask.

Juniper extends an elongated finger toward the blue circle around Alcatraz. "How much do you know about spatial magic?"

"Me? Not much. Nikon is the one gifted with that particular affinity."

Danika scoffs. "Nikon is nothing more than a glorified Uber."

I grip the table's edge to keep from jumping across it and tackling her to the floor. "Maybe you should excuse yourself. It seems your baggage is keeping you from being professional. Run along, now, little girl. The grown-ups have got this."

Danika holds her ground. "You're too caught up in his charm to know how doomed you are."

"Sweetie, I know him as well as anyone and love him to bits. It's you who doesn't have a clear picture of who he is and why he's done the things he has."

"Don't even pretend you know me, Red. You don't."

An electrical charge snaps as Juniper lifts her hand to silence us. "That will be enough. Danika, perhaps Fiona is right. You should step back if you can't focus on the problems at hand."

Danika turns her attention to the woman in charge and shakes her head. "That won't be necessary. I'm fine."

Juniper studies her for a long moment before shifting her attention to us and continuing. "What happened is relatively simple to understand and a great deal more complicated to correct."

She taps a button on the console in front of her. The blue boundary around Alcatraz fills in with a grid that covers the island and about half a mile around it. "Sixty years ago, when Alcatraz was closed as an island of incarceration for human criminals, several governing bodies of the fae in the human realm decided to convert it to a holding site for fae offenders."

I glance at Sloan and Nikon. "Did you guys know this?"

They both shake their heads.

"I'm not surprised you are unaware," Juniper says. "It was and has been a well-guarded secret only shared with the highest levels of fae law enforcement."

I make a mental note to ask Garnet if he knew about this. If he did, I think he should've mentioned it before sending us here.

"The wardings have been in place for decades, and the glamour hides the truth from visitors. This is what the prison looks like to humans, and this is how it exists in reality."

She taps the tips of her fingers against the glossy glass of the table. A series of three-dimensional buildings rise on the island in front of us. "To prevent the escape of detainees, the warding on the prison was cast by the heads of three local families of sorcerers and woven together with the help of a now-extinct order of fae called Light Weavers."

I cast a sidelong glance at Nikon and meet Sloan's gaze. His head shakes so subtly it's almost imperceptible, but still, I get the message to keep quiet about that for now.

"What was the exact purpose of the warding?" Sloan asks.

"To prevent escape and keep everyone in the prison restricted to this area." She circles the prison and the water beyond.

Sloan nods. "I take it, based on the inclusion of the water in the boundary spell, if by some chance, a fae inmate escaped the prison, he or she would be prevented from escape or captured in the surrounding waters."

"Exactly right," Juniper says. "The water of the bay and especially the warded area is patrolled by fae prison guards uniquely suited to prevent escape."

"You commissioned a selkie army." He lowers his chin and winks at me. "The sea lion shifters we spotted sunning themselves at the wharf are your last line of defense."

Juniper straightens and gives Sloan a wide-eyed look. "Very astute. Yes. Our selkie army, as you called them, have been in service for six decades and have never failed us. Not one fae prisoner has ever escaped."

I look at the orange boundary, and it falls into place. "So, when the veil dropped and the levels of fae prana in the water and the ambient power in the air went wonky, the wardings mutated."

Juniper nods. "Something like that, yes."

"The orange boundary line depicts what is now warded, and the entire city is now locked down to prevent escape."

"That's a simplified version, but yes, that's it."

"Now you're at a point where people and communications can enter, but nothing and no one can leave."

Juniper nods. "Now you're all caught up."

Danika pegs me with a shit-eating grin. "So, the question is, how exactly do you think you can help?"

The five of us take a moment to step away and confer. Under the guise of Manx needing to stretch his legs and get a breath of fresh air, we exit the headquarters and stroll down to the large fountain at the front of the property. "No offense, Greek, but your ex can be a Class-A bitch." I shrug when he frowns at me, but hey, I call it as I see it.

"It's not Danika's fault." Nikon picks up a stone and skips it across the massive fountain in front of the building. "She's hurt and angry and has every right to be. This is all on me."

"And the fact that she thinks ye and Fiona are together," Sloan says.

My head whips around, and I blink. "Hubba-wha? What makes you say that, hotness?"

"What are my primary disciplines, *a ghra?*"

"Healing and Spiritual."

"So, not only can I sense her pain but when she sees the two of ye together, I can read how hurt she is and how angry that makes her. She doesn't want to care, but she does."

"Well, I'm not going to apologize for being Nikon's bestie or being in his corner. She can suck it."

"Maybe set her straight." Diesel takes his turn skipping a rock across the top of the water's surface. "If she's unduly hostile because she believes you're with Nikon, tell her she's got her wires crossed."

Or maybe she sees what she wants to see and is a drama llama.

Yes, we share love, but I am one hundred percent with Sloan. He knows it, Nikon knows it, and I know it. "Whatevs. If you think it will help to dial down the hostility, I'm fine with that. I'd love to set her straight."

"Hard pass." Nikon shakes his head. "As much as I adore you, Fi, you don't test well with other women. You tend to get standoffish and aggressive when confronted by a female peer."

I shrug. "I admit, I prefer to spend my time with guys, but I have female friends. It's not like I have a problem with women."

"As long as they're beta or submissive. When you come up against another alpha female, you dig in, and your claws come out."

"No, they don't. You're exaggerating."

Nikon and Sloan share a conspiratorial look and laugh at my expense.

"All right, so I may not play well with some women, but I don't think the problem is mine. I'm delightful."

"Of course, *a ghra*." Sloan wraps an arm around my back and pulls me against his side for a kiss. "Yer a breath of fresh air—no argument—but let's let Nikon handle Danika his way, aye?"

I shrug. "Fine. I'm not one to argue."

They start laughing again, and I peg them with a look. "All right. Enough Fi-bashing. Let's get our thoughts together on what we are and aren't going to get into with Juniper. Sloan, why did you shake me off telling Juniper that Nikon is a Light Weaver?"

He tilts his head side to side and shrugs. "There's somethin' else going on."

"Other than the warding gone wild, you mean?"

"Aye, I can't put my finger on it yet, but somethin' in that war room set my Spidey-senses tinglin'."

Ha. I love that not only is he so integrated into my world but now he's adopting the way I think.

We are Borg. Resistance is futile.

"What was it that set you off?" I ask. "Something you saw or something you felt?"

He shakes his head, worrying his bottom lip. "I don't know. There's somethin' nigglin' at me. It's beyond my reach for the moment, but I'll figure it out."

"No one doubts that." Nikon brushes his hands clean. "If anyone can figure out the world's mysteries, it's you, Irish."

"So, in the meantime, what?" Diesel asks. "We're stuck in the city, we're not telling them Nikon's a newly ordained Light Weaver, and Sloan's not sure what the glitch is in the matrix. What's our game plan?"

Sloan takes that one. "Juniper said the original wardin' spells were set by the leaders of three sorcery families and woven by the Light Weaver. We need to know what that original spell was so Nikon can unweave it and end this."

"Will that leave the fae prison vulnerable?" I ask.

"Perhaps for a short time." Sloan nods. "A new set of wardin' spells can be put in place in short order."

"They can have the selkies on guard during the process," Manx adds. "Surely, they're not only in place to monitor empty waters. If the warding is as extensive as they led us to believe, what do they do all day?"

"Bask in the sun on bobbing docks?" I say.

Sloan strokes a hand over Manx's head and scrubs his cheek. "That's a good point, sham. It would help to know more about the prison, the capacity of inmates, and what would happen if we took the wardin' down."

"If we can take it down," Nikon says. "My Light Weaver training wasn't as extensive as Emmet's, and while I think your brother is a great guy, as an instructor he was rather like a cocker spaniel puppy with a ball."

That's accurate.

Sloan waves away Nikon's doubts. "Och, I think ye'll be fine, Greek. True, the light weavin' magic might be new to ye, but ye have the fundamentals. Also, I think the rate at which yer spatial magic is growin' will play into things too. Ye'll be grand."

Nikon doesn't look so sure, but if Sloan's confident, we all feel more confident. "All right, I guess our private confab is over. We better get back in there."

By the time we get back into the room, Danika is blissfully absent, and it's only Juniper, Val Ryn, and Trent left awaiting our return.

"So, what were you able to come up with?" Juniper asks. There is a quiet undercurrent of discontent in her voice, and I'm not sure if that is her being a little territorial or if it's more than that.

"We ended up with more questions, and we have answers. We'd like to learn more about the fae prison and how it works."

"The workings of the prison aren't the problem," Val Ryn says. "I think it's best if we keep things simple for the moment and focus on stabilizing the boundary spell."

"Stabilizin' the boundary spell? Is that what ye've been workin' on? I would think it easier to remove the boundary spell completely, ensure the city is again in the proper realm with the ability to come and go, and cast a new perimeter spell around the prison."

Juniper glances at Sloan and offers him a saccharine-sweet smile. "Your expertise on the matter is honed after a mere ten minutes of knowing what we're dealing with?"

"I meant no offense, Grand Governess. It's simply a fact that stabilizin' a spell gone wrong is more difficult than endin' it. Ye've been in a state of flux between realms fer three days. Perhaps yer approach needs to be revisited fer a quicker result."

"Again, you speak of things as if you understand what we've been going through. I have managed to stabilize the spell twice already for a short period. It was your use of unsanctioned portal magic which tipped things off-balance once more."

I raise my finger and shake my head. "I call bullshit on that. The five of us walked through the boundary and still stood on the highway when the city blinked back to the fae realm. Neither Nikon nor Sloan had transported us anywhere. It was only after we were pulled back into the fae realm that Nikon snapped us to Fisherman's Wharf and Golden Gate Park. Sorry, but the failure to stabilize the spell in flux has nothing to do with us."

Maybe I shouldn't have said that, but my father always taught us to speak our minds.

I'm sure Juniper is a skilled female and a wonderful leader, but I'm not going to let her pin her shortcomings on Sloan, Nikon, or our arrival.

"I don't need to stand here while you young upstarts barge in and act as if you know better than we do about our system."

"That's not what's happening here. Since we arrived, your people have attacked us, chastised us, and have now blamed us for what's going on. I'm merely saying that you're wasting time pointing fingers and pinning blame when you could be working with us to find an answer."

"What? Like we aren't working to find an answer? I've been pouring over this console for three days."

"Since you haven't fixed the problem, perhaps fresh eyes would help. Give us a crash course on the prison and the security protocols, and maybe we can help solve this problem."

"I don't have time to teach you about the workings of the prison. That's irrelevant. The key to the stabilization of the city is the warding spell."

"If the warding spell fails, it'll be good to understand what it was in place to do."

"Fine. If you think you know so much, I leave it to you. I'm tired and could use a long, hot bath." Juniper sweeps out of the room with a strong, cool breeze.

I meet the wide-eyed gazes of Trent and Val Ryn. "Believe it or not, it's not the first time I cleared the room by speaking my mind. I didn't mean to offend her, but if what she's been trying isn't working, it's time to at least consider trying something else."

The big blue guy, Trent, fields that one. "I'm sure it'll be all right. When she said she's been working on this for three days, that's true. She is overdue for some time away from the console. Maybe taking a break will do her some good."

"While Fi may have pushed Juniper's buttons, she wasn't wrong," Sloan says. "Our arrival had nothin' to do with the destabilization of the city. And I stand by my statement that to end the spell makes far more sense than tryin' to stabilize it."

"Which anybody who regularly casts spells would know," I add. Trent and Val Ryn share glances, and it's obvious they agree.

"Ye voiced this opinion to her already, haven't ye?"

They nod.

"So, why waste three days to stabilize it instead of ending it and forcing a factory reset?"

Val Ryn shrugs. "She's the boss. We voiced our concerns, she saw it differently, then she set our course."

"Well, now she left it to us." I grin. "How about you catch us up on the security protocols of the prison, the details of how the spell works, and we'll come up with a new plan."

They don't look convinced.

"Fine. Educate us on the system, and we'll talk about a new plan. No commitments…just us putting our collective heads together."

They check in with one another and nod. "Okay," Trent says. "That sounds okay."

CHAPTER SIX

"Do ye have a record of the original spell?" Sloan asks. "Because if ye do, that would be the easiest way for us to decide how to break it. As ye know, the wordin' and the intention are key."

Val Ryn nods. "We're well aware of that, but it doesn't matter what the spell was because we have no way to undo it. They wove it into the very fabric of the area. Without a Light Weaver, we have no way to unweave it."

"And Light Weavers are extinct," Trent adds.

I check in with the guys, and when they give me the nod, I hold up a finger. "Light Weavers *were* extinct up until December of last year. Not anymore."

Val Ryn's head turns so quickly that his blond braid strikes out like a whip from the side of his head. "What do you mean?"

"During our preparation for the Time of the Colliding Realms, our war party—which is my family and friends—were drawn back to the last Culling event. When the Light Weavers back then found out there are no Light Weavers in our time, they ensured there would be by training some of us."

"Are you serious? Because if this is your idea of a joke, it's not funny."

"For reals. Kyna and her sisters trained my brother—they were the guardians of the Hidden City on the island of Emhain Abhlach—and when we returned to our time, he trained Nikon and three others so they could unweave the spell and reveal the city."

"So, you've done this before then," Trent says.

Nikon straightens from where he's staring at the hologram table. "Not exactly this, but the basics remain the same. With experience and my gift in spatial magic leveling up over the past weeks, I think if we had sorcerers from the original three families and the spell, we'd be in good shape."

"You're so full of shit." Danika storms in to join us. "Don't you dare make promises like that to make yourself feel important."

"I wouldn't. Everything I said was true."

"Everything you say is a lie. You should never have come back here. We were doing just fine without you."

I snort. "Yeah, we could tell by how your city is flashing in and out of existence. You're doing amazing. Keep up the good work."

That earns me a dirty look.

Nikon steps forward to get between us. "Look, Dani, I didn't want to come here. I didn't want to stir up bad blood. But I work for a team that unravels problems other people can't fix, and this is where we are. Whether you like it or not—"

"I don't. I hate it."

"Fine. Even though you hate it, I *am* the most qualified person to help in this situation. I will do my best to work with your team and the sorcerers in your city. We will focus on unraveling the current spell, reestablishing a new spell, and getting out of your hair as quickly as possible. Then your city will be safe, and you'll never have to see me again."

"Then let's make that happen as quickly as possible. What do you need to get the job done?"

"We need to figure out the original spell, and it would help if we had access to the heads of the three original families. If by some chance there's a ninety-year-old sorcerer still alive who was there during the original casting, all the better."

I'm not sure if that's going to pan out for us, but yeah, that would be great.

"What does Juniper say about all of this?" She shifts her gaze to Trent and Val Ryn.

"When she left, she said she was washing her hands of things and left it to us to sort out," Trent says. "Honestly, I think the whole ordeal has drained her, and stepping back was a much-needed respite. She hasn't been herself the past three days."

Danika accepts that explanation. "All right. Two minutes to pull up the addresses we need, and I'll meet you out in the courtyard."

As tense as it is between Nikon and Danika, I'm glad she's tightening up and can work with us instead of against us.

As everyone files out, I hang back a bit.

Nikon eyes me up as he steps past. "Are you coming, Red? I think you should stay with us, yeah?"

I pat his arm as he walks past and wink. "I'll be fine, Greek. Just give the girls two seconds. S'all good."

He shakes his head. "I hear what you're saying, but I have a hard time believing this will work in anyone's favor. How about we stick to getting the job done? Seriously, Fi."

I pat him on the back and shoot him toward the door. "Two minutes, Greek. Trust me."

He rolls his eyes. "Famous last words."

I wait till we're alone and join Danika at the war table. She's tapping and typing on the surface of the glass, and I stay quiet so I don't disturb her.

"There's nothing you can say that I want to hear," she says without missing a beat.

"That's perfectly fine. I'll say what I have to say, and we'll get on with our mission. First off, yes, I love and adore Nikon. He's a very dear friend and I would die for him, but I'm *in* love with Sloan, and we're engaged to be married in less than two months. There is nothing romantic between the Greek and me and never has been."

Her fingers hesitate a moment as I'm having my say, but she doesn't look up or give me the satisfaction of a response.

"Second, I know the whole story about why he left, and it wasn't because he wanted to or didn't care for you. You're selling him, yourself, and your love short if you believe the worst of him."

Danika stops typing and glares up at me. "Don't talk to me about my feelings and experience with Nikon. You weren't there. You don't know what it did to me when he left. I may not have been able to see him clearly when we were together, but hindsight is twenty-twenty."

"I'm telling you, there's more to this."

She finishes her search in the system and takes a picture of the screen with her phone. "Even if there is, I don't care. It's been too long and too much has happened for me to forgive him."

"Fair enough. I just wanted to set things straight. If we're going to work together, we'll get a better result if we can at least be civil."

She gestures toward the door. "After you. We've got a city to save."

I flash Nikon an exaggerated smile as we join the men in the courtyard. "See, no drama, nothing to worry about. Despite what you boys think, I am capable of spending time with another alpha female without it devolving into a catfight."

"We stand corrected, *a ghra*. Yer the pinnacle of self-restraint and female grace."

I snort and wave his compliment away. "Now you're making fun of me. Be nice."

He shrugs. "I'm serious. Ye weren't long, there are no signs of a physical altercation, and if I'm bein' honest, ye both look a little less tense and aggressive than ye did when we left the room. Whatever it was ye wanted to get off yer chest, I think ye did well."

I smile and stand a little straighter. "Well, thanks."

What did you say to her, Fi? Nikon asks me.

Nothing private. Just that I'm with Sloan and you're a dear friend and that despite her being hurt and angry we need to work together to save her city.

And that's it?

Mostly.

He arches a brow at me. *And what else?*

Just that maybe you didn't leave because you didn't care about her but because you did.

I'm sure that went over like a lead balloon.

Nope. She didn't say a thing. I had my say and left it at that. S'all good.

Yeah, well, even if it's not, I appreciate you trying.

I look at him and wink. *I will always go to bat for you, Greek. You know that.*

Yeah, I do. Thank the gods for that.

The museum is closed by the time we step outside. The night is clear, and the air is crackling with ambient energy. The air here doesn't smell like cherry Coke. I'm not sure if that's a San Francisco thing or a fae realm thing…or maybe a combo platter of the two.

"We'll meet you by the fountain." Val Ryn points the way, and he and Danika go a different route to get the van.

"If the spatial energy of the city is already out of whack, does it matter if we portal?" I ask.

Trent shrugs, his massive blue arms hanging like sculptured

cabers from his shoulders. "Juniper's rules. She said we're only allowed to portal in the case of violations and criminal activity."

I figure we've rocked Juniper's boat enough for one day, so I let that go and stroll down the steps toward the fountain.

While we're waiting at the pickup loop by the road, I turn back and look at the Legion of Honor lit up for the night. "Dayam, this place has curb appeal."

"Are you dissing *our* building, Fi?" Nikon asks, turning to take in the scene.

"No. I love our building. It's completely functional and private and is the perfect place for us. I'm just saying this building has an architectural impact I find…well, impressive."

Nikon chuckles. "I know what you mean, Fi, and I'm not hurt. If you want a building like this to work from, you'll have to sweet-talk your other Greek. I've got bank but not this much."

"Nah. I'm good. I love our building. Although, I'd love the chance to sweet-talk Dionysus about anything."

Nikon wraps an arm across my shoulders and squeezes me against his side. "Yeah, me too."

"He knows we're thinkin' of him, *a ghra*. He'll be home as soon as he can be, I'm sure."

I accept Sloan's hand and let him pull me into his arms. "I hope so. I miss him."

A black Toyota Sequoia pulls up, and Trent opens the back hatch. "Will your companion be all right in the cargo area? It's going to be tight in the cab for seven of us."

Manx takes a couple of steps and launches into the back. "I'll be fine. Thank you for asking."

I relay Manx's words, climb in the SUV, and head to the back row. Sloan sits beside me, and Nikon slides in beside him. Trent and Diesel take the middle seats, and we're ready to roll.

Val Ryn twists to talk to us from the shotgun seat. "We heard back from Herman Humphrey's attendant. He's available and willing to see us tonight, so we'll start there."

Trent was right when he said things would be snug in the truck, so it's a relief when we stop in the guest circle of the Humphrey estate and we're able to get out and stretch.

"Holy huge house, Herman Humphrey." I blink up at the stone mansion. "When does a house become a castle, hotness? Is it like when a hamlet becomes a village when it gets a place of worship, and a town when it has a population over a certain number?"

"I don't think so, no," Sloan says.

"Because this is almost as big as Stonecrest Castle."

Sloan chuckles and wraps an arm around me and tugs me out of the way so Nikon can get out of the truck and close the door. "To be a legitimate castle, there must be fortifications."

I search the turrets, the belltower, and the dormer windows. No battlements. "All righty then. When can you call something a palace?"

Danika hits the hatch release, and Manx trots around to join us.

"All right, shall we?" Trent says.

A piece of paper flutters in front of Danika. She grabs it and frowns. "Wait. Annalise Templeton just got back to me. She's leaving for a fundraiser fashion show across town in an hour. Either we meet her now, or she's busy until tomorrow afternoon."

Seriously? "Busy? We're trying to save the city and the lives of everyone in it. Can't she be late for a fashion show for a good cause?"

Danika lifts a shoulder. "I'm reading the message I got."

"Yeah, not your fault. Okay, why don't you, Trent, Sloan, and Manx go speak to Ms. Templeton and Val Ryn can escort Nikon, Diesel, and me to hear what Herman Humphrey has to say?"

That seems to be an acceptable plan. Sloan brushes his lips over mine. "Stay close to Diesel and the Greek, luv. I don't want you lost in the city when everything is going haywire."

I chuckle and hold up two fingers. "Scout's honor."

He and Manx hop back into the SUV's back seat while Danika and Trent climb in the front. When they're driving off, we return our attention to the huge stone house. "All right, boys. Let's getter done."

Val Ryn jogs up the front steps, and I envy his natural grace. Being around Suede gives me the same hit to my ego. Elves are that fluid in their movements.

"Is there anything we should know about Herman Humphrey?" I ask.

"You like saying his name, don't you?" Nikon asks.

"Maybe." I shrug unrepentant and return my focus to Val Ryn. "Anything we should know?"

He stops on the platform of the top step and turns to us. "The Humphreys are one of the oldest and most powerful families in the empowered community of San Francisco. Not only in the sorcery community but all the empowered in the city."

"Are they amicable, difficult, entitled..." I hope for some inkling of what to expect.

He fingers the twin braids running down the side of his face behind his gently tipped ears and brushes a hand down his tunic. "Sorry. Juniper handles all the interactions with the prison, including the boundary spell and the prison warding. I'm rather stunned she walked away. It is unlike her to allow other people to have a say in her territory."

I'm not sure what to think about that. We didn't even dig in all that much. She threw in the towel quite easily. The sound of several metal deadbolts *clicking* open has us straightening and presenting a united front.

Except when the door opens, there's no one there.

"Hello?" I lean in the opening of the doorway. "Herman Humphrey?"

"Seriously, Fi." Nikon chuckles. "Stop."

I stick my tongue out at him and step inside. My shield isn't burning or tingling or anything, so there's no major cause for alarm. The door unlocked itself and invited us in.

That's totes normal.

"Anyone home?"

I take a couple of cautious steps inside the grand foyer and wander around the marble fountain. "How crazy is it that I've never considered putting a fountain in my front entrance?"

Diesel chuckles. "I was thinking the same thing."

"Of course, I'd have to get rid of a few pesky things like my table and chairs, but who needs those?"

Val Ryn and Diesel are looking at me.

I chuckle and shrug. "It's a Cumhaill thing. We prattle off on tangents sometimes."

Nikon nods. "Most times they're amusing though."

"Glad we keep you amused—oh!" I duck as the movement of a living projectile soars at me from the chandelier over the fountain.

CHAPTER SEVEN

I didn't duck far enough out of the way. A gentle *thud* to the side of my head precedes something landing on my shoulder and grappling my hair as it falls down my back. "What the hell is on me? Is it a bat? I think it might've been a bat."

"I'm not a bat," a voice says, climbing back to my shoulder. "Why would you think I'm a bat? I have fur and stripes and a tail." To punctuate his point, a long, beige tail curls around my shoulder and the end tickles my nose. "Prehensile tail, I should add."

I step deeper into the entrance and twist in front of what looks like a centuries-old gilded mirror. Shifting around enough to see the back of my shoulder, I chuckle at the little furball with round brown eyes and a stripe down his forehead that ends at his little pink nose.

"You are adorable."

"I am, aren't I?"

"And you talk."

"Since I was a toddler, yes. May I say, your hair smells lovely." The sugar glider adjusts its position on my shoulder, grips my hair, and pushes it up against his face. He pulls in a long, audible breath and sighs. "Divine. Is that ylang-ylang I detect?"

"It might well be. A girlfriend of mine made it for me for Yule."

"She has a gift."

"She's a tree nymph, so I expect she has more than a few gifts when it comes to natural products." Craning my neck to my shoulder to speak to him isn't great, so I hold up my flat hand for him to climb onto. "What is your name, sugar?"

He chuckles and ambles onto the platform of my palm. "A little play on words. Well turned. My name is Herman. Herman Humphrey."

"Named after your patriarch, are you?"

"Actually, no. I am, indeed, a one of a kind."

It takes a moment for my mental hamster to get its wheel moving enough to understand. "You're presently a sugar glider."

"Presently, yes."

"I take it you ran into a problem with a spell."

He sits back on his haunches. "How did you know?"

I chuckle and shrug. "A wild guess. A dear friend of mine was invisible for two days a while back. It wore off though, and he's back to normal now. How long have you been this way?"

"Five months."

"Oh dear, I'm sorry. That's quite a bit longer than two days."

"Considerably, yes."

"So, this happened at the time the veil first fell?"

"It did. I was working on a particularly complex spell and with the sudden flux and surge of power instability...well, things didn't exactly go as planned."

"Is there anything we can do to help?"

"I don't suppose there is, no. I've had more than a few experts try."

"Well, I'm sorry you're out of sorts. I hope the situation resolves itself for you quickly."

"Yes, well, I've stopped holding my breath. It's not so bad being a marsupial. Look, I have this nifty pouch to hold things in." He opens the little furry flap on his belly to show me.

"Very nice."

Val Ryn clears his throat.

Right. "As much as I'm enjoying this exchange, yes, I suppose we should get to the point of our visit so we can leave you to your evening."

"Very well, but don't think for a moment your presence is an imposition. I so rarely get visitors, and since my little mishap, I haven't been able to leave the house."

"Well, then, could we come in and sit? We were hoping to speak with you about the spell cast around Alcatraz back in the day. It seems it too has been affected by the fall of the veil."

"Really? Do tell. I haven't been able to stay up-to-date on the latest these days."

Herman directs us into the receiving parlor, and we take a seat.

"It's astounding to look at the world from a different perspective. Being this small, you look as tall as a tree, young man."

I glance at where Diesel is taking up and overflowing an antique chair. "It's not only because you're small. Diesel is a big guy from any perspective."

"Before we begin, can I offer you anything? A warm drink? A cold drink? My undying affections?"

I chuckle at the flirtatious tone and how he bats his eyes at me. "No, thank you. We're fine."

He hops off my hand, lands on the marble bust on the coffee table in front of me, and lays starfished over the statue's head like a furry toupee. Lifting his tiny hand, he props it under his chin and leans into his elbow. "So, tell me, Fiona, what brings you and your harem to my humble abode?"

It's a fight not to giggle. They aren't my harem, the house is in no way humble, and he's so damned cute laying there in front of me I can't stand it. Still, I let his comment pass in favor of forwarding progress.

Over the next ten minutes, we fill Herman in on everything the world has been through in the past five months. Some of it he's heard from his doorman and cleaning staff, but for the most part, it seems he has become disconnected from the world.

We explain about San Francisco phasing in and out between realms and how stabilizing it hasn't worked. "So, we intend to shut down the original containment spell to reestablish the city in its proper place. Then we can cast a new spell to secure Alcatraz. What we need to know is the details of the original spell. From what we know, your grandfather was one of the three sorcerers involved. Did he keep a grimoire or a journal where he might have archived the particulars of the spell?"

Herman waves his little tail through the air like a waggling finger. "Oh, no, no. Herman Humphrey the Second was much too committed to his oath of secrecy to write something like that down. Even if he had, your real problem is not having a Light Weaver to unravel the spell. That's your stumbling block."

"What if we know of a Light Weaver who could help? Do you think the other two sorcerers involved might've documented the spell?"

"It's possible, but if what you've told me is true, and San Francisco is locked in a phasing cycle with no way to communicate to the outside world, how could you send for your Light Weaver?"

"Assume that's not a problem. If we can get the spell and the Light Weaver, would you be willing to help us?"

His tail arches up and points at himself. "Me? You're asking me, a furry rodent with winged armpits, to help destroy one of the most intricate and powerful spells ever conceived? Are you making me the butt of your joke?"

"Not at all. You're here, and even in this form you have wisdom, and I'm sure some level of magic. Maybe you don't have the original spell, but you have access to your grandfather's life experiences and knowledge. You might still be able to help us."

"You sing a jaunty tune, Fiona Cumhaill. I'll give you that."

He doesn't sound convinced, so I sweeten the pot a little. "You can come with us while we speak to the other family heads. It'll be good for you to get out of the house. You never know, when this is over, I might be able to round you up a legendary wizard who could help with your current state."

"Oh? How legendary are we talking, Red?"

"A certain black sheep of Arthur's court. Wizard. Enchanter. Advisor."

Herman's round eyes grow impossibly wide. "Are you name-dropping who I think you are, little minx?"

I chuckle. "I never dropped a name."

"Well turned. I suppose that's true. Still, I follow your meaning and am captivated by your allusion. Yes, if you think he might help me in my time of—well, I suppose to call it a time of need is melodramatic. How about my time of not being myself?"

"I think that's fair."

He nods. "So, yes, if you're willing to help me in my time of not being myself, I will help you in your quest to stabilize the city."

"Excellent. We're off to meet with our counterparts, find a place to eat and sleep for the night, and will be back to pick you up in the morning."

His tail waggles at me again. "I have fourteen bedrooms upstairs and a keen interest in spending more time basking in your charms. You will, of course, stay here for as long as you're in town. I insist."

I check in with Diesel and Nikon. They don't seem to have an opinion one way or another, so I go with it. "That's very kind of you, Herman. Thank you for your hospitality."

"It is my pleasure. I'll inform Ms. Chanson we have guests.

How many rooms will we need prepared and how many mouths to feed?"

I think about that. "I'm sure those who live here in San Fran will stay in their own homes. My fiancé and—"

"A fiancé? Oh, some lucky chap has bested me. My hopes are dashed in one cruel word."

I chuckle and continue. "Yes, my fiancé and his animal companion are with the other team. So, we are four and a lynx."

"A lynx? The creature is housebroken, I presume."

"Completely."

"He doesn't make it a habit of consuming small marsupials?"

"No. He does not."

"That's reassuring. Very well. Give me a moment to confer with my staff, and I'll join you for a dinner out while you meet up with your party."

"Excellent. We'll wait right here."

He rises from his toupee sprawl over the marble noggin of a very dignified-looking man and looks around. "Sasquatch, any chance you can give me a boost? Crawling along the floor is demeaning. Carry me to the doorway and shotput me toward the back of the house, would you?"

I bite my bottom lip and try not to laugh. The look on Diesel's face is priceless. When he looks at me, I shrug. "Try not to shotput him into a wall."

"Do I look like a guy with no coordination?"

"No. You look like a guy who could free throw a marsupial sorcerer halfway across the city."

"Just a boost," Herman repeats, standing on his back legs and reaching toward Diesel. "I'll do the rest."

Good sport that he is, Diesel carries our host to the doorway of the parlor and launches him toward the back of the house. When he finishes watching the result, he comes back to join us.

"I didn't hear any crash or splat, so I assume all went well with the shot-putting?" I say.

"I assume so. He's an aerodynamic old guy."

Nikon laughs. "I bet when you woke up this morning wondering what your first day on Fiona's team would be like, you didn't imagine free-throwing elderly sorcerers through a mansion."

"Right you are. I did *not*."

I chuckle. "See? I told you this would be fun."

The four of us reconnect with Sloan over dinner at Tony's Pizza Napoletana. "Located in the heart of San Francisco's Little Italy, Home of thirteen-time World Pizza Champion Tony Gemignani. Tony brings his passion and perfection to North Beach, sharing his award-winning pizzas with us all."

I finish reading out of my tour guide, and Nikon looks at Sloan. "Tonight, when she's asleep, don't be alarmed if I sneak into your room and take that book."

I chuckle and tuck it back into my purse. "Rude. I'm enriching our experience of this fair city. Usually, Sloan is the one giving us the cultural experience, but he's never been here. Someone needs to take up the mantle."

He shakes his head. "You're ridiculous."

"I remind her of that almost every day," Sloan says. "She knows it and doesn't care."

"Live your truth, amirite?" The San Fran clan isn't jumping into this, so I defend myself. "I've never been held captive by a city before. If this is my forever home, I want to know what I'm in for."

Sloan wipes his mouth and reaches for his beer. "Throwin' in the towel, are ye?"

"Me? Not even a little. I still believe we'll getter done." I take another sip of my beer. It's a honey blond, and it's quite nice. When I set it back onto the table, I check in with our dinner guest. "Is there something wrong with your pizza, Herman? You're not eating."

"I wish it tasted half as good as it smells. Not being myself has its drawbacks, I'm afraid. The worst part is that if a bug flew past me, I might eat it. I am enjoying the pineapple. Might they have a little honey into which to dip?"

"I'll ask our server on my way back." Nikon gets up from the table.

Danika's icy gaze follows him as he pushes through the door to the restroom. Yeah, they have a major storm brewing.

I hope Nikon is ready to weather it.

"So, Annalise Templeton wasn't much help?" I paraphrase what Danika told us when we first joined up again.

"Not much, I'm afraid. We were an inconvenience."

Sloan nods. "She was much more interested in whether sitting down to speak to us would crease her dress before her event than helping us save the city."

"Just like her mother before that. Georgia Templeton was a goddess of a woman, but the past two iterations have been lackluster. Georgia's heirs have always thought too highly of their standing in society to realize the greatness of the woman who got them there."

"So, you don't get on well with them?" I ask Herman.

"Your two families co-host the All Hallows event every October," Trent says. "I got the impression you were all friends."

A sugar glider belly laughing is a funny sight.

"Oh, that's a good one, large blue man," Herman says. "The truth is, in public we are as thick as thieves while in reality, I've never had the patience to stroke Annalise's ego, nor her mother's."

There's a sharp tone in his words that points to a personal grudge between our furry old guy and the suave and sophisticated Templeton women.

Although, he seems quite fond of Georgia.

Maybe she gave him a cookie as a young lad, and he formed an attachment. With the age gap, he couldn't have been much more than a teenager when she died.

"So, Annalise doesn't have the spell either?" Diesel digs into his second cheeseburger platter. One thing about a guy his size... he can eat.

Sloan shrugs. "She says she'll have a look for it the first chance she gets but warns that this is a busy time for her and the industry she supports."

"The fashion industry?" I clarify. "She believes she supports the entire industry?"

Nikon returns with a small bowl of pineapple with honey drizzled over it and sets it on the table in front of Herman.

"She likely does," Herman says. "She is the queen of flitting around in shops all day spending money...that is, when she's in town. Her jet barely has time to idle on the tarmac before she's flying off to Milan or New York or lately it's been the UAE."

I can't imagine.

I enjoy having a couple of nice dresses for a fancy occasion, but I've never been one of the salon types. More power to them but paying someone eighty dollars every time I want to have my nails polished would be a personal kind of hell for me.

To each their own.

I'll pay fifteen bucks and buy a bottle of Blue Crush at Walmart.

I pick a piece of ham off the slice on my plate and pop it into my mouth. "All right, well, maybe Annalise will circle and get back to us. We still have a chance with Joseph McWinn."

"Joseph McLose, you mean," Humphrey scoffs. "That man doesn't have a magical bone in his body. If you look up 'riding the coattails of greatness' in the Grimoire of the Gray Lords, you'll see Joey's photo."

"Are you saying he's not a practicing sorcerer?"

"No amount of practicing will mold a sorcerer out of that lump of useless clay."

Oh dear. I take another long swallow of my drink and meet Sloan's grim expression. "We really needed one of the three to help us with that spell, didn't we?"

"Aye, we did. Fer Nikon to unravel it without knowin' how it went together is not only foolhardy but dangerous. On the other hand, if we don't try to shut it down, this city will be lost to the fae realm and likely us with it."

Thus, the grim expression.

"Wait, what?" Herman is shoving chunks of pineapple into his mouth. "You said Nikon would unravel it. How? Are you a Light Weaver, lad?"

"One of my hidden talents, yes."

"Very hidden." Danika scowls. "Like so hidden, it's hard to believe."

Nikon takes the insult in stride. "Some of my best skills are hidden and hard to believe. That doesn't make them any less impressive."

Before the tension between them devolves into a public scene, I lift my chin and raise my hand to signal for the server to swing by our table.

"On that note, the San Fran team is free to go home and call it a day, and the Toronto crew will take our uneaten pizza back to Herman's place and start brainstorming. It's been a long day. Maybe something will come to us in the witching hours. We'll reconvene at nine. If you don't mind swinging by Humphrey House to pick us up, we would appreciate it."

Val Ryn gets to his feet and tosses a twenty on the table. "See you in the morning. Sweet dreams."

CHAPTER EIGHT

"This is some house, eh?" I stare open-mouthed at the view outside our bedroom window. "Do you think there's a hunchback in that bell tower up there?"

I search the stone arches above, seeing nothing but the ancient bell.

Sloan chuckles, pulling our toiletry kit out of our duffle. "If Quasimodo comes to abscond with ye in the night, I'll fight to keep ye safe in my arms. Fear not, my sweet Esmeralda."

I chuckle. "I'm the kinda girl who fights to keep herself safe, hotness, but thanks for being my wingman."

He winks, returning his attention to unpacking while I sink into a moment of quiet contemplation and stare out the window.

The house was impressive this afternoon and is even more impressive at night.

Tall windows reflect the light of the two moons of the fae realm while ornate balcony railings guard darkened alcoves behind them. Above our room, three stories above, the complicated roofline follows undulating turrets, more windows, more balconies, and a bunch of wide stone chimneys.

This is prime real estate, but I suppose if the Humphreys have been here for generations, they got first dibs on a good spot to build their dream home. "This place is a bit more secret passageways and gothic horror than the stone erosion and Scottish heather of Stonecrest Castle."

He chuckles. "Tease me about my home all ye like, *a ghra*. I know it's growin' on ye. In fact, I'd say yer developin' a healthy respect fer the old-world charms of historic architecture."

"That's how brainwashing works. Over time, opinions get muddied, and one day I'll wake up and be a Stepford wife."

"I highly doubt that's possible." He finishes setting our clothes in neat piles on top of the dresser and saunters over. Standing at my back, he wraps his arms around me and rests his chin on my shoulder. "If anythin' *I'm* the one who is bein' brainwashed. The muddied opinion waters are mine. Ye've practically turned my world upside down and inside out over the past two years."

I turn my head and kiss his cheek. "Same."

We stand like that for a few minutes, staring at Alcatraz and the mauve haze beyond. "What do you suppose lays beyond the pocket of San Francisco in this realm? Can creatures and beings out there get in here? Should we be concerned?"

"I don't know. I suppose we should consider it, especially since the time spent here versus our home realm is heavily weighted toward us bein' here."

"For the moment, at least. Tomorrow's a new day."

"Aye, it is."

Bruin ghosts in and takes form in front of the fireplace mantle. Manx trots in soon after.

"Did you boys have fun exploring?" I ask.

"Aye, we did," Bruin says. "The grounds here are spelled much like the grove. We had a good run through green grasses and the wee labyrinth out back."

My shield tingles to life, and I pause to study our surroundings.

"Is something the matter, *a ghra?*"

"Nothing too pressing. Just a warm tingle...and sadly, not the good kind."

Sloan has experienced enough of my shield's interjections into our daily lives to know what that means. He frowns and raises his palms to start a sweep of the room.

I sit on the edge of the bed to get out of his way while he takes point on securing us for the night.

"One of those nondescript, not helpful kinds of warm tingles?"

"You guessed it."

I admire him as he moves around the room—both aesthetically and professionally.

Yeah, I'm a lucky girl.

He examines the rich walnut paneling of the walls, the pictures behind the overstuffed sofa, and the rows of spines lined up on the bookshelf. He screens the thick draperies and broad swaths of buttermilk marble that make up the fireplace.

"Anything?"

"Not that I can sense."

A note slides under our door and flutters up and through the air to find me by the bed.

Sloan finishes his search and strides over to listen as I read it to him. "If it pleases you both. I am enjoying a nightcap in my workroom. You are welcome to join me." I check the time on my phone. "It's almost eleven. Do you want to go for a drink or go to bed?"

Sloan lifts a shoulder. "I'm always interested in seein' the workrooms of magical folks. Ye never know what ye might pick up that could be of use."

"True. Mostly, I like the idea of a nightcap."

"That's because yer a wee lush."

"Says the Irishman who's never passed a pub without *stoppin' in fer a wee pint*," I say in a thick Irish accent.

"You two go." Manx jumps onto the end of the bed and curls

around in circles before laying down. "We'll guard the bedchamber and hold down the fort."

I chuckle. "Yeah, sure. You do that."

The invitation tugs at my fingers, so I let go and free it to fly away. Only it doesn't fly away. It flutters toward the door and hovers in the air.

"Is it waiting for us?" I ask.

The top edge bends and straightens as if it's nodding.

"All righty, then. Let the night capping begin."

"Do ye need me to come with?" Bruin asks.

"I don't think so, buddy. We won't leave the house without letting you know. Enjoy roasting your chestnuts by the open fire."

"Chestnuts? Rude. I'll have ye know—"

I laugh and get out the door before I have to hear the end of that sentence.

We scoot down a candlelit hallway and watch as the nightcap note dances in the air in front of us. It leads us to the narrow servant's staircase at the back of the house, up a flight, and over to the corner of the house and one of the large stone turrets.

"If I had a house like this, I'd make the turret room into my magic room too. It feels very sorcerery."

"Sorcerery?" Sloan repeats, his mouth quirked up at the side.

"You know what I'm saying."

"Aye, this is one of the rare times I do."

I give him that, and the two of us arrive at the end of the hall. The note abandons us and slides under the arched door. A moment later, it swings open.

I start to head inside, but a barrier prohibits my passage through the opening.

"Come in, friends. Come in."

The resistance to keep me out vanishes and I step through unimpeded.

"Welcome to my sanctuary." Herman stands on his back feet

and waves us in. His furry little wing flaps are so cute I can hardly stand it. If he wasn't a sixty-year-old man stuck in that cutie-patootie sugar glider, I'd be snuggling the hell out of him.

"Wow, this place is nice."

The stone wall of the turret rises two stories to a peaked ceiling. An iron circular staircase in the corner climbs to a platform above and gives access to an exit onto the roof.

The far wall is back-lit glass with an uneven surface.

Water trickles and splashes down the textured contours, falling from the top and making its way into a small pool of turquoise water.

"This is an incredible space, Herman," Sloan says.

"I don't generally allow people in here, but I hoped we could enjoy a dram or two of premium Irish whiskey and perhaps review the spell that brought me to my current state."

Sloan nods. "I'd be happy to take a look, but Fiona was right about the best option bein' Merlin himself."

"Yes, I agree that would be ideal, but that might take some time given that our city isn't even in the same realm of existence."

"True story," I say. The man has been a plush toy for five months now. I understand his need to get back to his previous life.

Sloan nods. "Let's see what we're dealing with."

Herman points at a bottle on the spellbook shelf against the wall. "Would you mind pouring? I don't think I could manage. Oh, and I'll take mine in a saucer if it's no trouble."

I'm not sure what the tolerance of a natural sugar glider is, but the Herman Humphrey sugar glider can really lap it up. The three of us spend the next hour going over the spell, and while I don't understand the specifics of magic that isn't based solely in nature, Sloan does.

The two of them strike off on a couple of very brain-twisty sidebars that I try to follow…and fail miserably.

"But yer intention was clear enough that it shouldn't be too difficult to undo," Sloan says. "Have ye considered askin' another local sorcerer ye trust to help?"

"The key point of that suggestion is a local sorcerer I trust. There isn't one magic practitioner in this city who I would trust to bring me my mail let alone try to reinstate me to my body."

"Maybe Nikon could help," I suggest. "He dated Hecate for years and studied everything he could to find a way out of his cursed existence. He knows a lot about witchcraft."

"Witchcraft and sorcery aren't the same things, luv," Sloan corrects. "Still, he might have some insight he could share with us."

"Do you want me to go wake him up?" I ask.

"No, no." Herman waves his little pink hand. "It'll keep until the morning. Speaking of which, the two of you should get off to bed. I don't want to be accused of being a poor host. You both need your rest."

I'd argue, but I am quite exhausted.

"We'll see you in the morning then?"

"Wouldn't miss it. I'll have breakfast ready for eight since we expect your counterparts at nine."

"You don't need to go to any trouble," I say. "We can pick something up as we drive."

He gasps, covering his open mouth with his paw. "Drive-thru breakfast? We're not savages, Red. There will be a proper breakfast for you and your party at eight in the main dining room."

There's no space for debate in his tone, so I nod and accept the hospitality. "Thank you, Herman. We look forward to it."

The moment my head hits the pillow, I'm out cold. Maybe it was the long day, the Irish whiskey, or the fact that the air in this realm doesn't make my skin tingle all day long. Whatever the reason, I black the hell out and am lost to the world within minutes.

My dream morphs into something "other" soon after.

One of the more useful side effects of being a Celtic shaman is that my mind and body have become acutely attuned to moments when reality bends and something magically influenced begins to happen.

One moment, I'm running through the wild forest of the Don Valley River System with my brothers, training and laughing, and the next moment, I'm tingling all over.

I stop running, and Calum and Emmet continue without me, laughing and ribbing me about being a loser.

My worldview morphs and I'm standing on a cobbled street outside an Italian restaurant, and a tall, dark and handsome god with brunette curls and a seductive grin is standing right in front of me.

"Dionysus? Is that really you?"

"What, you think someone could pull all this off without being me?" He waves a flourishing hand in front of himself and waggles his brows.

I close the distance and hug him with everything I've got. With every fiber of my being, I hope that whatever he needed to do has been done and he's coming home. "Thank you for saving Sloan, Tarzan, but—"

I'm about to say he shouldn't have done it when I catch myself. Losing Sloan to those hobgoblins would've crushed me. Nikon was right when he said that Dionysus knew exactly what he was risking and why.

"I love you, Tarzan. I love you, and I miss you."

"I love you too, but as much as I want to come home to my family, I still have penance to do and stipulations to live up to."

"After that, you'll be home?"

He steps back and holds my shoulders as he looks me over. "The very moment I'm released from my obligations I'll be there. We'll wear silly onesies and make umbrella drinks and spend frivolous amounts of time marathoning rom-coms for days."

"I can't wait."

A shadow edging into my dream is subtle at first, a feather brushing the synapses of my mind. The vibration of a gentle tap of a finger on a spider's web.

Dionysus shakes his head, so I don't let on that I'm aware of the intrusion. Instead, I relish in the joy of spending time, however short, with my dear friend.

"How are you?" I pull him to the table we shared on the patio the day we got pizza in Italy. "Are they treating you well? They aren't being mean to you, are they?"

His grin is sweet sorrow and makes my heart ache. "No one is being mean to me. It's not the same as being with my family but...well, I suppose that's not true. They *are* my family by blood but not my family by choice. I miss you guys and my loft and Contessa McSparkles and helping with Team Trouble work."

My shield fires to life and my instincts kick in. The shadow is edging closer.

What is that...or who?

I don't want to waste a moment of my time, so I return to Dionysus. "We miss you too, sweetie. So much."

He leans his elbows on the table across from me and takes my hands in his. The sun is hot where it rests on my skin, but I don't think I need to worry about burning.

This is a dream after all.

Dionysus reaches forward and brushes my cheek with his thumb. "Don't cry, Jane. I'm all right. Everything will be all right."

"You're suffering because you did something selfless. They shouldn't punish you for that."

He moves to the chair next to me and leans in, pulling me

against his chest. I breathe deep, relishing his scent—magic and summer sunshine.

The invading entity pushes further into our space, and I'm getting pissed.

First off, this is a private party, and we didn't send out invitations for anyone else to attend.

Second, whoever is invading my personal space isn't only probing my subconscious mind and spying on me. They're trying to get inside my head.

Too bad for them it's a jungle up there.

Dionysus eases back and frowns. "You need to go back, Jane."

"I don't want to. I've missed your face too much to give it up now."

He winks. "I'll find you again soon, I promise."

"You better. I'm heartbroken you sacrificed yourself. I'm thankful and proud of you and love you more than ever, but I'm heartbroken."

He kisses my forehead. "When I get back, can we go to Italy again for pizza for reals? Just you and me?"

"Anything you want."

"Can I have a kitten?"

Squirrel.

I laugh. "Yep. We'll pick it out together, and I'll help you get all the supplies you need."

He pulls me against his chest and kisses my cheek. "Don't forget me, Jane."

"Impossible. You're utterly unforgettable."

"Thank you for noticing."

"Tell Irish to take good care of you until I get back. He owes me that."

"I'll tell him."

His smile is as warm and real as always, and I drink in the sight of him. "Okay, then. It's time for you to wake up."

I gasp, my eyes flipping open as I reach for him.

Only Dionysus is gone, and I'm grappling Sloan. "What is it, *a ghra*? Did ye have one of yer nightmares?"

"No. It wasn't a nightmare. I dreamed about Dionysus…only it wasn't a dream. It was real. He was there. We were in Italy at our table where we got pizza when Loki was tormenting him."

"Ye didn't portal there, luv. I was holdin' ye here as ye cried."

I wipe my cheeks with the tips of my fingers, and yeah, I'm a mess. "Okay, give me a minute to splash water on my face and sort out my thoughts."

The room is mostly dark, the light from the two moons of the fae realm casting the only illumination into the space. I pad barefooted to the bathroom, navigating the furry mass of Bruin as I go.

I take a couple of minutes in the en suite and reset.

By the time I crawl back under the covers and sink into Sloan's awaiting arms, I've settled myself. "Tarzan came to me in a dream…only I'm sure it wasn't a dream. He wanted to check in and tell me he was all right. He misses us and is taking care of his obligations. Then he'll be home. It was real. I know it was."

"I have no doubt, luv. Ye've had enough adventures on the astral plane and walkin' dreamscapes to know what's real and what's not. It makes perfect sense that he'd visit ye that way when he's prohibited to come in person."

I know all those things myself, but hearing Sloan say so validates it even more. "Thank you for believing me and believing it was real."

He eases back so we're lying chest-to-chest and nose-to-nose. "Of course. Did he say anything else?"

"Just to make sure you take care of me…and that we're his real family and he misses us."

Sloan hugs me. "He'll be home soon. Ye'll see. Now. Close yer eyes and get a few more hours of rest."

CHAPTER NINE

I'm coaxed from bed by the succulent scent of bacon and the hopes of finding a pot of coffee brewing. I'm not disappointed. By the time Sloan, Manx, and I make it down to the main dining room, there is a full-out breakfast spread across the buffet against the wall and enough coffee and tea to get all of San Fran perked up.

"This smells wonderful." I nod at Diesel and Nikon already seated.

"Tastes that way too," Diesel agrees. "I worried we should wait for you, but Nikon said you wouldn't mind."

"No. Not at all." I head straight for the coffee and Sloan opts to pour himself some tea. "Growing up with five brothers and my father working a lot to keep the household afloat, it was elbows up and fend for yourself for most things in our house. I don't stand on formality."

"Fiona! You're here!" Herman launches off the shoulder of an older woman wearing an apron and carrying a tray of pastries. Being used as a springboard knocks her off her stride a little.

Herman either doesn't notice or doesn't care.

He lands on the table, knocking over the saltshaker and swiping his tail over the butter.

The look on his housekeeper's face is telling. She's not a fan of her boss at the moment. Maybe that's because he's a nuisance as a sugar glider or maybe she's never been much of a fan.

I set my cup and saucer at an open place setting and toss some of the spilled granules of salt over my left shoulder.

Diesel stares at me, looking confused.

"You don't do that?"

"Throw salt? No. Not usually."

I chuckle and accept the empty plate Sloan is offering me. "The superstition goes that to spill salt is bad luck. To remedy the gaffe, you're supposed to throw salt over your left shoulder with your right hand to blind the devil and keep him from taking your soul."

"If you believe in a devil," he says.

"Devil, demon, trickster, ghoul…there are many dark and dangerous sides to the same coin. Call it what you will. It can't hurt to cover your bases."

"Especially with the way things slide downhill fer us." Sloan strides to the table with a full plate.

"We may not be lucky, but we are very fortunate." I try not to tempt fate or piss off the universe. "In the end, everything generally works out."

"It just takes us a bit to get there," Nikon says.

I use the steel tongs to select a couple of poached eggs, bacon, and potato wedges and snag a slice of whole wheat toast before returning to the table. "Thank you both so much for the breakfast of champions. This is amazing."

Herman has crawled over to the head of the table and is sitting on his placemat nibbling on fruit dipped in honey. "It's amazing to have people here to talk to. If all it takes is a little breakfast on the griddle, I am pleased to make that happen."

I'm not so sure his house lady agrees, but hey, today she earned her keep.

Over the next ten minutes, I recount our conversation last night about Herman's spell and our thoughts about whether or not Nikon might be able to help.

"I might, but Danika or Val Ryn might be better. The power that's been leveling up inside me is amazing, but it's more like power than magic if that makes sense."

I finish chewing and take a run at that. "Your ability to manipulate spatial energy is growing, but it's not the same as spellcasting?"

"Exactly right."

"Okay, I'll talk to them today and see if they have any interest in helping us."

Herman reaches for another cube of kiwi and pauses. "Can we try to keep the conversation restricted to those who need to know? Other than Ms. Chanson, my butler Warren, and you and the others from last night, no one knows what's befallen me. If possible, I'd prefer to keep it that way."

The fact that he doesn't want the other members of his magical society to know is perfectly understandable. "We'll make sure to keep it between us, I promise."

"Excellent. I appreciate that."

After I finish with my plate, I set my dishes on the tray on the sideboard and pull out my phone to call Danika. Right. The black screen reminds me there's no checking in that way while no networks are available.

How did people survive before phones? Maybe we should lead the pack and coax the neighborhood pigeons to join us.

"How hard is it to train messenger pigeons?"

Sloan lowers his teacup and smiles. "Fer druids, likely not as difficult as it is for others."

"A-ha, we have an edge. I like it."

Herman sets his last square of passionfruit down and wipes his little pink hands on a cloth napkin. "I have some old cans and string we could use."

I chuckle. "We'll put that on the back burner for now, but a good idea."

Sure, I'm joking, but I don't relish the idea of being stranded here for much longer.

As if on cue, one of those long, melodious doorbell songs starts bing-bonging at the front of the house.

"It looks like the rest of team Save the City have arrived."

"Excellent." Herman takes a running leap at me and lands on my boob.

"Did you cop a feel, Herman?" I grab him and move him up to my shoulder.

"Heavens no. I would never. That was an honest navigational error."

Yeah no, I'm not buying that. "Well, let's try not to have any more navigational errors. My girls are not your landing cushions."

"Point taken."

Nikon is dying laughing, and I shoot him a dirty look. "You're not helping."

He shrugs and follows me out to the grand entrance with the others. "I give the man points for ingenuity. I bet you never thought you'd have a flying squirrel getting handsy with you."

"I'm a sugar glider, and I already explained it was a navigational error."

"Of course, it was," Nikon says.

Greek's easygoing humor falls flat the moment the door opens, and Danika pegs him with a glare. "Committed to the seriousness of the situation, I see."

Nikon sobers and offers her a smile. "Good morning, Dani. I hope you slept well."

There's an awkward pause while the two of them exchange terse glares, then look anywhere but at one another. "Trent, Val Ryn, good to see you both again."

I glance at Sloan, but as always, he has a polite smile that tells me nothing about how he's reading this situation. He's so damned polite.

"Thanks for swinging back to pick us up," I say. "Were you able to get in touch with Joseph McWinn?"

"McLose," Herman mutters under his breath.

"He's expecting us. Shall we go?" Danika gestures at the two vehicles at the bottom of the stairs behind her.

"Sure. Let me call our companions." My first impulse is to cup my mouth and holler up the steps, but I catch myself. When in a high-class mansion, do as the high-class would, amirite?

I close my eyes and focus on my connection with Bruin. *We're ready to roll out, Bear. Can you and Manx join us at the front door?*

On our way.

I nod. "Okay, they're coming."

Val Ryn looks curious about that. Did he not realize druids can communicate with our companion animals through mental communication?

Maybe I misread that, and he's simply wondering what surprises the day might hold.

Manx trots down the stairs and joins us. At the same time, a familiar breeze swirls around me and settles in my chest. Bruin takes his place, and when the flutter of his positioning ends, we're ready to roll.

"All set. Let's go save a city."

After the fashion heiress and the sugar glider eccentric, I'm almost afraid of what we'll find when we meet Joseph McWinn. The house looks innocent enough. It's a good size, but not a mansion like Humphrey House. Nothing seems odd, and my shield isn't weighing in.

That's a good start.

Trent plunges the button for the doorbell. It's a normal chime that ends after it's made its point.

All righty, maybe the third sorcery family will be easier to wrangle, and they'll have notes or a journal with the original spell.

When the door opens, a man wearing a collared cape greets us and dashes my hopes for normal.

Not that a completely normal sorcerer couldn't wear a cape… it's just less likely. Other than that oddity, Joseph McWinn is an average height, average build kind of guy. He's got sandy blond hair, dresses like an accountant, and has the kind of energy that would be lost in a crowd and forgotten soon after.

Maybe the cape is his effort to break out of the box?

Then again, Herman said he's a legacy to one of the three most established sorcery families in the city and doesn't possess magic.

If the magical gene skipped a generation, maybe wearing a cape is an effort to claim his heritage.

"Mr. McWinn?" Trent grins. "I believe you received a magical message last night asking if you'd be open to answering a few questions?"

"My goodness. You're blue."

Trent glances down at himself and meets the man's gaze once more. "This is true."

"Are you one of those awakening people?"

"No. This is me. The only difference now is that I don't have to glamour it."

He studies Trent's muscled frame as if considering that. "What a relief for you—to finally be able to be yourself, I mean."

Trent nods. "It has been different."

"Mr. McWinn," Danika says. "Was it you who responded to our inquiry about us stopping by?"

"You mean the little magical Post-it note that found me in the back garden?"

Danika nods. "With the phone systems out, that's been our best way of communication."

He nods. "Yes, I said you were welcome to stop by, although I'm not sure how much help I can offer you. What is this about?"

"We believe the surge of fae power during the fall of the veil has destabilized the containment spell your grandfather helped to cast over the Alcatraz holding station. We hoped he wrote the original spell down in a journal or grimoire somewhere that would help us correct the issue."

His gaze narrows as he casts a wary glance over our group. "That level of magic isn't for public consumption. I can't help you."

"No, of course not, but we're with the California Guild of Governors. It's not about public consumption. It's about reestablishing the balance between realms and saving the city."

He frowns, studying each of us in turn. "I don't know. My grandfather always said—"

"Oh, for the love of the gods." Herman leaps off my shoulder, glides the short distance to Joseph's shoulder, and, with his tiny little hand, smacks him upside the head. "Your grandfather wouldn't want his city flopping around between realms like a dead fish onshore. Stop being a noodge and take us upstairs. You're wasting time, Zorro."

The Zorro comment is pretty funny, but Joseph doesn't seem to share the humor.

I step into the convo and try to lessen the impact of the marsupial bitch-slapping. "Just think how well it will reflect on your family if you are the one who has the spell we need to save the city. You'll be a hero."

That lights him up.

All smiles, he considers things for a moment and agrees. "Right this way. I honestly don't know if I have what you're looking for, but you have my permission to look."

Turning on his heel, he rushes into the house and onto the wide staircase. "This way. Could someone please lock the door behind you?"

His cape flutters and flows out behind him as we climb, and I give the guy credit. He doesn't look like an athletic type, but he books it up two flights of stairs at a hasty clip and doesn't seem winded.

After the third flight of stairs, he crests the landing and leads us to a creepy red door at the end of the hall. "Right this way. Welcome to the McWinn Spellitorium."

He opens the door. Danika is keeping pace behind him, and I'm behind her. The two of them head inside, but as I get to the door, a rush of tainted magic hits me like a frying pan to the face.

My shield flares to life and my insides roll.

I throw up my hands and brace my palms on both sides of the door frame. Blocking traffic at the speed we were walking causes a chain reaction of bodies colliding. The force of the crashing almost knocks me into the room, but I lock my arms and hold firm. There's no way I'm going in there if I don't have to.

When the chaos of surprise settles down, I take a moment to reevaluate what happened. "Every instinct I have says we don't go in this room."

"Why, luv? What are ye sensin'?"

"I'm not sure."

Joseph turns back to study us all crammed up in the hall and frowns. "It's nothing. My grandfather was known to ward this room to keep out intruders interested in stealing his spells.

You're probably responding to that. Come along. We have a city to save."

I shake my head. "Nope. It's not the foreboding of a warding spell. I've encountered dozens of those. No. This is a run-for-your-life kind of 'do not enter' reaction. I'm not setting foot in that room and not letting any of you either."

"There's only one problem with that, Red." Nikon's voice is clipped. "Dani's already in that room."

I meet the concerned gaze of Nikon's ex and don't know how to put what I'm feeling into words. "Danika, can you come back out in the hall for a moment, please?"

"What kind of nonsense are you trying to pull?" Joseph snaps. "You asked for my help, I invited you into my home, and now you're getting all strange and distrustful? Do you want my help or not?"

"Of course, we do," Danika says. "I'm sure Fiona meant no disrespect. She's not from the area and is unaware of your family's reputation. We are grateful for you taking the time to help us and for allowing us to spend time in your family's private sanctuary."

"Which is hard to do if they don't come *into* the private sanctuary," Joseph says.

There's no mistaking the hostility lacing his tone. Sure, me blocking up everyone in the hall might seem strange to him, but why is he so angry about it?

"What does it matter to you if we all come in or if only one of us comes in?"

Joseph shrugs and feigns a look of disinterest. "Other than the fact that many hands make light work, nothing. I was doing you a favor. Do you know how many people in the magical society would kill to have access to this room?"

I meet Sloan's gaze and shake my head. "Not happening. Danika, seriously, you need to join us in the hall. There's something very not right going on here."

Danika looks more annoyed than concerned. "Fine. If the Toronto Rescue Squad is too wrapped up in paranoia and boogiemen to put the safety of our city first, we'll handle it ourselves."

Her attention shifts to Trent and Val Ryn, and she nods at them. "Are you boys coming in to help or buying into the delusions of a girl who's likely embarrassed to admit she's in over her head?"

"Don't be like that, Dani," Nikon says. "Fi's the real deal. If she's weirded out, there's a good reason."

As much as Nikon thinks he's helping, I'm not sure him defending me with kind words about me does any of us any favors. If I'm reading her right, it makes her dig in deeper.

"Humor me." I take a step back to give her room to exit the door. "If for no other reason than to prove me wrong."

Joseph stomps a foot like a petulant child and huffs. "If you entertain the ramblings of this hysterical child, I will take it up with Miss Juniper as a personal offense to my family and me."

Val Ryn pushes in beside me and raises his hands. "While we're all standing around talking, it should be simple enough to test your theory. If there is some kind of boundary spell on this room, whether it's a warding spell or something more devious, once we expose it, we'll know what we're dealing with."

"You insult me, sir," Joseph says.

His words fall flat because Val Ryn is already in the process of gauging the magic barrier between the corridor and the McWinn Spellitorium. As he speaks in tongues and works his hands through the air, his expression darkens. "Yes, I sense it. There's something here."

He pauses for a moment, and his scowl darkens. "Fi, come closer. Can you sense another entity here? Maybe an ancestral power?"

He steps to the side, and I slide in front. I hold my hands up to the open doorway and reach out with my senses. "I don't feel anything on the astral plane. Are you sure it felt like ancestral power?"

"My grandfather was a very powerful man." Joseph looks smug. "Of course, he'd be here. There's no putting down a McWinn."

"Until he McLoses," Herman says.

I glance at the furry grouch on my shoulder. "Are you helping the situa—"

Hard hands against my back shove me. As much as I don't want to go in there, there's no stopping the forward momentum as I stumble into the room.

CHAPTER TEN

I tumble into the sorcerer's workroom and fumble to catch Herman as he spreads his limbs wide and becomes a furry kite sailing toward the door of a cabinet. I catch him, preventing him from crashing, and spin to see what the hell just happened. "Humpty Dumpty was pushed."

My guys are about to push in, and I raise my hands. "Hold, boys. Seriously. Stay out. We can't all be inside the trap. Give me a second to sort this out."

I straighten and brush a hand down the front of my vest. "What the hell, Val Ryn. If you thought I was wrong and wanted to come in, you could've gambled with your own life. You had no right to force me and Herm—ione in here."

I check on Herman and settle him back onto my shoulder.

"Hermione?" Herman repeats.

"There's no sense trying to protect his identity, Fiona." Val Ryn turns to an amused-looking Joseph. "That's Herman Humphrey. He cocked up a spell and ended up a rodent."

"Forget about outtin' the man," Sloan snaps from the doorway with Nikon holding him back from entering. "What the feckin' hell gave ye the right to shove Fi into a space she obviously didn't want to go?"

Val Ryn chuckles, lifting his shoulders. "What she wanted is irrelevant. I need her and Humphrey in here. All of you would've been better, but it came down to a take what you can get moment."

Danika scowls at her teammate. "Take what you can get? Why? What's going on? Did Juniper tell you something about Fiona I don't know? You spoke with her last night. What did she say?"

"She said to extend all courtesies to the Toronto team and give them everything they need to succeed."

My gaze is ping-ponging from Joseph to Danika to Val Ryn, but I can't make any sense of this. "Can someone please tell me what the fuckety-fuck is going on because I left my decoder ring in my other weapons vest."

"I have no idea," Danika says. "I thought you were being a dominant bitch."

"Here I thought you were pretty cool. Well, other than you spitting venom at my bestie every chance you get. Even with that, I was willing to give you a pass out of professional courtesy. Now, you're off my Yule card mailing list."

"Focus, Red," Nikon says, beside Sloan standing in the doorway. "On task. The Count Dracula wannabe lured us up here. He and the double-crossing elf wanted us in that room. Why? What are you feeling? What set your shield off?"

I storm over to the door and try to join them on the other side. As I suspected, that's a firm no-go. "Part of it would be the evil intentions of duplicitous dicks."

"Agreed."

"Part of it was the trap lying in wait."

"No doubt."

"It's more than being trapped in this room," Danika says. "I bet it was those."

I follow her extended finger to the small black boxes mounted in the corners at the ceiling line. "I don't know what they are, but there's some seriously bad energy coming off them."

I raise my palm to connect with what's going on. The feedback I get zapped with is sharp and bites like an electrical shock. "Cat crap on a cracker."

"What is it, *a ghra*? We can't see."

I shake out the sting of my hand. "A black Rubik's Cube mounted in each of the blind corners. They gobbled up my probing energy like a shark on tuna. That's some seriously bad juju."

"Those are siphon vessels." Val Ryn grins. "I designed them. Genius, if I do say so myself."

"It's sad and needy to stroke yourself."

Nikon makes a face at me.

"I mean needing to have everyone's attention while he strokes…" I snort. "Damn, I miss Dionysus. He would have said something hilarious right then."

"You did tee it up for a line drive, Red."

Yeah, I did.

"What is wrong with you people?" Joseph shouts.

"They're too stupid to realize they're trapped mice in our maze," Val Ryn says.

I wave that away. Yeah, it's damned obvious that those little black boxes are leaching my power but that only makes me more determined to end this quickly. "Too stupid? No. Are we accustomed to shit going down like this on the regular? Abso-freaking-lutely."

Joseph grunts. "Those vessels will collect all the magical energy you possess until there is nothing left but two drained and mouthy women."

Well, that doesn't sound good at all.

"Mouthy?" Danika scowls. "How'd I get labeled in your tirade?

I think I've been amazingly calm, considering a part of my team totally backstabbed me."

"Calm, maybe." I jump in. "You could've been a little less judgy when I tried to help you earlier."

She gauges the measure of my fingers as I hold them up. "You're probably right, but who knew my right-hand man was working a side hustle with a guy who has a cape fetish? Seriously, guy, what's with the black silk?"

"Give him a top hat and a white rabbit, and the look is complete," Herman gripes on my shoulder.

"Is that it?" I ask. "You couldn't make it as a sorcerer, so you opted to be a magician?"

"I *am* a sorcerer!" Joseph shouts. "Soon you'll see how powerful I am."

My hamster is jogging along his wheel at a pretty good clip, and I think I've got what's going on. "You want to be a real sorcerer like everyone else in your family, so you enlist Val Ryn to trap a group of magically empowered folks in this room. The plan was for your ebony cubes to suck all our power, but then I stopped the train early."

"Yes, that was very unfortunate." Joseph glares at Val Ryn.

The elf shakes his head. "She shouldn't have been able to sense them. I don't know how she did."

"Because you don't know me, dickwad. You're trying to outmaneuver us, and you don't know who or what we are. It's a rookie mistake."

"I know you're the two most powerful people of the group," Val Ryn says. "I've fought at Danika's side for over four years, and the way you absorbed her power strike and slammed her into the ground was incredible."

"Aw…shucks, that was just some girl fun. I got pissed off at the witch who attacked my friend."

"The moment I saw that I knew you were the one we were

waiting for, and when you asked to meet Joseph, it was like the gods wanted our plan to succeed."

I chuckle at how stupid they are. "All right, so you see me slam dunk Danika into the grass, you think I'm the most powerful of my group, so you decide to try to leach my power. I guess you intend to transfer that power to Joseph so he can finally be a real sorcerer."

"I *am* a real sorcerer," Joseph snaps. "I know every spell my ancestors ever cast. I've studied and memorized and itemized. All I need is the magical energy to make it all coalesce."

"You mean the magic to make you a sorcerer," I correct. "Because without the magic part of the equation you're a researcher at best and a bookworm at worst."

Joseph's grin promises that he'll make me pay for that one. Too bad. He won't get the chance.

I shift my attention from Joseph to Val Ryn. "I understand the benefit to his side of this partnership, but what we haven't learned yet is what's in it for you."

Val Ryn chuckles. "Is that my cue to pull back the curtain and tell all?"

"I'd appreciate it, yeah."

He laughs and rolls his eyes. "This isn't one of those movies where the villain spills his guts because he's so sure he'll win. If the entire group was in the room, maybe, but the plan is in motion, and everyone is on a need-to-know basis only."

Well, that's disappointing. "So, he's not going to tell me where the original spell is for the containment of Alcatraz, and you're not going to tell me what your big plan in motion is."

"Sounds about right."

"You make interrogation much less fun when you don't participate."

"What makes you think you're interrogating us?" Joseph asks. "We have you held captive, and you can't use magic. We hold all the cards here."

"Do you, though? Do you *really?* I know magicians think they hold all the cards, but I've got a few tricks up my sleeve."

Joseph glares at Val Ryn. "What is she saying?"

Val Ryn rolls his eyes. He's casting a warding spell to keep the boys out of the room. "Nothing. She's bluffing. Running off at the mouth is her thing."

I chuckle. "Am I though? Are you willing to bet your future as a sorcerer on that?"

Danika's brow creases and I shift my footing to get into a better position. Yeah, fighting back might drain my power faster, but I'm sure as shit not going to stand here and let them suck me dry.

Bruin, we need to take these asshats down.

Down or out, do ye mean?

Down. I can't imagine the Great Pretender in the cape will put up much of a fight. Leave him to Danika and me. It's the elf we need to be wary of. If you have to end him, fine, but we'll learn more from him if he's alive.

Understood. When?

On my mark.

"I understand the pressure to hold up family greatness," I say. "I was a girl born after five strong, smart, and brave sons. They all became cops, like our dad. That's a lot to live up to."

I shift Joseph's focus to draw him away from Val Ryn by stepping closer to Danika.

This little weasel is mine.

Dani and I will have to take him on without powers. I already feel the effects of the siphoning and don't want to give them any more of my strength than I have to.

Val Ryn and Danika are bickering about loyalty and all men being liars. Keeping him distracted makes it easier for me to set things up.

"While I sympathize with you, some people are born empowered, and some aren't. You can't steal that."

"Wrong," Joseph says. "My grandfather always said being a great sorcerer was about more than power. He said cunning and having the guts to think outside the box was the true mark of a magical man."

I chuckle. "Well, siphon vessels are definitely outside the box. The only problem with your theory is that I *live* outside the box."

Now, Bear.

I tug Danika out of danger's path as my battle bear bursts free. Bruin materializes mid-air and takes Val Ryn down with a violent blow to the head.

While the two of them go at it, I lunge to cover the distance between the Amazing Dolt-zini and me, take him down and crash to the floor.

"You bitch," he sputters and grabs my hair, struggling for a good hold.

The moment I'm wrestling with him, I realize how drained I am and am thankful when Danika tags in to help me.

The three of us fight in a tangle of arms, legs, and nails. Joseph's elbow catches me in the cheek, and I pitch to the side.

Dani rolls on top of me and her arms are getting sloppy.

"You dare attack me in my house?" Joseph shouts.

"You bet your weirdo, wannabe ass I do."

"We're working on the warding spell, *a ghra*. Hang in there, luv."

I grip a fistful of black satin and yank back, choking the stupid ass with the ties.

He claws at his neck and yanks the string of the tie, releasing the bow. "You'll pay for that."

I chuckle, although nothing about this is funny. The boys are warded in the hall, my strength is quickly waning, and after fighting and beating some truly great foes, I'm going to be taken out by a hack sorcerer in a satin cape.

Danika grips his face, and her polished nails dig into his flesh.

A glint of sadistic delight flashes in her expression and I smile as he squirms and screams like a spineless little wimp.

He grabs my wrist and twists. The *pop* makes me wince and a spearing pain shooting up my left arm accompanies it. Yanking free from his hold, I throat punch him and vent some of my hostility.

The heel of my palm connects, and he grabs his throat and chokes as I roll to my knees.

"Motherfucker, I think you broke my wrist."

Bruin must feel my pain because he lets out a thundering roar and lands in front of Joseph McWinn. Lifting his mighty paw, he swings...

Bruin's attack swipes through empty air.

Joseph has already passed out and pissed his chinos.

I cradle my wrist and check in on Danika. "Help me find something we can use to bind them." I search the room and frown. "Where the fuck is the elf?"

"He bugged out when your bear started knocking him around," Diesel calls from the hall.

"Chicken shit piece of encrusted crap."

"That's very colorful, luv. Tell me about the siphoning?" Sloan says. "How bad is it, luv?"

"Not as bad as my fucking wrist." I stomp Joseph's crotch once and gross-out. Now there's coward pee on the sole of my boot.

"Rein it in, *a ghra*. I can fix yer wrist. I'm more worried about the siphon vessels. How do ye feel?"

I consider that and exhale. "I feel lethargic. Honestly, I could curl up right now and nap for a week."

"Same." Danika rolls Joseph over onto his belly and tugs his hands behind his back.

"Herman has taken the worst of it. I fear his size hasn't left him much chance to fight the effects." Sloan's comment has me searching the room.

I find poor little Herman lying starfished on the rug and kneel beside him. It's a great comfort that his chest fur rises and falls in slow waves. Being this small, having all his magical energy siphoned might be lethal.

"I can't believe Val Ryn did this to us." Danika drops to the floor next to me.

"Guys? Any luck on getting us out of here?"

Diesel hustles through the doorway carrying a handful of drapery tieback ropes. "Sloan broke through. They still can't come in, so I'll have to do. This is all I could find on short notice."

I check out the offerings and nod. "They'll do, thank you, but dude, you shouldn't have come in here. Now you're stuck too and will be drained."

"I'm where I should be. My power doesn't come from magic. It comes from genetics. I'm exactly who should be in here with you."

"Excellent point." Trent joins us. "Same applies to me."

I'm not going to argue. It feels like someone has a straw stuck into me and is sucking my energy down in greedy gulps. Having them in here to watch our backs is amazeballs.

"If that douche canoe wakes up, you have my permission to punch his stupid face."

Diesel finishes winding and weaving the curtain tie around Joseph's hands and brings the two ends together to knot things up.

"Further to yer point," Sloan says, "Diesel, can ye get those little black boxes down so we can take a look at them?"

Where I would've needed to find a ladder and climb at least three or four feet off the floor to reach the corners, Diesel simply reaches up, twists the siphon vessels, and plucks them off the wall.

"I need to see what yer dealin' with," Sloan says. "Fi, can ye pull that wee table in front of the door over so Diesel can set things up fer me to look?"

Rolling my eyes would take too much energy, so I don't

bother, but mentally, I'm rolling my eyes at him. "I don't think you understand how tired and weak I am, hotness. I don't think I can pull my body over there, let alone a table."

"I've got it." Diesel sets the vessels on top of the side table and carries it in front of the door.

"Grand." Sloan bends to get a look at eye level. "They've got a case on them. See if ye can figure out how to open things up."

I yawn and admire the rug, flopping over on my side. "I see why Herman collapsed here. It's much softer than the hardwood."

"It is." Danika joins me in an impromptu lie down. "You boys do your thing. Wake us up if anything exciting happens."

I nod, yawning and crumpling to the floor in a slow-motion descent. "Yeah, fight the fight, boys."

In a gesture of capture solidarity, Danika and I curl up on our sides like two kids at a slumber party and close our eyes.

CHAPTER ELEVEN

"Well, this day went to shit," I say. "And all before ten o'clock." Dionysus is lying on the settee next to me, grinning.

I chuckle. "Are you saying there's still time for it to get suckier?"

"No, but that's true."

I close my eyes and smile, liking this dream.

"Are you sleeping?" he asks me.

I crack one eye open and smile. "It's been a sucktastic day."

"Gotcha. Sometimes when things go wrong, I need to stop godding for a while, myself."

"Mhmm. I get that."

He takes my hand and kisses my wrist that Joseph broke. I'm thankful the pain is gone, at least in this dream.

Spending time with Dionysus feeds my soul. The simplest gestures, touches, or moments shared mean so much to him.

"So, what did I miss?"

I snuggle into the shelter of his chest and close my eyes. Over the next few minutes I tell him about what happened, why we're in San Francisco, and everything going wrong.

"Do you think the pee weasel knows the spell?"

I snort at the moniker. Yeah, pee weasel is a good one. "If he knows it, Sloan can pull it from him. If he doesn't, maybe we can find it in the journals his grandfather left behind."

"What about the other guy? The one that escaped?"

"Val Ryn. I'm not sure what his dealio is, but he's long gone. Whatever he's up to, we lost our chance at finding out when he ghosted us."

"Is he someone we need to worry about?"

"I didn't go up against him directly, but he wouldn't be on the first response team if he doesn't have game."

"So, we'll have Irish read the wannabe magician and keep searching the McWinn Spellitorium for the original spell. Sounds like a plan."

I hear the end of our conversation approaching. As much as I don't want him to go, I'm so tired. "I heart you hard, Tarzan."

"Right back at you, Red. Next time remember when the dark and deadly of the world is chasing you down and threatening to eat you, trip the guy next to you and run like hell."

I chuckle. "I'll remember that."

I close my eyes and let the healing energy of my time with him strengthen me enough to face the real world again.

Despite what people think, the hits I take hurt me as much as they would the next girl. Maybe I'm too stubborn to let it show, but it still takes its toll.

Those siphon vessels pack a wallop.

Keep on keeping on is what Cumhaills do, so I lock my shit down, draw a deep breath, and wake up.

Dionysus is still there, smiling at me. "That was a quick nap. I thought you said you were tired."

Hubba—wha?

I blink and look around. The room we're in has fuzzy wine-colored wallpaper and silver and gray drapes. We're lying on a rather hard settee, but at least it's softer than the carpet-covered hardwood I was lying on when I collapsed.

"Tarzan? Is that really you?"

Dionysus makes a face and presses his wrist to my forehead. "Are you all right, Jane? Are you having memory lapses? We just had a lengthy discussion where you caught me up on the San Fran sit-rep."

I blink, and my head spins a little. "I wasn't dreaming? You're actually here?"

"You weren't, and I am."

I throw my arms around Dionysus' neck and hug him tight. "Oh, I've missed you, sweetie. I've been so worried about you."

He chuckles. "Yes. We've been over that. It's like you're stuck in a time loop or something. Did those siphon cubes do more damage than Sloan thought?"

"Sloan? You talked to Sloan?"

He gives me a funny look. "Yeah, when I first manifested. When I told the sisters you needed me, they altered my penance and let me off early with good behavior. I'm here now. Really here."

I kiss his cheek and breathe him in. "Wait, you don't smell like you."

"What do you mean?"

"Magic and summer sunshine. Your scent has changed. Are you sure you're really you?"

He lifts a shoulder. "Mostly, but that part about the Fates altering my punishment…yeah, well, they took my magic from me. I'm wholly human. Cool, eh?"

I blink and try to wrap my head around that. "They dropped you here? In the middle of a phasing city and a battle with a corrupt sorcerer?"

He waves away my concern. "Stop looking so worried. I'll be fine. I'm more than magical powers, right? Remember when Loki messed with me? I did okay as a human."

The way I remember it, he was a trainwreck and hated every minute.

"Why don't you look happy? I thought you wanted me home with you."

I wave away his concern and hug him. "Oh, I'm ecstatic you're home, sweetie. I'm worried about you in battle. This is a dangerous situation we're in and god power enhances your skills."

"Not all my skills." He waggles his eyebrows while flashing me a suggestive look.

"I don't think sexual prowess can be considered an asset in battle."

"Oh, I think you underestimate my level of sexual prowess. I can charm someone into giving up information, I can distract someone from something we're doing, and I can detain someone as long as you need to get things done behind the scenes."

I smile. "I don't doubt that for a second. I'm only worried about you."

He nods. "That's what family is supposed to do, right? Worry about one another and try to keep them from harm."

"Yeah, it is."

"So, stop worrying. I'll be fine and still be an asset to the team. You'll see. Charm and seduction are great skills to have on the team."

"Well, you have both of those in spades, no question. You're here, and I'm glad about that. Just be careful. No one wants you to get hurt. You're too important."

He holds up two fingers and winks. "Scout's honor."

Nikon comes into the room with a tray of orange juice. "Oh good, you're awake. How are you feeling, Red?"

"Like someone sucked all the energy out of me. Where are we?"

"I brought you, Danika, and Herman back to Humphrey House."

"You transported us? You rebel. People are going to be pissed at you."

He shrugs. "I figured if the boss gave up on stabilizing things and the response team was with us, there was nobody else to object. Plus, I hated to see the two of you on that floor."

My eyes want to close again, but I force them to stay open. "Where's Dani?"

Nikon eases back, and I see her behind him on a plush sofa. Huh, I see how things are. Danika gets the cushy sofa, and I get the hard settee.

"Where's Bruin?"

"I'm here, Red." I follow his graveled voice to my battle bear lying in front of the doorway.

"Good. I know how testy you get when we're separated, and you get left behind."

"Not to worry. I've learned from experience and keep a closer watch on you now."

"I appreciate that." I draw a deep breath and lose the battle with lead lids. "I can't keep my eyes open one more minute."

"You rest, Jane," Dionysus says. "Bruin, Nikky, and I will watch over you."

"You're not going anywhere?"

"Where would I go? I belong here with you."

"Yes, you do. Okay, nap time. Love you, guys."

"Love you, back."

The second try at waking up goes a lot better. This time my stomach is rumbling, and all I can think of is butter chicken samosas. Man, what I wouldn't give for a bag of hot samosas right now.

"Ask, and ye shall receive, *a ghra*." Sloan sets a serving tray on the floor beside the settee. "Can I help ye sit up to eat?"

He grips my arms and tugs me forward while he swings my feet to the floor.

"I can manage," I say with no conviction.

"Fer the moment, yer as weak as a wee kitten. Let us help until ye regain yer strength. Then ye can fight yer fights and slay yer own dragons once more."

He knows what to say so I give in. I suppose that's the sign of a man who pays attention.

I draw a deep breath and let the savory bliss of hot buttered chicken samosas fill my senses. My stomach emits another long, demanding growl.

"Here, ye need fuel to refill yer tank." He opens the brown paper bag and holds it for me.

"How did you know? I didn't ask for these out loud."

Sloan arches a brow and Nikon chuckles. "It's all you've mumbled about for the past three hours. Maybe you didn't say it when you were lucid, but you said it."

I choose one of the triangles of delight and bite off one of the points. "Oh, my sweet petunia, these are good."

Sloan chuckles. "I'm glad yer enjoying them. How do ye feel otherwise?"

"Groggy and weighed down."

"Can ye access yer connections to yer powers?" He takes my free hand and turns it palm up. "How about a bit of faery fire?"

I pop the rest of my samosa into my mouth and focus on my intention. It takes a moment, but I get there. A small ball of blue flame forms in my palm. It's no bigger than a snowball, but it feels like I've conjured a giant boulder of flame.

Releasing it, I'm pleased to see Sloan's relief. "Excellent. Yer drained but will recover with a bit of rest."

I reach into the grease-stained bag and grab another samosa. "I'm done resting. Tell me what happened. How'd you get us out of there?"

"Diesel and Trent were able to open the siphon boxes, and I

talked them through how to destroy them. Once they were offline and there was no threat of us all ending up drained, Nikon created a spatial bridge to bypass the room's lockdown."

I glance at Nikon sitting on the coffee table and watching over Danika. "You opened a portal?"

"Yeah, one end of a portal in the corridor and another in the workroom. Then it was a simple case of using that to pass through."

"Yay you, Greek. You saved my butt yet again."

He shakes his head and winks. "We will never be even, Red. You gave me my life back. I will spend my immortal existence paying you back."

"Pfft, whatevs. You know I didn't do it for your unending devotion."

He chuckles. "Only the glory of being a savior."

"Exactly." I let that one drop, then get back on track and address Sloan. "What happened with Joseph? Were you able to do your Vulcan mind meld on him? Did you get anything?"

"Joseph is as useless to our cause as he is in the magical community. He has no idea if his grandfather took note of the spell we need because the man never trusted him with magic he could neither access nor comprehend."

"That's too bad...both for Joseph feeling inferior and for us trying to fix this."

"It is."

I swallow my second pocket of perfection and dive back into the bag. "So, stabilizing didn't work, and we have to consider the possibility there is no record of the original spell, so we can't undo what they did. What's Plan C?"

He shrugs. "I don't think we're there yet. There's one more thing I'd like to try before we give up."

"Oh? What's that?"

"Remember when Val Ryn asked you about the ancestral energy in the McWinn Spellitorium?"

I nod and take possession of the samosa bag so I don't have to keep reaching. "Yeah, I figured that was bullshit to lure me closer."

"Not entirely. After Nikon brought you ladies back here, Trent, Diesel, and I searched that workroom rug to rafters."

"But you didn't find the spell."

"No, but we found a very old and powerful Ouija board."

I stop chewing and shake my head. "Nu-uh. I don't like those things. You can't control what's going to come through. You might think you're talking to your dear Aunt Sally to ask her where the punch bowl is, and you get a seventh-level demon who wants to eat your eyeballs as after-dinner mints."

Sloan makes a face. "Sometimes less is more, *a ghra.*"

"You know what I mean."

"Aye, I do, and I don't disagree."

"So, you don't want to have a séance?"

"Och, no, I do, but not with the board."

I draw a deep breath. Maybe my hamster is still sleeping in my mental wheel, but I'm not following. "More words, please."

"The presence of the Ouija board got me thinkin' about a man like Joseph. With him so desperate to follow in his family heritage, I supposed he tried a great many avenues to connect with his grandfather."

"Did he have the goods to getter done?"

"I went back to my Vulcan mind trick and searched for the answer for that."

"And?"

He nods and plucks the samosa out of my fingers and takes a bite. "With the help of a local medium, he has spoken to his grandfather on more than one occasion."

"Okay, I follow you. So, if the three wizards who we need are dead, we perform a séance and see if we can conjure them for a chat."

"Exactly. Trent is tracking down the woman I saw in Joseph's memories at this moment. When he returns, we'll get things started."

I select one last butter chicken bundle and consider that. "If not the Ouija board, how are we calling the spirits of the dead?"

"Herman is handling the spell. The only thing he needed from us was a personal item of Georgia Templeton, Albert Humphrey, and Alistair McWinn."

I glance around but don't see our little furry friend anywhere. "Where is Herman?"

"He's preparing the parlor for the event."

I'm not sure how an animal that can fit in the palm of my hand can prepare a room for a séance, but I figure there's only one answer—magic.

"Cool. What do you need me to do?"

Sloan winks. "I need you to stay here and eat samosas for another fifteen minutes while I check on things. Then, when we're ready, I'll come to get the four of you, and we can go from there."

I glance at the sofa and see that Danika is awake now. "I'm stuffed, but I get your point. I'll be a good girl and rest while nothing's happening. Off you go."

He stands, runs a gentle hand under my chin, and lifts my face to kiss my forehead. "Try not to cause any chaos while I'm gone."

"I'll do my best."

He chuckles. "That inspires no confidence, but I suppose that will have to do."

When Sloan strides off, I gather my strength and extend my hand to Dionysus. "Help me up, Tarzan."

Dionysus makes a face. "Irish just told you to lie there and rest. Did you damage your ears when they drained you?"

I wave away his concern. "If we're going to do this, he needs to focus and not worry about me."

"I think he'll always worry about you, Jane. You're a bit of a disaster."

I chuckle. "That's rich coming from the god with no god powers."

He makes a face at me but, in the end, relents and helps me stand.

Getting my feet moving takes a bit of effort, but after a moment, the law of inertia kicks in, and what's in motion wants to stay in motion.

"Thanks for getting us out of there, Greek." I squeeze Nikon's shoulder. "See, I told you that double portal trick would come in handy."

The dark circles under Nikon's eyes have nothing to do with his guyliner smudging and everything to do with him being exhausted. "I still don't think we can take our magical inspiration from Disney movies, though."

Wrong. I hold out my crumpled brown bag of decadence. "Butter chicken samosas? You must be as famished as I was."

Danika is still in the weak as a kitten phase of recovery and looks like she's struggling to reach for the bag. "Yeah? You're sure?"

"Absolutely. I'm full." I hand Nikon the bag, so he can help her get sorted. She's at a point where she doesn't have the strength to argue or fight, so maybe he can explain enough that she'll call off the firing squad.

Leaving them to their business, I make my way over to Bruin and squat to rub my face in his fur.

Mmm...he smells like pine trees and spring breezes.

"Feelin' better, Red?"

"Quite a bit, yes."

"Would ye feel better if I took my place within ye?"

"I always do. If you don't mind lending me your strength."

"Not a bit." He twists around, licks the side of my face, and dematerializes. The moment he takes his place and settles in my chest, his power infuses mine, and the blood in my body starts to pump stronger.

Thank you, Bear.

Whatever ye need, whenever ye need it.

I pat my sternum and head across the hall to use the washroom and freshen up.

"Do you need me to come in with you?" Dionysus' grip on my elbow tightens.

"No, sweetie. I'm good. I've got this."

What does it say about my life that being able to go to the bathroom alone is a win? Sad face.

It's been a long couple of days, but if we don't get this sorted out soon, I worry we'll be stuck here.

The first time San Francisco made it back, it lasted less than fifteen minutes. The second time, it was less than that. I don't suppose we'll get too many more chances at securing the city where it belongs.

Sloan and Nikon were talking about it this morning over breakfast, and they figure likely one or two more blinks tops.

When I finish splashing water on my face and exit the powder room, Sloan is standing there waiting for me with his arms crossed over his chest. "Imagine my surprise when ye weren't where I left ye."

I chuckle. "Close enough. You said for me not to cause chaos. S'all good. No chaos here except for the heap we were already knee-deep in."

"Fair enough."

I begin the return trip across the hall, and he shifts our position so we're standing against the wall leading into the parlor and are out of the line of sight from Nikon and Danika.

With his hands flat on the wall on either side of my head, he looks into my eyes with too much emotion for mixed company. "Are ye really all right? Those siphon boxes didn't look to have any secondary purpose, but I need ye to tell me if there's more."

Caged in by him, I draw a deep breath and soak in the intensity of his worry. "I really am fine. S'all good. Thank you for loving me enough to worry this much."

He presses a kiss against my lips, and I wish I had the energy to drag him back into the washroom and have my way with him.

Sadly, I don't.

When we ease apart, I'm breathless. I cup the side of his jaw with my palm and remind myself how lucky I am. "I love you, hotness."

"I love ye right back."

Yeah, I know he does. It's in everything he says and does. "Okay, now. Let's go see dead people."

CHAPTER TWELVE

"Bring out your dead. Bring out your dead," I joke.

"I'm not dead yet." Danika plays along. Nikon's ex is walking with an old man shuffle as she enters the séance room, but considering what we've been through, I'd say she's faring pretty well.

"No, we're not dead yet. I guess we dodged a bullet on that one, eh?" I meet her gaze, and she smiles.

The two of us have come to a truce during our ordeal, and I'm glad. Despite what the boys said, I don't enjoy conflict.

Nikon directs her to one of the padded dining chairs and settles her in. She's not exactly friendly when she accepts his care, but she's no longer threatening to bash his beautiful blond head with a sledgehammer. "Does that make us the McWinners?"

I laugh and shake my head. "That was bad."

"In my defense, I recently had my life force sucked from my body."

I nod. "Me too. It must be going around."

"Let's hope not."

"Agreed."

"Welcome, please, come in." I follow the urging of a full-bodied brunette with the longest, sparkliest, candy apple red nails I've ever seen. "Take any seat around the table that feels right, and we'll begin."

Before us is a round antique oak table covered with a black silk altar cloth with gold and silver stars glimmering on it. In the center of the table is a bowl of water surrounded by candles. In front of the medium, there are three small velvet-lined bowls with an item in each: a brooch, a hand-carved pipe, and a leather bracer with runes engraved in it.

I'm not sure how the seat "feels" but when Sloan sits to the right of an ebony-haired fashionista, I sit next to him. Dionysus and Nikon sit on my other side, then Diesel, Trent, and Danika. Herman is crawling around on the table and settles in front of me. Joseph is gagged and tied to the last chair at the table.

Manx is sitting in the wingback chair in the corner, his ears perked and his eyes locked on the ceremony.

"Welcome, everyone. I am Grace Astoria, and I will be your guide on your journey today. For those who aren't aware, a séance is a means of connecting beings on this plane with those who have passed to the after. We connect with the spirit world to ask questions or seek guidance from those no longer with us. I'm told there is a very important question you need asked and hopefully answered?"

Danika nods. "Yes. A spell was cast over half a century ago, and the three sorcerers involved in casting it are deceased."

Grace bows her head. "Before us, we have an item which holds great personal meaning for each of the three spirits we are inviting to come through: the brooch of Georgina Templeton, the pipe of Alistair McWinn, and the leather cuff of Herman Humphrey the Second."

Movement on the water's surface draws my attention to the bowl in the center of the table, but there's nothing to see. Maybe it was a flicker of one of the candles.

"When you're ready, we'll begin."

A questioning look is shared around the table and we all nod.

"We're ready," Danika says.

Grace nods in return. "Friends and family of the spirit world, we come to you with pure intention and a dire need. Georgia, Herman, and Alistair, your experience and expertise are needed. For the sake and safety of your heirs and the city you loved, we ask that you come forward."

The flames of the candles flicker and dance with a rush of energy and my shield tingles to life.

It's not a warning, so much as my early warning system simply waking up.

"Go ahead and ask your question," Grace says.

I glance at Danika, and she gestures at me, so I take the lead. "Georgia, Herbert, and Alistair, if you can hear us, we need your help. The fall of the veil corrupted the containment spell you devised for the fae prison. We need to bring down the spell to stabilize the city."

"What's your question, dear?" Grace asks.

"Oh, right. Georgia, Herbert, and Alistair, do you remember the details of the spell you cast, or can you direct us to where to find it?"

Grace smiles. "A solid question with clear need. Will the heirs please press your palms flat on the table and close your eyes."

The fashionista beside Sloan, the sugar glider in front of me, and our prisoner, Joseph, each place their hands against the silk and stars of the altar cloth and close their eyes.

"Think about your ancestor," Grace says. "Call them forward with your will. Envision their spirits joining us in this room."

There is a moment of silence when I wonder if this will work. Then I feel a rush of power.

"Before the veil of magic dropped, it was much more difficult to call the spirits," Grace says. "With the abundance of magic around us these days, the dead are never far."

I think she means that comment to be uplifting, but that's not how I respond. Making it simple for the dead to interact with the living is fine in theory, but in practice, some spirits should stay on the other side.

"Annalise, my darling doll." The apparition of Georgia Templeton appears over the table and beams at her granddaughter. The woman has the same 1940s Hollywood starlet grace to her that my gran has, and I can't help but smile. "That blouse is lovely, dearest. It brings out the copper flecks of your eyes."

"I'm pleased you like it." Annalise smiles down at herself.

The next ghost to join us is a stern-looking man with cold, black eyes. "What have you gone and done now, boy? Tell me."

Joseph's eyes flare wide, but he's still gagged, so there's nothing he can tell.

I frown and tackle that one. "With the help of a real sorcerer, he trapped a few of us in your workshop and tried to drain our magic to steal it for his own."

Alistair's scowl is cutting, and if he could reach between planes and strangle his grandson, I have no doubt the boy would be gasping his last breath. "You cannot steal greatness. You're born with it inside you, or you aren't. When will you give this up? I told you. Sorcery is not your future. Find a woman who will settle for a poor excuse of a man like you and have a few children. Perhaps one of them will have power. Or perhaps your grandmother was more than a shameless flirt, and there's no McWinn blood in you. That's the likeliest answer."

Harsh.

Even though Joseph did me wrong and I'd love to throat punch him again for trying to steal my magic, his grandfather's words hurt me on his behalf.

Blood or not, family is a bond of acceptance...or, at least, it should be.

When people are raised without that, they search, covet, and flounder. I'm not saying they aren't responsible for their actions and how they turn out—they are—but usually, children of neglect and ridicule end up feeling angry and desperate.

I glance at Dionysus.

But not always.

Dionysus was desperate for love and acceptance, but he had a pure, loving soul and a heart that was waiting to find love.

I'm thankful every day to have him in my life and don't think for a moment that it happened by chance. The Greek Fates and their mother played their part in us finding one another, I'm sure.

"We're waiting on a third," Grace says. "Herman Humphrey Senior...if you can hear us, please come through. Your grandson is here to greet you."

He might not look exactly like you remember, but he's here.

Herman is sitting on the table smiling up at Georgia Templeton as if he's starstruck.

I don't blame him. She's a classic beauty.

"It doesn't look like Granddad is coming through," Herman says. "Maybe he's busy, or he doesn't recognize my energy with me like this. I don't want to hold up the results. We should proceed."

I don't disagree. I don't know a lot about seances, but I assume the energy wanes, and eventually, the spirits have to return to where they came from.

I start us off. "Welcome, Alistair and Georgia. I'm not sure if you're aware of the current state of the world, but shortly after Winter Solstice this year, the veil between the magical realm and the human realm dropped, and there was a powerful surge and imbalance."

Georgia curls her hair behind her ear and smiles. "Yes. We felt the effects of that occurrence here too."

"Is that why Herman is a rodent?" Alistair chuckles.

"I'm glad you find it funny, Alistair. I live to amuse," Herman says.

"It's good to have a purpose, Humphrey."

Georgia tilts her head and gives Alistair a patient look and an arched brow.

He sobers and turns his attention back to me. "My apologies, please continue."

"In the past five months, many things have gone sideways, but the problem we're faced with right now is tied to the containment spell you cast over Alcatraz to secure the fae prison. The power surge corrupted the intention of the original spell and is holding the entire city hostage."

"Oh, my." Georgia's fingers come up to pat the base of her throat. "How unfortunate."

"It is. On top of that, because the spell's energy is so out of whack, the city is blinking between the human realm where it belongs and the fae realm."

Alistair scowls. "One has nothing to do with the other. Your connection between the two events is flawed."

"How so?" Sloan asks. "The spell is incredibly powerful. Isn't it possible it could be affecting the phasing of the city?"

"No. I don't believe so." He glances at Georgia.

For the first time, Georgia looks more like a woman of force than a lady of leisure. "I don't see the connection either. What has one to do with the other? The magic for the spell was grounded in a self-renewing power—the current of the water was the conduit with the power of the selkie guards reinforcing the spell. It had nothing to do with spatial energy."

"Then do you believe we're dealing with two problems?" Danika asks.

Alistair considers that and nods. "I believe so, yes. Tell me exactly what's happened from the moment you were aware things weren't right."

I let Danika take that one because she knows what was happening before we got here. Most of it we knew, but the details of Juniper's efforts to stabilize the city were new to us.

"There's no reason the city should be suffering a shift like that," Alistair says. "What do the magicals say?"

Danika looks from him to us and her expression drops. "Val Ryn handled the discussions with the witches, wizards, and sorcerers while Juniper and I worked on stabilizing the containment spell."

"Who is Val Ryn?" Georgia asks.

Danika sighs. "He was a member of our guild team. It turned out he was a traitor. He was the one who designed the siphoning devices to steal our power for your grandson."

Alistair shakes his head and scowls. "Why would a man who obviously has skill help Joseph with such a scheme? What benefit would it offer him?"

"I asked him before he escaped," I say. "He wouldn't say, and so far we haven't figured it out."

"Well, the motives of men are simple," Georgia says. "Money, power, love, or revenge."

That sounds a little oversimplified but whatevs.

Alistair turns toward his grandson. "Joseph, look at me." Joseph meets his gaze without hesitation. "Remove the cloth from his mouth so he can speak."

Trent gets up, steps around the table to stand behind Joseph, and removes the gag.

"Joseph? Why did their guild sorcerer agree to help you? What was the bargain?"

He lifts one shoulder looking terrified. "Nothing much, sir. I got the better end of the negotiation."

"I'm quite sure you didn't. Now, tell me exactly what the terms of the agreement were and how this arrangement of yours transpired."

I watch Joseph as he explains to his grandfather what happened. Sure, he's a little afraid of the man, but he genuinely adores him. How heartbreaking it must be to know he doesn't have power and is essentially letting down the importance of his family line in a community where the McWinn name is respected for greatness.

"You did *what!*"

Joseph flinches and bites his bottom lip. "Don't be angry, Grandfather. That old mantle clock never worked anyway. I figured if he wanted a broken antique and I got to make you proud, that was a McWinn win."

Alistair rolls his eyes and draws a deep breath. "That antique mantle clock isn't broken, you dimwit. It's a Port Gate. It regulates space and time on an entirely different level of existence."

As always, when something like that goes over my head, I turn to Sloan to wait for him to be my Clarica agent and explain.

"What does that mean, hotness?"

"It means that the plan in motion Val Ryn mentioned is likely the very reason the city is phasing." He turns from me to Alistair. "What exactly are the limitations and parameters of the device, Mr. McWinn?"

If the ghosts were in full color, I have no doubt Alistair would be red in the face furious. "I couldn't tell you. The Port Gate Clock was something I confiscated during a particularly dangerous arrest of another sorcerer back in the late eighties."

"Arrest? You were in law enforcement?" I ask.

"I was part of the California Council of Sorcerers. For six months, I investigated the disappearance of young witches who later turned up dead and exsanguinated."

"Blood magic," Sloan says.

Alastair nods. "Yes. It's a vile practice, but the lure of dark power is strong and well…you know elves. Anyway, we tracked down our suspect, and it was fortunate we found him when we did. We barely stopped him before he leveled the West Coast."

"How?" I ask.

"With that damnable clock. I don't know what it was designed to do if it was working properly, but I saw what it could do if it wasn't."

"And now it's back out in the world," I say.

"You stopped him?"

Alistair nods. "Not before he drained a coven of witches and used the blood magic power he gained to open up a portal vortex that nearly swallowed the California coastline."

"What was the name of this sorcerer mastermind?" Nikon asks.

"Rilios. Brynali Rilios."

Danika curses under her breath and shakes her head. "Val Ryn is a Rilios."

"Well, there's no way that's a coincidence." I don't like the sound of any of this. "So, Val Ryn made a deal with Joseph. He would siphon power from us, and in return, he'd reclaim the device his father…or maybe grandfather invented."

"Likely father," Sloan interjects. "He's an elf, so he ages much slower than we do."

"Okay, so, he gets back daddy's device, and what? He starts kidnapping and slaying witches to follow in his father's footsteps?"

"No way," Danika says. "I've known Val Ryn for four years. He's never once said or done anything that sounds remotely similar to this. He's a good guy."

"Who trapped us in a room and tried to juice box our magic," I point out. "Yeah, he's a real charmer."

"So, if he *does* plan to finish what his father started, what does that look like?" Nikon asks.

Alastair shrugs. "I can't say. I studied that clock for months with two of my counterparts. We never figured out how it worked. We couldn't activate or destroy it, so we decided to shelve it and keep it close."

"Now Val Ryn has it back," I say. "Lunatic daddy will be so proud."

Sloan's got that familiar look when he's solving problems I don't see coming yet. "What are you thinking, hotness?"

"I'm wonderin' if Brynali Rilios was sentenced to the fae prison on Alcatraz and if maybe us plannin' to take down the containment spell was part of his plan all along."

The logic slips into place, and everything starts to make more sense.

"Bam, drop the mic. Oh, Henry! bar for you. We now have Val Ryn's motive. He's planning a jailbreak."

"There's not much time left," Grace says. "You need to conclude your conversation."

"Are you serious?" I say, checking with her just in case she was yanking our chain. "There's so much we still need to work out. We haven't even gotten the spell yet. Without that, Nikon can't unweave it, and we can't save the city."

She gives me an apologetic shrug. "I can't help you. Your time is almost up."

"This isn't some collect call to the afterlife where we ran out of change. We need more time."

"Perhaps we can give that to you," Georgia says. "What if we join you while you work out the worst things?"

"Join us how?" Danika asks.

Alistair meets Georgia's contemplative look and nods. "That's a fine idea, Georgie girl. A fine idea indeed."

"I'm still not following," I say.

"We'd have to act quickly," Herman says. The sugar glider sorcerer hasn't missed a beat. "Annalise and Joseph. Will you host your ancestors for a bit while we save the city?"

"Host them?" Annalise says, her eyes wide. "Host them how?"

"Like a possession?" Joseph asks.

"Similar to that but not permanently and they wouldn't overtake you. There would be the two of you in there together."

Annalise makes a face of sheer horror.

If we hadn't tied Joseph to his chair, he'd be jumping up and down right now. "Yes, I accept. I welcome him."

With that, Herman raises a tiny pink hand, his furry side wing flapping with effort. He mumbles something in tongues, and the Alistair apparition floats over and dives into Joseph.

Joseph's eyes roll back, and he bucks for a moment as if he's being electrocuted, but the struggle is short-lived. A moment later, he holds up his hands and smiles as he tests out his limbs.

Annalise breathes a sigh of relief. "Then you won't need my body, correct? You have a volunteer."

Georgia frowns at her granddaughter. "One is good, but two would be better. You will do this for me, darling. I have given you everything you ever wanted for your entire life. You will give me this."

"But Gigi...my schedule is full. I couldn't possibly fit in—"

"Annalise Margaret Templeton," her gran says in a hushed snap. "Don't you dare say no or I will haunt you morning and night for the rest of your shallow life. I'll be the poltergeist at your parties, the apparition at your appearances, and the ghost that haunts your groups."

Annalise's eyes widen. "You wouldn't."

"Try me."

There's not an ounce of bluff in her words, and we all know it.

Annalise huffs and pouts like a twelve-year-old and crosses her arms. "Fine. I accept, but only for a short—"

Georgia doesn't wait for the end of that sentence. She leaves the center of the table, floating through the air with purpose until she merges with her granddaughter.

When the shock to Annalise's body subsides, she opens her eyes and waggles her brows. "Hot diggity. This is going to be a gas."

CHAPTER THIRTEEN

Trent ushers Grace to the door and sees her out. Our medium is both shocked and appalled at the turn of events. She doesn't abide spirits being allowed to overtake the living, but hey, what's done is done.

"Honestly, having two of the three original spellcasters is better than we could've hoped for," I say to Sloan.

His gaze narrows and I see the wheels of his mind turning.

"What?"

"I'm not so sure we have two of the three," he says.

"You think either Georgia or Alistair is a fake?"

"Och, no. I believe they're real enough and were two of the three original conjurers of the containment spell."

"But, you just said…"

"I think we have all three of the original spellcasters. If I'm right, the reason Herman Humphrey Senior didn't come through to speak to his grandson is that he's not dead. They are one and the same."

"Very astute, Mr. Mackenzie." Herman leaps off Diesel's shoulder to glide across the room and land on my arm. "People

I've known for decades haven't figured that out, and here you are for two days, and you've exposed my secret."

"I have no interest in exposin' yer private business. My interest sits solely in the benefit it offers us to have all three of the original spellcasters here to help us fix this mess."

I hold up a finger. "Wait. If you are *the* Herman Humphrey, why couldn't you give us the spell in the first place? All of today's running around was to find the spell. You cost us a whole day."

"Forgive me, Fi. To live a lifetime when all your friends and family pass and leave you behind is a lonely existence. I figured if you were all so inspired to find the three original spellcasters, there was a chance I might be able to spend a moment or two with old friends."

"So, you anticipated we'd hold a séance?"

"Or something of the sort, yes."

"We're dealing with something very serious here. The entire city is locked down and displaced."

"I would've given you the help you needed with the spell before anything dire happened, I swear."

"Of course, you would, darling." Georgia winks at the sugar glider. The woman possessing her body has a lot more sway to her hips than Annalise does. It's honestly not as difficult to see who's driving the train as I thought it would be. "We mustn't negate your part in this, young lady."

I blink. "Me? What did I do?"

"Herman has always been absorbed by the beauty of a redhead. I should know. I used to be one."

Herman makes one of his leaps, climbs up her arm, and sits on her shoulder. "Hello, Georgie girl. If I had lips right now, I would lay one on you."

She arches a sultry brow and grins. "You would try."

"Any chance you and Al might want to restore me to my former glory?"

She chuckles. "That depends. Do you mean being a man or

being twenty-five years old again?"

"Oh, I think our twenties are better left in the past. No. I meant me walking on two legs and being able to waltz a beautiful lady across my ballroom floor."

The sparkle in her eyes tells me the two have waltzed together and it was a good time. "I'm certain we can arrange that. We might be a bit rusty, but I'm sure we'll manage." She holds up her hand and Herman climbs onto her palm.

The two of them walk off chatting, and I blink at Sloan. "I've been replaced."

"It seems so."

"Have you noticed the two in the corner?"

Sloan glances at where Nikon and Danika are talking quietly. "Don't start concocting happily ever afters that aren't there, luv. Nikon wanted to set things right. Let him have his moment without pressuring it to be more."

I chuckle. "I don't have to pressure anything. Look at them."

"I see two adults having a quiet conversation."

I roll my eyes. "Amateur. I see a man and a woman standing less than a foot and a half apart, their heads bowed toward one another, and their bodies turned toward one another. The fire is still burning."

"Stop. He's yer friend. Let him find his way."

"How can you be such a hopeless romantic with me and a stick in the mud when looking at others?"

Sloan chuckles and pulls me against his chest. "Because us bein' romantic is my business. Them bein' romantic isn't."

I push up to my toes and kiss him. "Fine. I'll focus on the mess that is our mission and let things happen naturally."

"That's a wonderful idea. I think that's best. Now, back to work." He takes a step back and raises his hand to signal Diesel, Dionysus, and Trent to come inside from the back patio and for Nikon and Danika to join us.

When we're all assembled, I draw a deep breath. "Okay, from

the top. What's on the to-do list?"

Danika nods and takes the lead. "We need to find wherever Val Ryn has the Port Gate Clock, seize it, and stabilize San Francisco back into the human realm. We also need to take advantage of having the three original spellcasters and a Light Weaver, so we can take down the faulty spell and release the containment on the city."

"During that time, we're leaving the prison vulnerable," I add.

"And Val Ryn will be keen to make his play to spring daddy from the big house," Nikon says.

"So, we're to find the Port Gate Clock, end the spell, stop Val Ryn from liberating his father, and... Is that it?"

"Return the ghosts to the spirit realm?" Diesel suggests.

I nod. "Yeah, that goes into the cleanup column."

"Can the stabilization of the city be done at any time or only when we're in our home realm?" Nikon asks.

I frown and look at Sloan. "Good question, Greek. What say you, hotness? If we cut the spell when we're in the fae realm, what happens?"

He shrugs. "How would I know? This is my first spatial instability. I assume doing it when we're in California would be best, but we don't know if we'll get that chance again."

I breathe deep and exhale. "The first time it flipped back was the third day for fifteen minutes. The second was the same day for less than ten. There's no way to predict when or even if we'll blink back to California."

Sloan frowns. "Yer right. Since we have all three sorcerers and Nikon and the spell, I say we get that done as soon as possible. We have a good idea Val Ryn will make a play for his father, so we'll notify the prison to be on heightened readiness and inform the selkie guards as well."

"Juniper will help with the prison communications," Danika says. "She's in constant contact with the warden and knows the most about their procedures."

I'm not sure looping Juniper in now when everything is in motion is a great idea.

I understand Dani's motivation. If we were in Toronto, I'd want to tell my boss too, but we're not, and Juniper is no Garnet Grant.

"What if she tries to shut us down again? She wasn't very receptive to the idea of us working together to take the spell down."

Danika meets my hesitation with a shrug. "She didn't know Val Ryn was working against us. She also didn't know about the Port Gate Clock being the cause of the second issue. She was working under the assumption that everything happening was one problem. Being exhausted and frustrated, she handled the situation poorly, but she's new to running our branch office. She only got the appointment after the veil fell and puts a lot of pressure on herself."

I know that feeling and can sympathize.

Fine, we can give her another chance.

"I'm still a little fuzzy on the whole Port Gate Clock thing," I say. "How does it work?"

Dionysus grins. "I picture it like the Port Key boot to get Harry and the Weasleys to the Quidditch Cup. Only it doesn't just take people from two places in the same realm. It also takes people to places in different realms."

I hold up my finger. "First, point to you for the Harry Potter reference, Tarzan. I'm proud of you. Second, if that's true, we really need to get that clock back."

There seems to be a consensus of agreement on that.

Danika is the next to speak. "If we find out what kind of energy it uses, we might be able to track its signature or output with our systems back at the Legion of Honor."

"Alastair might know," Nikon says. "He confiscated the thing and had it in his possession for forty years."

Sloan nods. "That's solid, Greek. I bet yer right."

Danika nods. "I'll ask him and head back to the Legion. I'll start tracking and update Juniper."

I'm still a little apprehensive that Juniper joining us in the eleventh hour might be a backward step, but that's not my call. "Okay. Once we have an idea of how to pinpoint the clock's signature, Sloan can transport you and Trent to the Legion. You'll catch Juniper up, tell her about Val Ryn, and start tracking for the clock. At the same time, Nikon, Diesel, Dionysus, and I will work with these three on taking down the containment spell."

Trent shakes his head. "I agree we should update Juniper and start tracking the signature of the clock, but then I think Sloan should take me to Pier 39 to inform the selkie guards. When we're ready to do this, we'll need all able bodies in the water to prevent prisoners from taking advantage."

That makes sense. "Sounds good. Sloan can drop Dani at the Legion and take you to the pier. We'll work with the sorcerers and Nikon is here as our Light Weaver to undo and reset the containment spell."

Danika rolls her eyes. "There are a lot of working parts on this."

"So much to do. So little time."

Nikon puts his fist into the circle, and we all reach in for a bump. "It's musketeer time."

Danika and I walk through Humphrey House, searching for where the three old friends have gotten to. It takes me a minute, but I figure it out. "He wanted them to try to restore him to his former self. I bet they're upstairs in his workroom."

I gesture at the stairs, and because Sloan and I went there from our room last night and there are so many twists and turns in this mansion, we go to our room so I can navigate from there.

Envisioning the little note fluttering before us, I retrace my steps from last night. "Thank you for calming down enough to work together productively."

Danika nods. "Thanks for leading the charge against Val Ryn and getting us free from that crazy room."

"I caused the fight, but Nikon got us free."

She doesn't say anything, but hey, she's not spitting nails at the mention of his name either.

"Has he talked to you...about why he left, I mean?"

She nods. "He told me about being stalked by Hecate and how you and your brother risked your lives to free him."

I wave that away. "He's saved me a dozen times in return. Did he also tell you about the time a trickster was haunting me and I rammed my spear through him and killed him?"

Her eyes widen, and the flare of anger and protectiveness warms my heart. "You killed him?"

"It was a total accident. I was a snotty mess for days...even after he sent word that he was recuperating and would be fine."

She shakes her head. "He said you two have a complicated relationship."

"Nah, not really. A lot has happened, but the relationship is simple. I love him to bits, and he feels the same. We're friends and family, and we've got each other's backs."

"I'm glad he found that kind of a friend in you."

"I'm just as lucky."

I find the narrow stairs that lead up another flight and lead the way. "Did he tell you that the few times he let himself love or be happy in his life that Hecate killed the women?"

"He did."

"And when he realized the two of you had fallen in love, he ghosted you because he knew she would come, and he would be the cause of your death?"

"That doesn't make it hurt any less."

"Doesn't it?" I stop at the top of the stairs and wait for her to catch up. "He didn't leave because you meant nothing to him. He left because you meant everything."

She sighs. "Maybe that will help in time, but for now, I'm still hurt and very angry."

"Fair enough. I'm not telling you how you should feel. I just want to make sure you have the whole story—for both your sakes."

Danika offers me a tired smile. "Thanks, Fi. Now, let's get the job done so everyone can get home."

"Sounds good."

The two of us arrive at the closed door of Herman's sorcery workroom and hesitate. "Is it a bad thing to interrupt sorcery in progress?"

Danika makes a face. "Probably."

"Well, I don't want Herman to go from a sugar glider to a toad or anything. Maybe we should wait." I step closer and listen at the door.

"Anything?"

"No. If this was my magical sanctum, I'd have it spelled for privacy."

"So, we wait?"

I hear the stress of impatience in her voice, and I don't blame her. We've got too much pending to stand in this hallway for any time.

"Right. This isn't going to work." Thinking maybe entering quietly would be less of a distraction than knocking, I try the door handle.

It isn't locked.

Twisting it, I ease the door open and peek inside. Three people are standing by Herman's worktable. They're chatting about best-laid plans and laughing like old friends.

"Knock, knock." I rap my knuckles on the door. "Sorry. We didn't want to disrupt your process, so I thought I would peek inside."

"It's fine, Red." A distinguished-looking man with salt and pepper hair and beard beckons us in. "It's good to finally meet you properly. I'm Herman Humphrey."

I accept his hand, and the moment our palms meet my skin tingles. Wow. His being a cute little fuzzball really dampened his power. "It's good to meet you too. Congrats on being your old self again."

"It's all because of you and your friends. I know the circumstances are dire, but I'm grateful you happened along."

I don't think we deserve the credit, but I suppose everything happens for a reason, so indirectly, we had something to do with it. "Speaking about the dire circumstances, Danika has a question about the power signature the mantle clock gives off. She's going to try to track it so we can stop the phasing."

Dani steps in beside me and focuses her attention on Alastair. "You were the one who confiscated it and stored it for decades. I assume you can tell me a bit about how it works."

Alastair grins. "I can. Come over here, and I'll explain what you need to do."

When they break off, I'm standing with Georgia and Herman. "While they do that, we need to recover that spell so we can take down the containment on the city."

"There's a problem with that, dear," Georgia says. "A Light Weaver bound our spell and since they are no longer—"

Herman waves her worry away. "They have that sorted. Apparently, the Light Weavers are extinct no more."

Cue the graceful arch of a manicured brow. "Surprises. Surprises. Very well, we can certainly do our part to right the wrongs of the time."

While Georgia and I look on, Herman goes to his bookshelf, selects a particularly thick text, and brings it to the table. He flips open the heavy cover and goes through the pages until he finds the one he needs.

"Page eight hundred and twelve." He winks.

She smiles at the number and winks at him. "Such a romantic."

I'm not sure what the number has to do with romance, but I don't care. Stepping close I glance over the spell on that page and frown. "I'm no sorcerer, but even I can tell that isn't the spell for a high-level containment spell."

"Right you are, Red," Herman says. "It's a placeholder. We sorcerers love to hide things in plain sight. It's a bit of a joke with us."

I take a closer look as Georgia passes her hand over the weathered cream parchment and the words of the original spell dissolve and fall away, replaced by a new spell appearing in its place.

"Et voila," Georgia says. "The well-guarded spell to ensure containment of fae prisoners of Alcatraz."

Nikon has joined us, and he steps close to my side and looks over the spell. When he flashes me an annoyed grin, I know exactly what he's saying. We wasted hours and days trying to track this spell down, and they had it here all along.

That's the problem with working with other people who don't share the same motivations as you—they don't share the same motivations as you.

"Excellent, well, onward and upward." I try to look at the bright side. "Nikon, do you want to go over this with them, so we can all get on the same page?"

He nods. "Yeah, I suppose that would be best."

Herman holds out a hand to Georgia and pulls her into the conversation. "We're happy to help, aren't we?"

Georgia grins. "I've been sitting on a shelf gathering dust for twenty years. I'm happy to be put to work."

I gesture at the cushy chair in the corner. "Excellent, and while you're doing that, I'll be right here, thinking with my eyes closed."

CHAPTER FOURTEEN

I must've dozed off because I jolt awake to the rowdy congratulations of Herman, Georgia, and Alistair. It takes a moment to get reoriented, but I'm still in Herman's workroom, and the three sorcerers are patting Nikon on the back, seemingly quite taken with the Greek's mad skills.

I'm not even a little surprised.

Nikon has had greatness in him since the first moment I met him. I'm only happy that he's starting to really shine.

"I take it you did it?" I wipe the sides of my mouth dry of any drool and go to the worktable to join the celebration.

"We did half of it," Georgia says.

"The more difficult half," Herman says. "We got it down, which will be the more difficult task by far. Due to the instability of magic right now, it was a feat in and of itself."

I hug Nikon, pleased that his skin isn't vibrating with electrical barbs or rotating through the colors of the rainbow doing his lava lamp light show. "Excellent work. Now we need to put it back up, right?"

"Right." Nikon exhales. "Now that I've got a sense of how the spell works, I'm not anticipating any issues. It should be smooth sailing."

Thank goodness. Finally, we catch a break. "That's great news. While you guys finish up, I'll go down and give everyone the update. You guys keep on keeping on. You're doing great."

Between the success with the containment spell and my little nap, I've got a second wind and a burst of optimism. Things are finally turning around on this case.

Dionysus, Diesel, and Manx are having a beer out on the back patio, staring at the pink sky and two moons. "Hey, how are things down here?"

"Strangely peaceful," Dionysus says.

Diesel grins up at me. "We decided to take a breath and get ready for the next shoe to drop."

"I see. You're catching on already."

I pull out one of the other patio chairs and join them at the glass table. "The others haven't gotten back yet?"

Dionysus shakes his head. "They've been gone for almost an hour. Sloan said they wouldn't be much longer than that, so we expect them any time."

I take the elastic out of my hair, rake through the waves and tie things back up. "So, Diesel, what do you think about being part of our team?"

He nods. "I'm enjoying it. I don't think I've been too useful yet, but like you said, it'll take a bit to settle in."

"Useful is subjective." I reach for Dionysus' beer, and he slides the glass into my palm to share. "I think you've done fine. You've been solid all along."

I feel the air surge with Sloan's wayfarer signature and turn to find them rushing in with purpose. They're wearing triumphant grins, and I'm hopeful we might just have scored another win for the team. "Let me guess. You found Val Ryn?"

Danika grins. "More importantly, we found the location of the mantle clock. But yes, I'm sure Val Ryn is there with it."

"I'm sure you're right."

"We need to move quickly." Sloan accepts the beer from my hand and takes a long drink.

"Why? Is he on the move?"

Danika shakes her head. "He's locked down in one of the outbuildings on Alcatraz. We think he's about to make his move to break through the spatial shielding and access the prison."

"Oh, dear," I say.

Sloan frowns. "Oh, dear, what?"

"The sorcerers took the containment spell down about fifteen minutes ago. They're working on putting it back up right now. If Val Ryn is already at the prison, we might have done him a favor."

Sloan nods. "Aye, we need to go."

Nikon and the three sorcerers come downstairs to join us. "Huzzah," Nikon says, grinning. "Broken containment spell down. Proper containment spell reinstated."

I look at Alistair. "Let's suppose Val Ryn succeeds in getting his father out of his cell and out of prison. How dangerous is the man? What should we expect?"

"That depends on whether or not his son gets his collar off. The prison suppression collars negate powers and render prisoners much less lethal. Brynali was a skilled fighter but a nightmare of a dark sorcerer. If his collar is off, he's every dark impulse you can imagine."

"Then let's hope his collar remains on and he's found some kind of inner Zen while in the clink."

Alistair frowns. "He was a violent murderer when he went into that prison. I expect he'll be even stronger now with years of venom to fuel his black soul."

"That's not the only problem." Sloan frowns at me. "The best way to ensure his father's escape will be to cause enough chaos so they can get away."

I roll my eyes. "He's going to let everyone out."

"Aye, that's my thought. After workin' with Dani to track the energy, I doubt Val Ryn could focus the power of the Port Gate enough to affect only one holding cell, even if that were his intention."

"So, how many inmates are we talking?"

Danika frowns. "In total, there are one hundred and seventy-five prisoners in four wings and on four floors."

"That's a lot of ground to cover," Nikon says.

I peg Trent with a look. "What about the selkie guards?"

"They have been notified and are calling in reinforcements preparing for an imminent breach."

I hate the sound of an imminent breach, but I suppose that's where we are. "How will we know when that's happening?"

Trent holds up a black disc and a ring of lights begin to flash across the top of it.

"So, that's what it'll do when the shit's hitting?"

Trent cursed. "Yeah. Exactly this."

From the reactions of both him and Sloan, I get a bad feeling. "This isn't a demonstration of how it works, is it?"

Sloan shakes his head. "No, luv. This is a real prison break crisis."

"Of course, it is."

CHAPTER FIFTEEN

Since we now know portaling had nothing to do with the destabilization of the city, we're back in business and unhindered by travel. Nikon snaps all of us there in a blink.

When we arrive on the island, I'm not sure where to begin. The old concrete and sandstone buildings might've been suitable to house and hold human prisoners in the past but not empowered prisoners of the present.

"How do we get through the glamour to the fae prison?" I ask. "We can't defend something we can't access."

"Allow me." Georgia takes Herman's hand and raises her palm.

A moment later the dull, whitewashed, and run-down prison disappears, and we're standing in front of a glossy black mammoth. "Wow. That's damn ominous."

Danika and Trent look as awed as my crew does, while Herman, Georgia, and Alistair have obviously been here before.

There's no time to admire the architecture, though. There is a prison break in progress.

With the glamour removed, the roar of the klaxon is deafening, and the immediacy of the situation is front and center.

"How do we get in?"

Danika is about to speak when the wall seam glows, and a door appears where there was a solid wall moments before.

When the door swings open, Juniper leans out. "Get inside. Even with our warning, the guards have been caught unprepared."

Our group hustles inside, and I take a look around. The place is massive.

"Break into groups and grab a prisoner pad," Juniper commands, pointing at a wall with silver tablets slotted in cubbies. "The system tracks the prisoners and the permissions they have. Anyone outside their allowed area is a flashing red dot."

Trent is grabbing tablets and handing them out.

"The prisoners locked down or staying within their areas are black dots."

I accept a tablet and study the layout of the prison. It's a hollow rectangle with a center row going through the middle and two corridors crossing it from side to side.

A man joins us. "The first-floor houses non-lethal offenders, the cafeteria, and access to the outdoor yard. Floors two through four are the more dangerous inmates as you go up."

Juniper gestures at the man. "Warden Wells has given you all full access to the prison. Place these patches on the muscle of your shoulder, and you'll have no trouble getting from section to section or floor to floor."

She starts handing out a stack of stickers and we pass them around. "Your animal companions will have to stay with one of you or get locked out. The warding between cell blocks will negate portaling, dematerialization, and all other methods of magical transport."

"Ye better release Bruin now, *a ghra*," Sloan advises. "The corridors and doorways are wide enough fer him to navigate with us."

I raise a finger and get the attention of the warden and the two guards at the door. "I'm releasing my battle bear. He's on our side, so please don't mistake him for an enemy."

The three nod, and I free him to come out and join us.

The rush of trepidation from the onlookers makes me proud. "Bruin and Manx, engage your battle armor. We have no idea what we'll be facing."

They do as I ask, and the onlookers grow even warier. Yeah, they really are that badass.

"We're tracking the device responsible for the current mayhem." Danika glances down at her watch. "Alistair, Trent, and Nikon, you're with me. We'll take the fourth floor."

I blink but don't say anything. Fine, she can set her course and take one of my guys. It's a bit assuming, but whatevs. I suppose, on a personal level, it's good for her to want Nikon around.

Yay Greek.

"We'll take the third." I glance down at the screen before sliding the tablet into the thigh pocket of my pants. "Looks like we've got four to put back into their cells. Bruin, Dionysus, and Herman, you're with me. Diesel, Sloan, Manx, and Georgia, you're on two."

I see the worry in Sloan's eyes and know he prefers to be at my side when the shit hits, but one of us needs to be with Diesel. I've already got Bruin as a battle beast and having two of the three strongest men on the same squad doesn't make sense.

What happened in Montreal can't happen again.

No part of my away team is a red shirt.

Sloan's got strategic thinking, magical skills, and healing. Diesel has the strength, and Georgia has the sorcery abilities.

It's the right call, and when he nods, he's telling me he understands and agrees.

I flex my palm and call Birga forward at the same time I enact my body armor. "All righty then. Let's do this."

Based on the flashing red dots on my prisoner tracker, there shouldn't be any enemy forces taking us on when the elevator door opens. The good news is that the elevator car walls are clear, so we can see what we're dealing with before they open.

Even still, I stand in front of the doors and erect a shield to protect Herman and Dionysus behind me. "Are you ready to do this, boys?"

Herman is grinning like a fool. "For the first time in five months, I'm standing on my own two feet. I'm ready for anything."

I love the ring of joy in his voice and am excited for him that everything worked out.

"What about you, Tarzan?"

"I've been battling since the beginning of civilization, Jane. I'm always ready."

Yeah, but this is the first time since the beginning of civilization that he's battling without immortality and god powers. I frown at the stun stick the warden gave him. "I wish you had a sword."

"You and me both."

I hear the slight quiver of nerves in his voice and understand his trepidation. Facing your mortality is a humbling and scary thing.

"You've got this. Stay close until you find your rhythm. It's just another battle. We've fought dozens of them together and always come out in one piece."

He swallows and nods. "I'm good. I won't let you down, I swear."

"That's because it's impossible." I wink and give him as much support in a smile as I can. "Here we go."

The elevator bumps to a stop, and I pat the reinforced leather of Bruin's armor. "Safe home, Bear. I love you."

"Love ye right back, Red."

Let the games begin.

The elevator doors glide open with silent ease and my shield flares. "On our toes, guys. My early warning system just came online."

Bruin takes the lead, and I'm caught wondering if Dionysus and Herman should go next, leaving me as the last man on the line or if I should stay in front of Dionysus and Herman?

Considering escaped prisoners could come from several directions, I decide on the first scenario and become the sweeper.

"Move out, boys. I've got your backs."

I smile as our procession moves through the first hall and think about Manx and Sloan. The boys love fighting with one another. Manx might not have the strength and ability to ghost out of places like my bear, but he's got speed, agility, and endless heart.

"On your toes, Bear. We've got a wandering soul six feet down the corridor on your right and coming fast."

I check for the others on our floor and pause. "Herman, we've got someone coming our way from behind. Are you ready?"

He pivots with me and raises his hands. Swinging his hands through the air in a series of practiced motions, he creates a geometric shield of symbols in the air. The magic ignites and crackles with power.

"Not bad for an old guy."

He chuckles. "Oh, it feels amazing to be able to do that again."

I imagine his little sugar glider persona doing the same thing and laugh inwardly. It would be super cute but not nearly as effective as what's happening here.

Dionysus nods. "I remember one time when I was transformed into a goat. Sure, it's fun to bounce around and kick over the other goats, but I was glad to get my hands back. There are certain things a man can only do with a palm and the ability to form a grip."

"And on that note..." I'm not the least bit interested in him continuing that train of thought.

Bruin's roar breaks the silence around us.

I check the screen one last time, slip the tablet into my pocket, and settle in for the fight. *"Bestial Strength."*

The guy that comes around the corner could never pass as human. I'm not an expert on all the empowered races but judging by the fact that he's literally on fire, I'm going to go with some kind of ifrit, elemental, demon, or fire dragon.

Not that it matters.

When a human torch comes barreling at you, there are only a few ways to respond. *"Ice Storm."*

I call to the moisture in the air and convert it to pellets of ice. It would be helpful if there were a large pond or fountain in here to siphon from, but beggars and choosers and all that.

My efforts are barely holding back his advance. There's no way I've got enough chill to douse him altogether.

"You need to go back to your cell, dude. There's no escape. Even if you could get outside, which you can't, we've got all the guards swimming the waters and circling the island. You won't get anywhere."

Our opponent doesn't seem put off by that.

"You're not trying to escape?"

He shakes his head and cracks a flaming whip at me. "No. Just stretching my legs and having a little fun."

I spin out of the way to avoid getting pegged by the fiery rope.

Damn, he's good with that thing.

"You've got a real future in front of you." I adjust my footing so I've repositioned to defend. "What are you thinking? Ringmaster or Dom?"

He grins. "Hit me with some more of your storm, little girl. It tickles."

I chuckle. This guy knows how to sass.

I respect that. "I'd go Dom if I were you. Then you can start building up your clientele in here. Ringmaster would be too tricky. The whole point of a traveling circus is that they travel. You're currently grounded."

"I don't think we're supposed to be flirting with the prisoners, Red." Herman fires intermittent blasts of magical energy.

I laugh and shrug. "Why does battling have to always be about death and hate?"

The ifrit—or whatever he is—sobers and turns his attention to Herman. "She's not wrong. I don't hate you two. I don't even dislike you. You're simply the two people I found when I was out on my freedom stroll. Now Mountain, on the other hand, is a different story."

He gestures behind me, and as much as I don't want to get caught turning away from an enemy, my shield is ramping up its burn.

I sense Mountain behind us and step to the side to turn my back to the wall so I can see both opponents.

Not that I want to see the second one.

Damn, the guy must be close to nine feet tall...eleven if I count the bull horns. My guess would be that he's part centaur and part giant...is that a thing?

Not that I want to imagine how that happened.

He walks on four legs and has long tufts of ebony and white fur covering his legs and arms. In his hands, he's swinging what looks like the leg of a human man. He's got a hold on the ankle and from what I can tell, ripped the limb off at the hip joint.

Based on the blood down his chin and chest, he may have also eaten the owner of that leg for a snack.

"Mountain, I take it? Is that leg you're swinging from a guard or a prisoner?"

The beast grunts at me, swiping the leg through the air from side to side and spraying a line of blood from wall to wall.

Cleanup on aisle two.

"Hilarious. I love the face you just made." The ifrit chortles. "It'll be worth the repercussions for leaving my cell to have that image in my mind."

I scrunch up my face. "I'm so glad to amuse you. I think the fact you don't find that gross says more about you than me."

He laughs again. "That's probably true."

Mountain storms forward, swinging the dismembered leg at my head. I get Jackson Pollock'd and groan.

Oh, it's on. I raise Birga and ready for his attack. "Fi-fi-fo-fum. That leg wasn't, by any chance, from an Englishman, was it?"

I'm not sure my question registers. It certainly doesn't slow him down.

The downward strike is bone-rattling, and I'm thankful for the strength feeding my cells. I block his hit by bracing Birga in both hands and locking my elbows over my head.

The spray of blood hits me a moment later.

Gross.

"Herman? A little help?"

A large golden serpent rises behind Mountain and attacks. It coils around his horse body, its tail immobilizing his legs while its head continues in slithering circles, constricting around his chest and arms.

The serpent wraps and spins, covering more of the beast with each winding circuit.

"Where does he belong?" Herman asks.

"Oh, I'll show you," the ifrit says, extending a fiery finger back the way he came.

I stare the man down. "Why would you show us?"

He laughs, absorbing his fire whip back into himself. "I've had my fun. I'll show you where the big guy belongs and return to my cell. Maybe you could mention to the warden that I was helpful."

I'm not sure what he's playing at, but I don't sense any deception, so I let it go.

It takes all kinds.

"Sure. I can do that. Help us get this one put back, and if you don't try anything, I'll mention to the warden that you were helpful."

The ring of fire sheathing him flares and he gives me a wide smile. "And a good time is had by all."

Yeah, peachy.

Herman and I follow the ifrit's lead, get the Mountain back into his cell, and use the touch screen on my tablet to resecure the cell.

Once we repeat the process with the ifrit, we follow the sounds of fighting and set off to search for Bruin.

We weave through the space until we find evidence that my bear has been here.

"Is he dead?" Herman asks as we come to a body.

I frown at the man with no head and look at Herman. "I'm pretty sure. Yeah."

"Your bear is fearsome."

"That he is." I check that he's good and get us going again. "That he is."

When we find Bruin and Dionysus, I raise Birga and get back to business. It's three on two, and while my boys are holding their own, the arrival of Herman and me tips the scales in favor of the good guys.

After that, it doesn't take long before we're forcing the disgruntled prisoners back into empty cells.

Without the help of the ifrit, there's no way for me to know who belongs where, so I don't try. We shove bodies into empty cells and lock the door.

I'm not sure what to do with the dead prisoner, so I do the

same thing. I drag the body into a cell while Dionysus tracks down the head. When we find it, he sets it inside the cell, and we lock things down.

Pulling out the tablet, I check that the third floor is clear. It is. The second floor is too.

"The warden and the guards can figure things out later." I release Birga to her resting place on my forearm. "How about we head upstairs and check on the others?"

"Sounds good to me." Bruin grins.

I chuckle. "Try not to have too much fun, Bruin. This is a battle, after all."

He swings his boxy head and wiggles his black nose at me. "These men know how to put up a good fight. It's hard to find qualified opponents."

I search for a clean patch of fur and pat his head. "I'm glad you're enjoying yourself, buddy. Hopefully, you can kick some more butt upstairs."

"Hopefully."

The time we wait for the elevator gives us a chance to catch our breath. I wish we could all be like Bruin and gain mana from fighting.

Studying the tablet for what's going on in the prison break, I watch as the blinking red lights outside the prison get corralled and funneled back to the entrance.

"That must be the selkie guards doing their thing." I point it out to Herman and Dionysus.

"Have I ever told you about the time I got invited to a selkie wedding?" Dionysus waggles his eyebrows.

"No, but I'm afraid it'll have to wait. It looks like two prisoners are still free on this floor. This is the floor for the most dangerous criminals. Remember to watch your backs. No one dies today."

Dionysus sobers and smacks his stun stick into his hand. "Right and tight. Got it."

I slide the tablet away and draw a deep breath. "All righty, here we go again."

The moment the elevator doors open, Bruin and I race forward and follow the sounds of magical warfare. I flex my palm and faery fire burns bright in it. That's both good and bad. If the dampeners are down, we can all access our powers…including Val Ryn and possibly his father if he's free of his collar.

A thundering metal *slam* echoes down the hall to our right, and Trent slides down a steel door and crumples into a heap like a ragdoll.

The dude got air. It's scary even to consider who or what could toss him around like that.

"Bruin and Herman, help Trent."

"Aye, I'm on it."

"On our way."

They veer off to help Trent contain one of the escaped prisoners, and I continue on our original course with Dionysus. "Stay close, Tarzan. The magical dampeners seem to be offline. We don't know who's coming at us or what they've got in their arsenal."

Downstairs the battle went okay, but I'm not confident in Dionysus' abilities to defend himself if things go sideways. Honestly, if I knew he'd end up on a supermax prisoner floor, I would've thought twice about bringing him.

A pulsing silver glow shoots out from behind the next corner, and I slow our pace. "Someone can cast here."

"It could be Nikky's witch, the possessed pee weasel, or the sorcerer elf."

"Or his father if he's got his suppression collar off."

"Yeah, that too. Although, that possibility is less to my liking."

Mine too. I ease up to the corner and give my shield a moment to weigh in. It's active but not going haywire.

That's a good sign.

I listen to what's happening around the corner and get a

clearer picture. Nikon is closest to us, and Danika and Alistair are farther up the corridor.

Nikon has a few magical talents in his bag of tricks but mostly he portals and fights with a sword.

Sadly, no swords are available at the moment.

By the sounds of it, Brynali Rilios is not only free from his prison cell, but he's also free from his collar and casting.

"Well, shitters." Based on the grunts and the sniping, I pinpoint where I think everyone is, then I draw a deep breath and round the corner.

It's worse than I thought.

Somehow Val Ryn has Nikon and Danika separated. Team Rilios has made it to a locked common area farther up the hall, and the purple-haired witch is pinned in Brynali's empty cell and unable to go after them.

Where's Alistair?

"Detect Magic." It takes a moment to find him. He's camouflaged himself to match one of the cell doors and is hiding in plain sight. Nifty trick. "Mind if I join the party, fellas?"

The shift in attention is exactly what I was hoping for, and it gives Nikon a chance to retreat and fall back to join me. "Hey, Greek. How're things?"

"I've had better days. My ex is currently locked in a prison cell and being targeted by her ex and his maniacal father."

I blink. "Her ex? She was seeing Val Ryn?"

"Yeah, right up until he locked her in McWinn's room and tried to suck her dry of magic."

"Well, that's a breakup to remember. So, how is she, anyway?"

"I think she's fine. She said it was pretty casual."

I roll my eyes. "Not about Val Ryn, goofball. How does she fare in this fight?"

"Oh, fine, she's just pinned."

"Excellent. Can you flash, Greek?"

"Nope."

"Why is magic online and portaling not?"

"Maybe it's a by-product of the prison security?"

"That doesn't seem fair."

He chuckles. "No, but I don't suppose fair matters."

True. My armor is still active from our third-floor conflict, so I take a chance. "Come on, Greek. In my world, the guy always gets his girl. Stay behind me. We're going on a field trip. Alistair, I need you to back me up with some fireworks and light show action. I want a chaotic distraction."

"I can do that."

The moment I start spinning Birga, fireworks start going off. The *squeal*, *crackle*, and *pop* of the pyrotechnic light show give me cover, and I can feel my spear's excitement as Brynali and his son start firing bolts of energy at us.

In high school, I was always a field hockey girl, but I could hold my own on a baseball diamond. Bolt after fireball after energy charge, Birga connects and returns fire.

The redirection of their magical attacks makes them sit up and take notice and gives us the chance to push forward.

Swing after swing, I return fire, and we move closer to the cell. When we get there, Nikon slides in behind me and checks on Danika. "Are you all right?"

Dani straightens and scowls. "Other than being pissed, yes. We're the good guys, and they've got the higher ground."

They definitely do. "Bruin, if you're available, we could really use you, buddy."

I get no response from my bear.

"He must still be indisposed helping Trent."

Danika nods. "That's fine. Trent and I are both pissed at Val Ryn's betrayal, but I wouldn't mind being the one to bring the asshole down."

I grin, liking her more and more.

Movement on the floor inside the common room brings my attention to two guards lying in view of the open doorway. I'm not sure if they're injured, but they don't seem interested in this fight.

I begin to tell Nikon to snap in and get them when I remember his powers are blocked.

"Okay, Greek. When I say go, your job is to—" My thought is interrupted as one of the guards makes a break for it. He's running straight down the hall toward us, and Val Ryn is firing to take him down.

"That kooky kid is going to get himself killed." I rush out of the cell, grab him, and turn to take the hit against my back. My shielding can take a couple of hits from this range, so I block the fire and run him to the corner.

Bruin is rushing up toward us. "Excellent timing, buddy. Dionysus, you take care of—"

A thunderous explosion detonates, and the entire building shakes.

I lift my arms to shield my head and throw myself at Dionysus. There's no time to erect a barrier as we crash to the floor. My heart is racing as the prison collapses on top of us.

CHAPTER SIXTEEN

I don't think I black out completely. There's a moment or two when I'm not tracking, but once the fog clears, my mind is not only working but buzzing. The explosion came from behind us. Maybe Val Ryn and his father blew themselves up.

We can hope, but I doubt we'd be so lucky.

Nikon is back there with Danika and Alistair. Could something Alistair did cause an explosion like that?

I doubt it. The force of the blast felt more like a bomb going off than a magical spell.

The dark space entombing me is full of the sounds of stone shifting, metal clanging, and growls of frustration.

Pushing to get up does me little good other than to make Dionysus grunt and cough beneath me.

"Sorry about that, Tarzan. There's a building lying on top of us."

"It's fine. It's been months since anyone has tackled me to the floor and pressed up against me."

I half laugh and half groan. "You can't help yourself, can you?"

I try again to move, but something seriously heavy is pinning me down. "Bruin? Are you with me, buddy?"

"Aye, I'm here." His voice is groggy and somewhere to my right.

"What about you, Herman?"

I wait, but there's no reply.

The lack of response hangs heavy in the silent air. "Herman? Talk to us. Give us anything. Are you okay?"

Still nothing.

"Bruin, are you still unable to ghost out? Are the wards still up?"

"Whatever the warding is here, it's still in place and preventin' me from ghostin' out, aye."

"Are you pinned?"

"Not so much pinned as worried if I move, things will shift, and I'll end up hurtin' one of ye."

"I don't know that we have much choice in the matter unless Herman wakes up."

"Did I hear my name on the lips of a lovely lady?"

I smile and breathe a little deeper. "Good to have you back, old man. Can you magic us a fix somehow?"

"Not while I'm flat on my face in a heap of rubble. Sorry. I'm good, but like your friend said, there are a few key things a man needs his hands for. Casting spells is one such thing."

Dionysus wriggles beneath me and reaches around my shoulders. "I can try to brace our position if you think you can get free."

"With the weight holding me down, I can't see that working. Bruin, you're our best bet. Try to stand, buddy—very slowly—and we'll take it inch by inch."

"That's what she said," Nikon says somewhere in the distance.

I bark a laugh, my relief a warm rush at the sound of his voice. "Yeah, she did. Glad you're alive, Greek. Are Danika and Alistair all right?"

"Alive to fight another day."

"Good. What about Trent?"

"I'm here, Fi." The deep voice of the blue warrior is a relief to hear. Maybe with his strength on our side, we can get free of this mess.

My head is throbbing, so I close my eyes and breath deeply for a few minutes.

"What about Sloan, Diesel, and Manx? Did they finish on the second floor? We could use the manpower."

"We're here, *a ghra*," Sloan calls from below. "The elevator shaft collapsed, but we're climbin'. Where are ye, luv?"

I struggle awkwardly to move a hand and try to make it to my knees. Debris shifts around me.

"Whoa, don't move yet. Let us work our way to ye."

"Don't worry about me. Herman doesn't have armor. Help him first. He was on my left when things went kaboom."

"And where's Dionysus?" Sloan asks.

"Oh, don't worry about me, Irish. I'm enjoying myself beneath our girl." Dionysus' words are playful enough, but there's something off about the tone of his voice. "If I must be human and meet my end, this is how I want to go. Go ahead and rescue Herman first."

I stay very still and lower my voice. "What aren't you saying, Tarzan? Are you hurt?"

"In fact, everything in me hurts. It's a strange feeling, pain."

I don't like the sound of that at all. "Let's not wax philosophical. What's wrong? Are you speared by something, crushed, broken?"

"Yes, I think so. All of the above."

"Where? By what? You gotta give me something to go on. I have some healing skills. Nothing like Sloan's but I can plug holes and patch up damage until he digs us out and can heal you up properly."

"I don't know that we have that kind of time," Dionysus says. "Maybe I was never meant to be human."

I feel sick. I thought I had him shielded. Did I miss something? Did I mess up and make things worse?

"Sloan, you gotta get us out of here. Dionysus is hurt. Bruin shouldn't be that hard to spot. He'll be under the large mountain of rubble."

"Ugh, don't say mountain," Herman groans. "No man should ever use another man's appendage as a weapon."

It *was* gross, but I don't have time to think about that. "Find Bruin. Dionysus and I were a bear's length closer to the main corridor at the time of detonation."

I zone out as the grunts of men and the groans of a battered building sound all around me.

With all my focus on Dionysus, I reach into his system and search for whatever injury he's suffering from. I'm not sure if it's the dampening of magic from the prison or I'm still drained from the siphoning, but I've got nothing.

My hands are braced against the concrete floor so I can't feel around in the dark and check him out. I can only reach out with my powers. "Hang in there, Tarzan. They're coming."

My panic over Dionysus is an inflating balloon of pressure building in my chest. "How's it coming, guys?"

"Slow and steady, Red," Nikon says. "The world up here is a tangled mess of steel and concrete. We're working on things."

"I've got her," Manxy says above us. "I found her scent. She's here."

"Good find, sweetie." I'm relieved.

"Humphrey, are you finally dead and ready to join us on the other side?" Alistair shouts in the distance.

Herman chuckles. "If I'm dead, at least I went out as a man. Much better than spending my afterlife as a fuzzy critter. Although, I did enjoy my furry pouch."

I roll my eyes. All this talk about dying and the afterlife is doing nothing for my current state of anxiety.

"Hotness?"

"We're coming. Almost there."

"One moment, darling," Georgia says. "Alistair and I shall set you free."

I'm not sure if she's talking to Herman or me, but it turns out I don't care. Any progress in our unearthing is welcome.

Moment by moment, more of the rubble shifts, and bits of the concrete avalanche off it. I lay very still, not wanting to disturb the process. Whatever Georgia is doing, it's working. The weight pinning me down is lessening as debris lifts.

When I'm able, I roll off Dionysus and struggle to stand. He lets out an ungodly shout and the floor sways beneath my feet. "I'm so sorry, sweetie."

A head rush hits, and I slide backward.

Strong hands catch me, and I twist to see who prevented my fall. "Hey, Mackenzie. Good catch."

"Hey, Cumhaill. If ye fall, I'll always be there to catch ye." He presses his forehead to mine and pulls me into a hug that crushes me almost as much as the rubble.

With my feet back under me, I regain my bearings. "Dionysus, you have to help him."

Sloan hands me off to Nikon and returns to the spot where I was lying on the floor. "Okay, Greek. Let's see what we've got, shall we? Can ye tell me what hurts and where?"

"Everything," he groans. "It's bad. I didn't want to scare Fi, but it's really bad."

Sloan lifts Dionysus' shirt and begins moving his palms slowly over his core, radiating outward in gradually bigger circles.

I cling onto Nikon's arms, my entire body shaking.

Long before I expect the healing to end, Sloan gets off his knees and offers Dionysus an extended hand. He pulls him to his feet, and I lurch forward to hug them both. "Are you finished? Is he healed?"

Sloan nods, and I can see he's fighting off a smile. "Aye, I got to him in time. All is well."

Dionysus gives both of us a strong hug and moves off to hug Nikon and celebrate his miraculous return from the brink of death.

I meet Sloan's gaze and frown. "What am I missing? I take it he wasn't as near to death as he thought himself to be."

Sloan chuckles close to my ear. "No. He had a wee fracture in one of his ribs and a sliver in his thumb. Crisis averted."

I exhale a laugh and pound my chest. "I suppose a cracked rib might feel like he's dying to a guy who's never felt pain."

"The important thing is that he's not. All is well. I think the fact that ye covered him with yer armor on was the savin' grace this time around."

A grumble and a grunt draw my attention to where Bruin is sitting on his haunches shaking his head. Beside him, sitting up unscathed is our lynx companion.

Sloan helps me over the shifting rubble, and I plop beside them. "Hey, boys. I'm sorry you got caught up in yet another dangerous debacle."

Manx nuzzles my thigh with a throaty purr.

While the world slows its spin, I run my fingers through Manx's soft coat and stroke the long, ebony tufts of his ears.

Harried voices and low grumbling curses of men grow louder as guards and prison staff make their way toward us. "Let's hear it, people. Is everyone okay?"

"A couple knocked unconscious for a bit," Alistair says. "I think everyone is alive and accounted for."

"Not everyone," Nikon says, his voice tight. "Danika made a run for Val Ryn before the explosion. He got the upper hand, and the three of them disappeared just before the place detonated."

I scramble to get to my feet. "They took her?"

"Och, Greek, I'm sorry."

"We'll get her back," I state with conviction. "The moment we get out of this mess and regroup, we'll put together a rescue plan."

Rubble crashes and crumbles as people dig to us. "Can we get some more light in here?" one of the guards asks.

Sloan calls faery fire to his palm and tosses it to the roofline to illuminate the space. The destruction of the scene is extensive.

Dayam. It looks like a bomb went off.

Freed from our pocket of devastation, we head around the corner to search Ground Zero. Nikon gives us a quick recap of who was where at the time of the explosion, but the landscape of the building has changed considerably since only a few moments ago.

"What do you think blew up?" I try to make sense of the carnage.

"I think it was the Port Gate itself," Alistair says.

"We're wasting time," Nikon snaps. "The longer we take, the farther they get."

"Not if we find the device," Sloan says. "If the explosion didn't destroy the Port Gate Clock and we find it, you may be able to track the destination. A detonation of that size would discharge a considerable amount of spatial energy."

I understand where Nikon is coming from, but his state of mind is currently locked in fear and not strategy. "Sloan's right, Greek. We find the clock, so we have a better chance to find her."

He knows I'm right.

The short delay in acting will bring us the info we need to find Danika quickly.

"Do you think they are still contained in the city somewhere?" Diesel asks. "They'd have to be, right? With the containment spell still in place, they'd be stuck like the rest of us, wouldn't they?"

Sloan frowns and keeps working with Manx and Bruin to sniff out the old clock. "Unless it was the conflict of power that caused the explosion. If the city and this prison are so heavily warded to prevent portalin' and they were able to get the Port Gate open usin' the clock, the resultin' power conflict would likely cause an explosion like this."

"So, the explosion was because they opened a portal to breach the containment," I say.

"I expect so, aye."

"It might well be," Alistair says. "When we first took down Brynali and confiscated the device, the spatial instability around him was incredible."

"Aye, ye mentioned the California coastline bein' in jeopardy," Sloan says.

I'm still confused. "What do killing witches to drain their power and a portal device have to do with one another? What was his plan?"

"We never learned that," Alistair says. "It's a question that remained unanswered no matter how long or hard we worked on him."

"Do you think whatever he was planning is long over or might he still have plans to finish what he started?" I ask.

"There's no way to know," Alistair says, "But knowing Rilios, I wouldn't be surprised if he picks up where he left off. The man is driven."

"Got it." Manx pops his head up from the search. "Well...I see it, anyway. It's a little stuck."

We make our way over to where Manx made his discovery, and I stare at the place he indicates.

A little stuck is an understatement.

The magical mantle clock is fused with the concrete of the prison structure.

Pressing my palms flat against the wall, I focus on softening the surface trapping the clock in place and releasing the Port Gate.

Nikon is right there with me. He's got a hold on the old clock and eases it out of its prison.

Once we have it in our possession, we leave the messy aftermath of the explosion to the prison's emergency staff and return to the meeting room downstairs.

Trent is there, speaking to Juniper, and by the look on her face, he just told her about Danika getting kidnapped by Val Ryn.

"We'll get her back." For her sake as much as for Nikon's. The Greek has unfinished business with her and deserves his chance to set things right. "With Nikon's power in spatial magic and our team's track record with getting the job done, we'll get her back."

Herman meets my conviction with a nod. "With the Port Gate Clock in our possession, Alistair can track its signature to the last destination it opened, and we can use it to track them down."

Alistair contradicts him. "This device won't be getting anyone anywhere. The explosion destroyed it. Wherever it sent them, we can't follow."

"Not by the power of the clock," I point out. "Maybe if you track the magical signature, Nikon can open a portal for us to follow and get her back."

Alistair, Herman, and Georgia turn to look at him.

"You can open portals between realms, son?" Alistair asks.

Nikon nods. "I can. I've never tried to direct the opening location, though. That will be new."

"Alistair can take care of that," Georgia says. "With all three of us powering his triangulation, we'll be able to pinpoint where they took your girl."

The four start a side conversation, and I circle back to Bruin. "Are you sure you're all right, buddy? We've all taken hits in battle, but it's really important not to downplay your injuries."

"What's this now?" Sloan arches a brow. "Are ye really preachin' the importance of full disclosure of yer injuries? What have ye done with Fiona Cumhaill?"

I wave his words away. "Har, yeah, fine, but I don't want Bruin hurt and trying not to worry us."

"No, neither do I, but the same sentiment applies when yer the one who's takin' a knock."

"What are you implying?"

He chuckles. "Not a thing. I'm sayin' outright that ye tend to gloss over yer injuries to avoid a fuss."

He's not wrong.

"I tell you if it's important."

"Aye, fer the most part, ye do."

"Fi? Can you two join us?" Nikon waves us over. "I think Alistair has what he needs. Are we ready to give this portal thing a try?"

"Not from within the prison," Juniper says.

"No, of course not," Nikon agrees. "But if we're done here, I want to leave and get started as soon as possible."

I glance around at our party, and everyone seems to agree. "Yeah, we're done here. Let's leave so we can portal back to Herman's house. There's a massive back lawn where we'll have room to open it without sucking in unsuspecting citizens."

Nikon portals us to Humphrey House and we gather on Herman's back lawn. The grounds of his estate are as impressive as the house itself. I'm thankful our paths crossed, and we've had the opportunity to get to know him…even if he's not a cute and furry sugar glider anymore. "Who's coming for the fae realm rescue?" I ask.

"Until Danika is safe, I'm with you," Trent says.

"Same," Nikon says. "I owe her that much."

"We wouldn't let ye have all the fun," Sloan says. "Would we boys?"

"Not a chance," Manx says.

Diesel shakes his head and rolls his eyes. "Why you insist on calling this fun, I've yet to understand."

I chuckle. "Trust me. Once you get attuned to the ebb and flow of things, you'll think it's fun too. At least, I think you will."

My question hangs in the air, and it's the sorcerers I'm not sure about. Alistair and Herman seem gung-ho, but Georgia is shutting them down. "I can't risk my granddaughter's life by taking her body into the fae realm when there is imminent danger. Annalise means too much to me."

I understand that.

"You shouldn't go either, Alistair," Georgia cautions. "You may not share the same concerns regarding Joseph's well-being, but the only point that matters is he's your grandson. Yes, you did a lot of good when you worked for the council, but for all the adventures you led in your life, he deserves the same opportunity."

Alistair nods. "Exactly right. That's why I *will* be going. Joseph hasn't the skill to have the adventurous life he craves. If I do this and help take on Brynali Rilios and rescue the young witch taken, he'll be living an adventure he couldn't otherwise."

"No, you'll be living the adventure you've missed and craved."

"I won't deny that I'll enjoy it too, but the boy has craved greatness his entire life. It'll do him good to experience the rush of danger and responsibility."

Georgia isn't happy with that answer, but she's not going to win the argument, so she lets it go.

"It'll be all right, Gigi, you'll see." Herman runs a gentle hand over her shoulder. The action is intimate and familiar to him, and I wonder how long they were involved. "I'll watch his back and ensure he and the boy survive to live separate lives once more."

"I suppose that's the best I can ask for, considering."

"It'll be fine, beautiful," Alistair says. "I promise I'll be careful with the boy and have heard everything you say."

With that settled, he gestures at Nikon. "All right, let's go get your friend."

CHAPTER SEVENTEEN

The only time I slipped behind the Faery Glass to the fae realm was when a witch hexed Sloan, and Dillan, Dart, Bruin, and I went to break the witch's hold on him so he wouldn't die.

That time we didn't portal.

We rode the rainbow Patty called for us, and the entire process was magical and quite peaceful...at least until I ass-planted on the hard ground on the other side and centaur guards chased us.

This time, Nikon is the man of the hour.

With his newfound spatial magic power boost, instead of sealing a portal rift like he's been doing so often over the past couple of weeks, he opens one.

With Alistair and Herman on navigation, Nikon focuses on creating the doorway between Herman's back lawn in our pocket realm and where Val Ryn and his father took Danika.

As we draw close to one another, the air grows warm and tingles against my skin. I breathe deeply. Mmm...the magic here smells like cotton candy.

It's little wonder that since the fall of the veil, the air in Toronto has smelled this way too.

Nikon's portal rift bursts into existence, and the air snaps alive with magic. Transporting into the fae realm proper this way isn't the same as transporting with wayfarer, immortal, or Moon Called magic. It's much more powerful than that. It's like the air is alive with energy snakes and they're slithering all over my skin.

It's less than ideal, but the discomfort is short.

Once we're on the other side and gain some distance from the air undulating with power, Nikon closes the rift, and we're ready to take stock of our surroundings.

"Okay, which—" Something sharp pierces my ass, and I spin, grabbing the shaft of a dart. "Ouch!"

I pull the tip from my flesh and release Bruin before calling my armor. It's too late to avoid the one that already pierced me, but no one says I've gotta make it easy for the fuckers trying to pincushion me.

"Bruin, Manx, armor up. Someone just pegged me with a dart. I'm pretty sure it was drugged because I feel odd."

I glance around, and it takes a minute before my brain catches up. Someone shot me.

They point-blank shot me.

In the ass.

"Okay, limp-dick," I shout toward the vine-covered trees behind me. "That is no way to welcome a guest to your realm."

My mind is a muddle.

What am I doing here? Did I come alone? I look at the faces of the people around me, and everyone seems oddly familiar and at the same time, like dangerous-looking strangers.

My shield burns hot on my back, and I flex my hand and call Birga to my palm.

I'm surrounded.

I swing to keep everyone at a distance and back away from the mass of people encircling me. They're shouting and scurrying around like ants while furry little creatures with wide eyes are chittering and waving stubby arms at us.

The walking teddy bears are smaller than Ewoks but bigger than Mogwai…and are holding dart shooters.

I glance at the dart clasped in my non-dominant hand and remember the pain in my butt.

Ah-ha! The Ewoks shot me with a dart.

But why?

I struggle against the fog blanketing my mind. It feels like someone has a finger on the backspace button of my brain and is wiping out sections of my memory.

Line after line of understanding is deleting at an alarming rate. The dart was tipped with something.

That has to be it.

"Yub-nub, assholes. That wasn't nice."

I swing Birga again to keep everyone away from me but can't figure out what the hell is going on or why I'm alone in the forest of Endor.

"Try more," one of the furry troublemakers chitters.

"It no good. Bounces off."

"Give me fun-gun."

I follow the chitter-chatter between a green teddy bear with a black patch over his eye and a blue one with white paws.

The green one takes possession of the dart shooter and points it at me. A projectile shoots out, hits my body armor, and bounces onto the ground.

"See. No good." He tries again, but again, the dart bounces off the armor and sticks into the dirt. I pick it up and frown at the sticky slime-green liquid coating the needle-sharp tip. "Rude."

I throw the dart from my butt and the one from the ground and hit the dart-happy fuzzballs with their method of attack.

"Ow!" the green guy screams.

The blue one pulls the dart and swoons.

Good. At least I'm not the only one woozy. Speaking of

woozy...I lay on the grass and close my eyes. The world is spinning, my body playing the part of my very own amusement park fun house.

The roar of a ferocious beast startles me bad enough that I pee a little. What was that?

I scan past the chaos of strangers rolling around and flailing their arms through the air. A giant brown grizzly bear is stomping and snarling through the turmoil. A sleek lynx accompanies him.

As strange as it seems that they're friends fighting together, stranger still...they have matching battle armor.

The giant grizzly swats a fuzzy purple teddy bear through the air like a screaming golf ball, and I giggle.

That is my kinda bear.

If I felt better, I'd launch a few Mogwai myself, but I don't. I'm achy, muddled, and feel like cat hack.

Speaking of cats, the lynx is dodging through a mass of teddy bears, tackling them to the forest floor and snapping up their dart shooters.

The grizzly swipes a few more with his massive paws and—wow, he can really get air. Now it's the little furballs screaming and running around like mad.

Can ye hear me, Red? The voice in my head is both strange and comforting. I glance around, and the massive bear is looking right at me. *Focus, Fi. Whatever they've done to ye, yer stronger and smarter than these yappy rainbow bears from Hell.*

The grizzly is gruff but charming, his voice floating to me like distant music on the breeze.

I watch the horde of harried Ewoks and the strangers fending them off looking rattled, and all of this seems familiar to me somehow.

Have I been here before?

I don't think so.

Why am I here now?

I feel like there was something important I needed to do. I stare at the light of the pink sky and push at the blanket wrapping my mind in wool. It's pretty here...in an "I'm gonna eat you" sort of way.

Fiona. Focus, lass. Sloan and the others got hit by many darts while yer only affected by one. Ye need to clear yer mind and help them.

Sloan?

I follow the scramble of men fighting off furballs and scan the faces of the strangers. Are they strangers? A couple of them tug at my heart when I look at them.

The black man in the fine clothes—yeah, he's delish—but something tells me he's even more incredible inside than out. I feel like we're partners somehow...

Then there's that one. I study the slim blond with a Mediterranean complexion brawling with the colorful bears behind me. He's a pleasure to look at too, but I feel like we share something more.

Like we get into trouble together.

Then there's the tall, regal-looking one with the brunette waves. When I look at him, I can't help but smile. He makes my heart happy. He's also too beautiful to be real.

Maybe he's *not* real.

Am I dreaming?

It's getting a little easier to focus with every passing moment. Whatever drug tipped those tranq darts, the effect of being poked only once is wearing off.

I glance at the others.

They are in trouble.

Whatever took hold has a tight grip on them.

I turn to the grizzly racing around keeping as many attackers off us as he can. "What do I do, Bear? I can't think. How do I fix this?"

"Call on yer druid powers. Castin' the druid spell Detoxify *would work best since yer not sure if it's a poison or a natural drug."*

"Okay. How do I do that?"

"Ye set yer intention to detoxify first yerself, then the others from the effects of the drug. Intention is the key. Yer magic will do the rest."

Hilarious. A talking bear is telling me I have magic. Maybe I'm more drugged than I thought. Perhaps I'm not clearing the cobwebs but getting sucked further down.

"Detoxify, Red. Trust me."

As cray-cray as it sounds, I do trust the talking bear.

Closing my eyes, I go with my instincts and focus on my intention to detoxify myself from whatever these demon Care Bears have done to me. *"Detoxify."*

I feel the power of my intention the moment it takes hold. Is that me? Did I do that?

Holy shit, I'm powerful.

My spell takes hold, the film of confusion peels away, and everything becomes clear. These little furry fae freaks attacked us the moment we came through Nikon's portal, and instead of rescuing Dani, we're the ones who need a rescue.

"Faery Fire." Calling the blue flames of faery fire to my palms, I target our annoying persecutors. "Nice try, fellas, but your ass is grass now."

"That's my girl," Bruin says. "Glad to have ye back, Red. Ye had me worried there, fer a minute."

"S'all good, buddy."

My perspective of the world around me clears with each passing moment, and I take in the chaos. The forest is wild with fighting, and while everyone is holding their own…if we were fighting as one, this would be over in a heartbeat.

I focus on Sloan, Nikon, and the others. *"Detoxify."*

Repeating the spell as I fight through the battle, I set them free one by one. I know from my experience it took a few minutes for the mind muddle to clear, and I was only shot by one dart.

Bruin said the others were shot by many.

So, while I wait for them to get back to the regularly scheduled program, I take my frustrations out on the furry assholes who haven't quite realized the tides have turned.

I'm not sure what they intended to do with us once we were in their thrall, but they never expected Bruin and Manx to foil their plans.

"What the fuck?" Nikon grumbles behind me.

"Welcome back, Greek. We were drugged and derailed by evil Ewoks."

"How long were we out?"

"No idea."

"No more than ten or fifteen minutes," Bruin says. *"Not too long."*

I relay that to Nikon, and he seems relieved.

I jog forward to help Sloan with the green bear and a yellow one. Despite the cleansing of my mind, it still feels like I'm running in water.

My legs feel heavy, and I can't get enough oxygen in my lungs to get my groove on.

Doesn't matter.

These hunters aren't fighters. The little furballs use their numbers and the immobilization of their prey to keep the upper hand.

Only that won't work anymore.

"Fi? What's goin' on?"

I meet the confusion in Sloan's pale green gaze and wink. "The furball horde wanted to make you into their private love slave, but I fought for your honor. You can thank me later."

He looks so confused I bust out laughing.

"Sorry, hotness. I have no idea what they wanted, but I've neutralized the drugging of their attack. Let's end this and get the hell gone."

"Good enough."

Five furballs are trying to get control of an irate Diesel. He's big and can defend himself, but that's just rude. I change direction to help. I spin Birga in my hands and crack one of his attackers with the blunt end of her staff.

The guy spins like a top and hits the ground.

I sidestep him and go for the next one.

"Fi? What's going on?" Diesel grabs the scruff of a golden bear and chucks him twenty feet into the trunk of a tree.

"This is our fae welcoming committee. They shot you with darts and drugged you. Having fun yet?"

He chuckles and grabs the next closest bear. "The chaos is growing on me. It's much more interesting than being a night watchman at a bank."

"Right? I told you it would be great."

He laughs. Herman and Alistair come back online, and we're fighting in full force.

When energy bolts and electrical shocks start permeating the air, they sound the retreat and bugger off.

We stay on guard for a minute or two more before we consider the battle well and truly over, but after that, we're all about regrouping and getting back on track.

"Is everyone all right?" I scan their faces.

"Thank the goddess ye got yer armor up in time to avoid gettin' caught up in their snare," Sloan says.

I wave away his praise. "Nah. It was all Bruin and Manx. They are the heroes of the hour."

"Our armor helped." Manx grins. "Those darts couldn't penetrate our gods-given armament."

"Well done, boys. Ye saved the day," Sloan says.

"They sure did." I'm proud of them. "Now, let's figure out where to go from here. Herman? Alistair? Have you still got a lock on where they took Danika?"

"It's a little more complex than having a lock on her. I tracked the destination of the portal. I have no way of knowing where they took her after they arrived."

I understand the storm brewing in Nikon's eyes, but it's not

Herman's or Alistair's fault. "You two got us this far. Maybe Manx and Bruin can help. Can you smell Danika's scent?"

"I'm not a bloodhound, Red," Bruin says.

"No, but you and Manx both have great sniffers."

"We do," Manx agrees.

"Aye, we'll do our best, of course. I'll do recon. Manx, go ahead and try to catch her scent and we'll see where we end up."

Bruin ghosts out and swirls around me once before rushing off.

The look on Nikon's face says he's not happy with where we're at. I loop my hand under his elbow and hug his arm. "It'll be fine, Greek, trust me. We'll find her, get her back, and she'll be berating you and breaking your back before you know it."

He arches a brow and chuckles. "As far as pep talks go, that one sucked."

"Doesn't matter. At least you're smiling again."

He leans over and kisses my forehead. "Thanks, Red. Now, let's go find her."

CHAPTER EIGHTEEN

Our rescue party might be a bit of a mish-mash, but it's got heart. We've got the senior sorcerers, the Toronto crew, the animal companions, and one large blue guy from the San Francisco crew.

It hasn't escaped my attention that we haven't fixed the phasing issue yet.

We're one for two.

I'm scanning the surroundings, watching for any trace of a returning Manx or Bruin, when Sloan comes over to join me. "How's Nikon doing?"

"Not great, but he's hanging in there. It's hard for him to know someone he loves is suffering. It's even harder on top of the guilt he already feels for breaking her trust and heart."

"He's lucky to have yer friendship. Sometimes all a person needs when the world is crashing around them is a sympathetic ear and a friend they know will have their back no matter what."

"Agreed. Nikon's good people."

"He is at that."

I meet Sloan's caring gaze and his words ring true in my

heart. It's like that for me too...with him, the Greeks, my brothers, and my friends.

People often see me running the team and think I run the show.

That couldn't be further from the truth.

There is no I in team, and my team is my support system. "I love you, Mackenzie."

Sloan winks and leans forward for a quick brush of our lips. "I love ye right back, Cumhaill."

I hug him, and my world resets so I can focus on what's to come. "Do you think Manx and Bruin will find her trail?"

Sloan shrugs. "Unless Val Ryn anticipated us having animal companions follow their scents and spelled the area to make that impossible."

Yeah, that would suck.

I'm about to voice that opinion when Manx gallops back. His armor is still engaged, and it's glistening in the sunlight. "I found her scent. Come. This way."

That's all we were waiting for.

I reach out on the mental wavelength I share with Bruin and relay the information.

"And away we go."

We follow Manx at a steady pace, weaving through the strange growth of green and purple leaves, spotted grasses, and the multi-hued tree trunks that remind me more of a military camouflage pattern than something we'd see in nature.

Manx leads us back to where he caught Danika's scent. "It's strong here, and it goes this way." He indicates with the tilt of his head and keeps moving.

"Well, it seems my second trip to the fae realm promises to be as disturbing as the first."

It feels like we're characters living in *Jurassic Park.*

Discarded huts lay broken and abandoned, left to the cruel whim of the wild things growing through them. The forest is overgrown with bizarre foliage, and even the ground gives off an unpleasant magical vibration.

"This place is royally messed up." Nikon scowls at our surroundings. "It's like we're caught in a movie remake of *Planet of the Apes.*"

"I was thinking *Jurassic Park.*"

Sloan brings his wrist up to check our progress. "If the passage of time here is similar to our realm, we should have enough daylight to get to the rim of the next valley before things get dark and dangerous."

To call what he's pointing at a valley is generous. Ahead of us, the ground gives away in a series of dips and rises that create craters a mile across and eighty feet deep. Some are steaming and releasing a yellow fog, and some set off my shield's warning system just by looking at them.

Regardless, his point is sound.

Getting as far as we can before it's too dark to see what's coming at us is a good idea.

With our eyes locked on that next rise, we push our pace to make it before daylight is lost. Halfway there, Bruin catches up with us and takes form to tromp through the long grasses.

"What does it look like around here?" I ask. "Anything we should know?"

"Other than the fae realm bein' feckin' bizarre?"

I chuckle. "Yeah, other than that."

He swings his boxy head around to meet my gaze. "Well, there are more of those Skittles-colored bears in every direction, I saw a patch of carnivorous flowers lift their roots out of the ground and chase down a groundhog-lookin' thing and devour it, and I'm pretty sure the water veining through the creek is acid."

"What makes you say that?"

"Because I saw two animals fightin' and one got knocked into the stuff. It was screechin' before it hit the surface and made one helluva noise when its fur and muscle burned off while I watched. Death was welcome, from what I could tell."

"All righty then. No impromptu dips to freshen up."

"Agreed." Sloan bends to the forest floor and picks up a stick. After checking it over, he runs his palms down its length, strengthening it and smoothing it out like a staff.

"It's creepy, that's for sure." Diesel flashes the canopy above the ocular version of a middle-fingered salute.

I know exactly how he feels. "Yeah, I hated it the first time, and I'm still not a fan."

"Same," Herman says. "When we get back, we'll have a huge dinner party to celebrate surviving this."

I want to say *if* we get back, but figure that wouldn't be helpful. "That would be lovely, Herman, thanks."

Before we crest the rise of the next crater, my shield burns hot, and I raise my hand and signal for us to halt and fall silent.

I take a beat to listen to my instincts.

While none of this is good, I don't get the impression that there's anything immediately wrong either.

After a long moment, my shield neither amps up nor dies down, so I take that as a sign to proceed with caution. I continue forward on the main path, crouching low as I crest the crater's rim and look over the drop of the concave bowl.

When I reach the lip, I drop to my hands and knees to peer over the ridge.

What the fuckety-fuck?

When Nikon said this place is royally messed up, he hadn't even seen this yet. It takes my mental hamster a moment to register the town details below.

It looks like the illegitimate love child of a glitzy casino on the Vegas Strip and a rootin'-tootin' Wild West town.

As lights blink and music plays, fae dancing girls in bustled silk dresses are coaxing patrons through the swinging doors of a saloon.

A gun-slinging man wearing a heavy black slicker and a silver star badge is glaring at the men strutting down the sandy streets.

Six dead bodies are twisting in the wind, hanging by their necks from the town's welcome sign.

"Do they realize welcoming people with dead bodies is an oxymoron?" Dionysus asks.

Diesel snorts. "Forget *Jurassic Park*. This is *Westworld*…after the AI has taken over and is killing people."

"You're sure Val Ryn took Danika in there?" I ask.

Manx nods. "Aye, I'm sure, unless he cast a spell to deceive us."

So, does that make him sure or not?

"I doubt he anticipated us following," Trent says. "Val Ryn has always been too cocky for my liking. He always considers himself the smartest man in the room."

"Humble."

"Not in the slightest."

"That works in our favor." Nikon scowls at the metal gridwork keeping us from entering the Wild West town below. "He won't be expecting us or in a hurry to get rid of Dani."

"Agreed," Sloan says. "Overconfidence is a spectacular weakness to exploit in an enemy."

Trent sighs and shakes his head. "Enemy…I can't wrap my head around that. Four days ago, I'd never have believed Val Ryn was the enemy."

"Except this is where we are." The hostility in Nikon's comment isn't only in his words. It's in his eyes too. "If you're not committed to taking your friend down, say so now. Any hesitation in battle could mean Danika's life or the life of one of us."

Trent shakes his head. "There won't be any hesitation, but tonight, when this is all over, I will mourn the friend I held in high esteem."

"That's fair. Now, let's get back to the rescue. We need to

figure out how we get in there and get Danika out with minimal chaos."

Nikon snorts. "When have we ever gotten the job done with minimal chaos?"

I shrug. "Maybe today's our lucky day."

He arches a brow. "Yeah, sure. Maybe."

The fae *Westworld* town in front of us sits at the bottom of a crater, and a flat metal mesh entirely seals off the top of the valley. Based on the level of power snapping over my skin and the ice-blue glow of magic radiating off it, it's safe to assume the entire system is heavily warded.

Built on the crater's outer rim are two outpost buildings that seem to be the official gateposts for those who wish to enter.

I rake my fingers through my hair and pull it out of my eyes. "We could go the direct route and declare our intentions. Maybe they'd see we're out-of-towners and welcome us in."

Diesel snorts. "Right, because the dead people pinatas prove how welcoming they are."

"How far does the warding run beneath the ground?" Nikon studies the long grasses beneath and behind us. "If it's not far, you guys can move the earth and make us a tunnel."

Sloan considers that a moment. "Should we try to portal in?"

"Hold off on that, hotness." I raise my hand. "If they've got the juice to light up the warding across the ceiling of an entire valley town to keep people out, they've anticipated people being able to portal."

Dionysus nods. "Yeah, let's try not to be the next welcome sign pinatas. Death isn't a good look for me."

"Deal."

"What about opening a rift?" I glance at Nikon. "Portaling is a fairly common ability and happens enough to expect and ward against. For a person to be able to open a spatial rift is much more uncommon. Maybe they haven't warded against that."

"I think ye've got a solid point there, *a ghra*, but as well as gettin' inside, we must consider how we navigate the rescue. Who are the people of this town? Will they know we don't belong on sight? Will they care? Do they report to a higher power?"

"You think there's a god of Vegas Bonanza?"

He rolls his eyes. "No. I meant perhaps there is a corrupt sheriff or a wealthy tyrant in charge of things."

"I vote we don't stay long enough to find out."

"I second that." Herman raises his hand.

Nikon and Dionysus raise their hands too.

I consider all the options. "Okay, Sloan, and I can do some druid poking around in the last few minutes of daylight. We'll test the boundaries of the warding. If it's a matter of it extending ten feet out and ten feet down, we can certainly move the earth out of our way and make a tunnel that lets out under the mesh ceiling."

"And if not, I can try to open us a rift," Nikon says. "Is it wrong that I hope this lands on you?"

I chuckle. "Considering how much you hate rift energy, not at all. I hope it lands on us too, for your sake."

"Thanks, Red. You're the best."

While Sloan, Manx, and Alistair explore a little to test the parameters of the warding, Bruin, Nikon, Herman, Dionysus, and I scope the town below to find our optimum point of entry.

Do ye see how the buildings cluster along the center of the dip? Bruin asks.

I scan the main street and yeah, other than a few outlier buildings branching off on smaller side streets it's just like Vegas and all about the Strip down the main thoroughfare. *Yeah, I see.*

Well, whoever designed the town positioned those outposts up top so everyone would come in that way and have easy access to the main path.

But that's not what we're doing.

Och, no. Never do what's expected.

I relay the exchange.

"I live by that motto." Dionysus grins.

I chuckle. "Agreed. Always keep them guessing."

"What about over there?" Nikon points at several outbuildings below us and against the slope we're on.

Bruin nods. *"Aye, that's the spot. Once night falls and we gain access to the other side of the warding, we'll have a straight shot down to those buildings."*

I scan the sloping walls of the valley and frown. "Do you think they'll have guards? If so, they'll have a direct line of sight to us coming down that hill."

"I didn't see any in the daylight, so I doubt we'll see any at night. That doesn't mean they aren't there. Just because it's an old-fashioned setting doesn't mean they don't have modern modes of surveillance."

"Once we're inside the valley, Sloan or I can portal everyone down behind the saloon." Nikon points at the two-story building at the main intersection of town.

Bruin nods. *"I'll ghost around and watch in case they have guard animals or fae with night vision that home in on ye."*

"Maybe there's nothing to worry about." My words sound hollow even to me. "Maybe they're a group of fae LARPers obsessed with the human Wild West."

"Who harbor fugitives and aid in the kidnapping of witches," Nikon adds.

"A little darker than what I was going for, but sure."

Bruin says, *Well, whatever the situation, there's no scenario in front of us with zero risk. All we can do is consider the possible obstacles and plan things to allow fer the greatest chance of success.*

I take another look at the bustling street. "There is enough activity to hide our arrival as long as they don't peg us for strangers."

I'm still thinking about that when the shuffle of footsteps brings the return of Sloan, Manx, and Alistair. "How'd things go with the warding?"

Manxy gives me a wide smile and Sloan waggles his brows. "I think we're in good shape, luv. The warding is strong, but it doesn't extend far into the surrounding land around the crater. It should be no problem to create a passage to get to the underside of the mesh."

I glance at Trent and Diesel. "It'll have to be a fairly big passageway to get everyone through."

Nikon shakes his head. "No. We don't need a full-sized tunnel. If you create a physical open-air passage between here and there, we can portal through."

"That's excellent news. Keeping things small makes it less likely anyone will stumble upon our tunnel too."

Everyone falls quiet, and we exchange glances. It seems that's the end of the questions and concerns.

"Excellent, so unless anyone objects, let's get this infiltration party started."

CHAPTER NINETEEN

Sloan and I discuss how we want to handle creating the opening and decide that while I pull the soil out to create a passage, Sloan will focus on making sure no earth trickles down the slope to alert anyone to our presence.

Easy-peasy.

Facing each other a couple of yards from the edge of the lip, we kneel and press our palms against the earth. It's the work of a moment to create a connection with the fae power running so strongly beneath the surface of the wild grasses.

"Move Earth." Supercharged as my fae connection is in this realm, the earth heaves and shifts without hesitation. With the two of us working on the tunnel, we create a mound of moving soil, pushing the earth away from the crater and hardening the outer edges to keep it from collapsing.

While I pile the soil, Sloan ensures no loose dirt tumbles down the slope.

Then it's done.

It doesn't matter how good the warding is if you can bypass it. Which we have.

Easing back from the edge, I straighten, brush off the knees of my pants, and scrub my palms together to get rid of the dirt.

"All righty then, let's get locked and loaded."

Dionysus raises a fist for a knuckle bump. "Let's getter done, boys and girls."

Nikon comes over and extends his hand. "Good luck everyone. Watch your asses. Saving Danika won't mean much if we don't all get out of this in one piece."

A look of agreement passes between each of us as we stack our hands on top of Nikon's. When we're ready, he transports us through the small tunnel and into the crater area.

When we materialize at the base of the slope, we're behind the saloon. Everyone goes silent.

Manx and Sloan are the sweepers, taking up the rear to ensure nothing unexpected comes from behind.

Short scrub covers the valley's slope. It's moist and thick enough to absorb the sounds of our progression but too low to conceal our presence.

There's a small outbuilding and our group slides inside and peers between the wooden slats as we get our bearings. I war between calling Birga and being ready to battle and trying to blend in as one of the locals.

I suppose the right answer depends on how likely our discovery is. I glance down at our clothes and frown.

"Alistair and Herman," I whisper. "Can you magic us some clothes so we pass ourselves off as locals?"

By the look on Alistair's face, that's child's play.

A stack of clothes appears on the dusty table against the wall by the door, and we all begin a hasty change into our local personas.

I hold up the emerald green silk with black lace and frown. "A dancing girl? Seriously? Does anything about me suggest I've got saloon dancing girl blood in me?"

Alistair shrugs. "If your friend is in any of the private rooms upstairs, you have the best chance of gaining access wearing that."

I hear what he's saying and don't disagree, but I'm not buying that his motive was solely strategic.

Turning away, I undo the Velcro straps holding my weapons vest and pull my shirt over my head. I make quick work of pulling the satin bustier on and lifting the girls to sit in the high cups.

Glancing down at the fleshy swells, I roll my eyes. "I'm going to get even for this."

Sloan chuckles behind me. He gathers my hair and sets it over my shoulder to the front before tugging on the laces crisscrossing over my back. "I don't know, luv," he says quietly by my ear. "I think the look suits ye. We haven't done much roleplay, but I've got visions of 'dancin' girl seduces her piano player fillin' my head."

Mmm. Now I do too.

I hold my arms up for the next layer of my dress and unbutton my jeans and shove them down my thighs. The kiss of cool air on my backside tells me just how short the skirt is. "Yikes, I'll be mooning people all over town."

"No one will complain," Dionysus says behind me.

Nikon chuckles. "No. In fact, it's the perfect way to keep men from looking at your face and realizing you don't belong here."

I roll my eyes and ignore the encouragement.

Sloan has taken a knee in front of me and slides a thin layer of stocking over my foot and up my thigh. Reaching under the short skirt, he tugs down the garter clip and dutifully continues putting me together.

"I can do this, you know." I flash him a look.

The contentment on his face is answer enough. "I don't mind, *a ghra*, honestly." He finishes with the elastic at the back of my thigh and gives it a ping.

The snap against my flesh draws the attention of the other men, and every one of them has the same smile on their face.

I wave and stop the staring. "Okay, enough. Show's over, boys. Heads in the game and minds out of the gutter."

Nikon and Dionysus share a look and say something in ancient Greek.

"Do I want to know what you just said?" I peg them with a look.

Dionysus blushes.

Nikon shakes his head. "Not unless you're finally opening up to the idea of embracing hedonism. Then yes, yes, you really do."

I swallow and shake my head. "No, I'm not open. I'm very closed. Try to remember we're here to rescue your ex-lover who you're trying to make amends with."

Nikon shrugs. "You say that like I can't multitask."

Dionysus chuckles. "I have spent more than a few salacious moments with Nikky. I can verify that he is very adept at multitasking."

I blush and turn to Alistair. "Do you see what you started? This is your fault."

A noise outside has our entire group stopping to hold position. I bend to look out the crack between two boards and realize too late I'm now flashing my party the rounds of my ass.

Straightening, I turn and glare at my gawkers. A woman has come around the building with an empty produce basket propped on her hip.

I glance around at the bags of vegetables and frown. This isn't going to be good.

Dionysus holds up his finger. *I've got this,* he says directly into my mind. *Get everyone behind the door.*

Seriously? He wants six men, me, and a lynx to get behind the door? I would protest, but he's already out in the night air and intercepting the woman.

"What's he doing?" Nikon hisses.

I shake my head, grab all the clothes, and throw them into a burlap sack. I toss that to Diesel, shooing the entire group as quickly and quietly as I can.

I grab my boots off the ground—again realizing I'm flashing my ass—and hustle behind the door.

Bruin dematerializes, and I join the others.

In no way are we hidden, but there's nothing to be done about that because Dionysus is already leading the woman inside.

Standing at the edge of the open door, he screens the view to us, all the while making small talk and flirting with her. When she goes over to set her basket on the little table, he steps in behind her and proceeds to suck on her neck.

"How long has it been since a man treated you like the angel you are?" he asks. Even without his god powers, he's got a velvety tone to his voice that could dampen any female's panties.

Her groan says she's all for being seduced by the handsome stranger in the storage building. "Too long," she breathes.

"Then close your eyes. I'm going to rectify that right now." As Dionysus continues to taste the column of her neck, he waves, indicating it's time for us to leave.

It's a risk.

If she looks up, she'll see seven people and an animal companion hurrying out of the building.

Honestly, though. I don't think she's got anything on her mind except what's going on with the god of a man grinding up behind her.

He gently grips her throat and tips her mouth up to meet his. Yeah no, he's got this covered.

I stand corrected, Tarzan. Charm and seduction are useful battle skills. Have at it.

The woman doesn't notice us take our leave and by the time we're out of the building and hustling deeper into the shadows, I'm giving Dionysus the win.

We're barely out of sight when two men in black fatigues

come around the corner. They look intent on something, but I don't think it's us because they have their sights set on an iron railing that leads up to the second and third floors of the building opposite the saloon.

We hold position while the dispatched soldiers close the distance to whoever or whatever they're after.

Both of them climb the stairs. One sneaks along the balcony looking in the windows. The other unlocks the door and slides inside.

I'm about to suggest we continue and get gone before they return, but the one on the balcony stops and pulls out his gun.

"Whoever they're after, I think they found him."

Balcony guy lifts his weapon and presses it against the glass of the room he's peeking into. He taps his ear as if he's got an earpiece in. Then the quiet *snap* of glass breaking gets swallowed by the night. When he steps out of the way, he moves back to the stairs.

A moment later, the guy who went inside comes back, dragging the body of a man killed with his pants around his ankles.

"A rather humiliating way to die," Herman whispers.

I shrug. "Not our circus. Not our monkeys."

Nikon is staring intently at the scene. "Maybe we'll be lucky, and they took out Brynali Rilios. Makes sense, doesn't it? He's been locked away for decades. The first thing he does is find himself a willing female and sets himself up for the night."

I chuckle. "I think that's wishful thinking, Greek."

"Well, nothing ever works out smoothly for us. I just thought, for once, maybe the Fates could smile on us."

I know how he feels. It's hard when someone you love is in danger, and nothing goes right to get them back. "We'll get her, Greek. Hang in there."

The two men don't bother to carry their man down the fire escape steps. They dump him over the rail, and he hits the ground with a hollow *thunk*.

They gather him up, dragging him twenty feet in front of where we're hiding in the shadows as they round the corner and take their kill to go.

"Sadly, that was not Brynali Rilios," Alistair says.

No. I didn't think so either.

"Likely another body for the welcome sign," Manx says.

"You might be right, buddy."

When the coast is clear again, Nikon leads us toward the side entrance of the saloon, and by the time we get there, Bruin is breezing around me, lifting my hair in his wake.

Upstairs. Third floor. Last room on the left.

I relay that information to the others.

"Is she all right?" Nikon asks. "Hurt? Drugged?"

Spitting mad, gagged, and bound with a cloth bag over her wrists, he says.

When I relay that, Alistair nods. "Yes. Brynali did that with the witches he drained of power as well. The bag over their hands is his way of ensuring the young witches can't access their powers and fight back."

"I still don't understand why he drained an entire coven of witches," I say. "What did that gain him?"

Alistair shrugs. "We never figured that out."

"To consume the power of a working coven through blood magic would create a huge amount of power," Sloan says.

"Like how much?" I ask.

Sloan frowns. "Like slaughter a city, move a mountain, change the course of a river system kind of power."

"Could he have used it to make the Port Gate Clock?" I ask.

Sloan shakes his head. "That's like equating the impact of an elephant landing on you versus a ladybird. It would be a waste and overkill."

"So, what did he use all that power for?"

"Nothing," Alistair says. "We assumed that he either transferred the power to someone else and we never caught his partner, or he stored the power in a vessel for future use."

I don't like either of those scenarios.

"These are all things we can work out after Danika is safe," Nikon snaps.

I nod. "Sorry, Greek. I just want to know what we might be walking into."

"What about Val Ryn or his father?" Sloan asks. "Were either of them up there watching over Danika?"

Val Ryn is in the same room. I didn't see the father, Bruin says.

Sloan relays that last bit. "I suppose we're as ready as we can be. Thanks, Bear."

With the intel in, we set our strategy the best we can. "Nikon and I will enter through the side door and go upstairs posing as a randy client and his saloon girl."

Sloan nods. "I'll make my way to the piano to keep an eye on the main hall."

"Diesel and I will each watch an exit from the shadows," Trent says.

"What shall we do?" Herman asks.

"You two will order a drink at the bar and lay low in the saloon to back us up. There's a good chance not only Val Ryn but also Brynali will recognize us. We've got to be ready to take whatever comes at us."

"What about Dionysus?" Diesel glances back at the storage hut behind the saloon.

"He's the god of good times. Let him do what he does, and maybe we can keep him out of harm's way."

Sloan and Nikon seem to agree with me.

"Okay, let Operation Westworld Rescue begin."

CHAPTER TWENTY

The saloon's interior is pretty much like I expected...well, sort of. Instead of being a Wild West saloon, it's more like the cantina in *Star Wars* with odd-looking fae and sketchy-looking characters wheeling and dealing in the corners, back rooms, and shadowed tables. But there are tables, serving girls, and guys slamming back drinks and getting rowdy.

It's not so different that we're at a loss.

From the side entrance where Nikon and I came in, we need to step into the main room briefly to get to the stairs.

Bruin said third floor, last door on the left, so that's where we're heading.

With my arm looped through his, I lean in, flutter my eyelashes, and pretend I'm hanging on his every word. We're up to the first landing and turning to go upstairs when we're joined by a third.

My adrenaline pulses and I glance back to see—"Alistair? What's wrong? What are you doing?"

He wraps a hand around my lower back and scoops me along at his pace. "On second thought, I'm the one who took him down the first time. I think it's best if I stick close."

I'm fine with modifying plans but not usually when the cogs are already moving and everyone understands what their part is to play.

To stop and argue the point would only draw attention, so there's no use putting up a fuss.

We ascend to the second floor, round the landing, and climb to the third. When we get to the top, we run into another couple coming out of a room. The guy shuffles off toward the stairs, smiling like he won the lottery, and is on his way.

The woman isn't so quick to vacate the area.

I turn my face into Nikon's neck and giggle, hiding my features, but when Nikon stops walking, I figure the ruse fell short.

"Who are you?" the woman asks.

I straighten and meet her gaze. She's a little more crone than maiden, but I figure it takes all kinds with the clientele here. Her purple and orange wings are nice, and I wonder what kind of draw they brought in when she was in her prime.

"I'm new," I say, offering her a sweet smile. "Just started tonight."

"You don't say. Do you expect to get paid?"

That stumps me a bit. "Uh…yeah, that's the plan."

"Then I suppose you shoulda spoken to the woman in charge before ye got all gussied up and put your ass on display."

It hasn't escaped my attention that her red satin dress hangs a great deal longer than mine. Alistair did this on purpose, and I'm not too pleased about being made into a female sex symbol.

"The woman in charge?" I repeat, getting a sinking feeling. "Let me guess. That would be you?"

The smile on her face holds no kindness, and I curse. "Well, you caught me. My guys here like to play naughty games and tonight was saloon night. You wouldn't want to ruin our fun, would you? We'll rent the room. Whatever you need."

She looks Nikon over, and he gets a smile of approval. When she checks out Alistair, she frowns. "A bit of a twig, isn't he?"

Despite Alistair's power and presence, he's still inhabiting his grandson Joseph's body.

"He's a bit of a late bloomer but a dynamo between the sheets," I say. "No complaints, I promise you."

Nikon rolls his eyes, glaring at Alistair. "Can you please fix this so we can get going?"

"Of course. All you had to do is ask."

Alistair trails a finger down the woman's bare arm, and her champagne orange eyes flutter. "Why don't you go up to the third floor and have your fun? I'll make sure you're not disturbed."

Alistair's words ring heavily with the magic of suggestion, and my shield wakes up. "Off you go. Leave your cash on the table when you finish."

It takes only a few seconds. Then her eyes go bright again, and she looks us over. "Why don't you go up to the third floor and have your fun? I'll make sure you're not disturbed. Off you go. Leave your cash on the table when you finish."

Scary cool but it worked.

"Thanks so much," I say. As much as I want to take that as a win, something about the resonance of Alistair's coercion niggles my nerves.

Maybe it's that he didn't stick with the plan.

After all, he got us out of a jam and did exactly what Nikon asked.

I tuck that away for another time because we're cresting the landing on the third floor and heading down the hall. *Are you with us, Bruin?*

Right here, Red.

Perfect. Keep an eye on Alistair for me, will you? I've got one of my feelings.

Will do.

We reach the last door on the left without issue, and I pause and raise my finger. "If Val Ryn is guarding, I bet he has warding in place. Alistair, you're up."

Alistair may have been dead for twenty years, but he didn't get rusty. Or maybe he did, and he was even more skilled before he died. I'm not sure which but honestly, I don't care.

Within a minute, he nods, and I crank the handle and push into the room.

Bruin gusts past me and both Danika and Val Ryn turn wide-eyed. Bruin materializes and takes Val Ryn down in a tackle that would crush most men.

Nikon goes straight for Danika, and I wait for Alistair to get inside and close the door.

By the time I turn, Nikon has the gag off Dani and is freeing her hands from the suppression bag.

Alistair says something in tongues, and I turn in time to see him releasing a ball of energy. My shield fires to high alert and I follow the trajectory of Alistair's focus. "Bruin! Ghost out, now!"

Bruin feels my emotions when they're heightened and reacts immediately. Despite being embroiled in a melee battle, he ghosts out leaving Val Ryn as the sole recipient of the spell thrown at them.

The elf's death is instant and shocking.

Val Ryn has no chance to escape or to defend himself. The curse hits, and he stiffens and fragments to ash.

The world is locked in one of those slow-motion moments when it takes time for everything around you to catch up and make sense of things.

"What the hell?" I shout, the adrenaline thrumming through my system making my head spin. "You didn't need to kill him, and you nearly killed Bruin."

Alistair gives me a noncommittal smile. "Sometimes when

dealing with high-level criminals, you have to make hard choices in the split second that could mean life and death."

"Bullshit," I snap. "Val Ryn wasn't a high-level criminal. His father was. Yes, he screwed us over and needed to answer for that, but you annihilated him. Not cool. Very not cool."

"I didn't realize you valued his life so much. My mistake."

I blink at him. "Do you really think an, 'Oops, I didn't realize,' is going to cut it? You could've killed Bruin. You targeted them both and things were well in hand."

Alistair lifts his chin. "From where I stood, Val Ryn was about to get the upper hand. I couldn't risk escape or him possibly taking down the entire group. I did what was best and won't apologize for it."

No. It's obvious he won't. Nor does he care.

Red. You've got men in black fatigues coming up the stairs to the third floor.

"Dammit. We've got company coming." I extend my hand to Nikon. "Get us out of here, Greek. Back to the storage building, if you please."

Nikon grabs my hand and pulls Danika against his chest. He looks at me and tilts his head. "What about the sorcerer? Does he get a ticket on the outgoing train?"

I'm tempted to leave him behind and let whoever is coming find him with Val Ryn's remains. Unlike Alistair, I'm not cold-blooded, and I don't end people's lives without cause.

"Yes, he does." *Bruin, ghost downstairs and tell Sloan to get Herman and get out.*

This rescue op has left a bad taste in my mouth. Something's not right, and I want to put some distance between us and this place to figure it out.

In the blink of a moment, Nikon snaps us back to the storage room. The good news is that Dionysus has completed his distraction and we didn't interrupt the god taking one for the team.

The bad news is, he isn't where we left him.

"We'll be fine here," I say to Nikon. "Go see if you can round everyone up."

Nikon nods. "Back in a flash. Try not to miss me too much."

"Impossible." I chuckle and stride around the rickety room, peering between the boards. By the light of the two moons, I can make out enough of the surroundings.

I'm pretty sure the coast is clear, and we have a moment to regroup. "Are you all right?" I ask Danika. "They didn't hurt you or try to drain your powers or anything, did they?"

She shakes her head. "No. Val watched over me to make sure nothing happened. I'm not forgiving the betrayal, but he was pretty twisted up about his dad and the choices he felt he had to make."

I glare over to the corner where Alistair is wisely staying out of my way and out of my line of sight. "I'm so sorry about what happened."

"Me too. He didn't deserve that."

"No. He absolutely didn't."

My fingernails are biting into the flesh of my palms, and I honestly don't know if I've ever been so angry. The two days we spent working with Val Ryn gave me a glimpse into the man's character.

Sure, maybe he felt pressured into making a few seriously bad choices, but his path wasn't irredeemable.

He didn't deserve to die and certainly not that way.

Diesel is the first to arrive, and he's got Dionysus in tow. I hug them both and grin at the giant sack of clothes Diesel is carrying. "Thank you, baby Groot. I want my clothes back on."

By the time Sloan and the others are approaching, I've

released the garters and have my pants, socks, and boots back on. Sadly, when they arrive, they're running full tilt.

"Get them out of there, Greek," Sloan shouts. "I've got the others."

Nikon grabs Dani and me, and I grab Dionysus and Diesel. Alistair grips Diesel's shoulder, and I guess he's coming for the ride. We materialize back in our little forest spot above the crater, and I wait, heart hammering until the others arrive.

"Is everyone accounted for?" I search the faces as Sloan *poofs* in with Manx, Herman, and Trent.

Sloan comes over to pull me into his side. "Aye, we're all here. Danika, it's good to see ye safe and back with friends."

Dani looks a bit shell-shocked. Whether that's because of the emergency evacuation, the murder of Val Ryn, or her kidnapping, I couldn't say.

There's so much to choose from.

"We're not done yet," Danika says.

We all turn and give her the floor. "No?" I say. "Why, what's up?"

"Val's father has some big plan to shift the balance of power. Val was telling me a bit about it before you guys burst in, and he murdered him." She throws Alistair a scathing look.

"Murdered him?" Sloan repeats, his brow pinched tight. "I take it Val Ryn was killed during the rescue, then?"

I tilt my head from side to side. "More like exterminated without cause. Alistair threw some kind of death curse while Val Ryn and Bruin were fighting. It could have been both of them in a pile of ash on the floor, but as it turns out, it was only Brynali's son."

All eyes turn on Alistair, and as much as I hate ganging up on people and judgment, I'm having a hard time being charitable to the ghostly sorcerer.

"That's neither here nor there right now." I file that away for a more appropriate moment. "How much of Brynali's plans did you learn?"

"It all ties back to the crimes that sent him to prison. Val said he didn't know much about his father's dealings growing up, but when he was arrested and sentenced to prison, he made it his business to dig up everything he could. That's what led him to become part of the Guild of the Empowered."

"He wanted access to the records about his father," Trent says.

"Yeah. He said he learned about the mantle clock a few months ago from a file on Juniper's desk and started putting his plan together."

"So, was any of it real?" Trent asks. "We served with him every day for years. Was it all a cover? He came out for drinks. We were friends—hell, we were family."

Danika lifts a shoulder but doesn't seem to have an answer. "I guess we'll never know."

I'm sorry they're going through the loss of a friend both because of betrayal and death, but we're not in the clear here. "Brynali is still out there, and if he plans to resurrect his original scheme of forty years ago, we need to focus."

Danika turns to me and nods. "Right. Yes. That's where the Port Gate Clock comes in. You still have it, right? I'm hoping you retrieved it from the prison after the explosion."

I nod. "We did. It's back at Humphrey House with Georgia."

She frowns. "Then we better get back there because Brynali needs it for his plans to unfurl and we've had enough senseless death for one day."

CHAPTER TWENTY-ONE

Nikon opens a portal, and we get back to Herman's place as quickly as we can. From the back lawn, everything seems calm, but my shield is tingling, and I've got a bad feeling I'm missing something.

"Gigi, darling, are you here?" Herman jogs through the French doors that lead out to the back patio, and we follow. "Georgia, please answer me."

"I'm here. What on Earth is the matter?" Georgia is sitting at a large worktable in the back corner. She has a dozen texts set out, a notepad covered in beautiful cursive notes, and the mangled and burned Port Gate Clock.

"Crisis averted." I draw a deep breath.

"What's the crisis in the first place?" Georgia asks.

We explain to her about the rescue, what Val Ryn said, and how this all ties back to the clock.

"Brynali wasn't there keeping you prisoner with his son?" she asks.

Danika shakes her head. "I don't know what happened to him. He was with us in the prison. Then Val warned his father the clock was overloading and was about to blow. Then, Val and I were outside that town. He took me through the gates, explained his father would be coming, and they gave him a place to hold me while we waited for him to catch up."

"He didn't come through the portal with you?" I ask.

Dani shakes her head. "No. That's why it was so senseless to kill Val. He wasn't hurting me, and I don't think he would have. He was waiting for his father to get something. Then they'd be reunited."

"He told you a great deal." Alistair frowns. "The California Council of Sorcerers worked on Brynali for months with every manner of torture, and the man never disclosed a single thing. Val Ryn was obviously made of lesser mettle."

I roll my eyes. "Which makes it even more upsetting that he's not here with us. If he were, maybe his connection with Danika and Trent could have borne fruit."

He doesn't seem impressed by that idea.

"So, what is it about the clock?" Georgia asks. "Did he tell you what it was supposed to do?"

Danika shakes her head. "No. Only that he needed to get something before he could move forward with his plans. And another time that his father tasked him to get the clock from Joseph McWinn at all costs. He said the key was the clock."

I shuffle over to look at the clock, and Georgia frowns. "What on Earth are you wearing, dear?"

I glance down at myself and chuckle. I'm half saloon girl and half Fi-warrior. "I was in the midst of changing when we had to make our escape. It wasn't a conscious decision, by any means."

"Thank the stars. I worried I might have to incite an intervention."

I'm still chuckling about her reaction when I lean in to get a closer look at the mantle clock. "It's hard to believe this is the root of all this trouble, isn't it?"

I reach forward to pick it up. My hand sinks through the side of it, and I grab nothing. "Hubba-wha?"

"Oh, that isn't the real clock, dear," Georgia says. "I made a magical copy of it when your boss came to collect it."

"My boss?" I repeat. "Who would that be?"

"A lovely high fae woman, Juniper Ravello."

I glance at Trent and Danika. "Why would your boss come here to collect the clock?"

Dani shrugs. "It's not that odd. Maybe she was concerned about it being out in the world, and she wanted to secure it and lock it in the vault back at the Legion of Honor."

Sloan nods. "Not a bad idea."

Of course, he'd approve. That's what he does with the enchanted objects and powerful antiquities he gathers at his shrine in Toronto.

I meet Diesel over by the leather sofas and rummage through the burlap sack with our clothes. "Okay, so everyone finish changing, and we'll head over to your headquarters to see what we can learn from the mantle clock. Sound good?"

There's a general nodding of agreement around the room, and we all grab our stuff.

The Legion of Honor is no less impressive today than it was on the first afternoon we were brought here by Danika, Val Ryn, and Trent. A lot has changed in the past couple of days, but that seems to be the way of things in these times.

"What do you think, Tarzan?" I ask as we stride through the colonnade toward the back corner entrance to the branch office of the California Guild. "Impressive, isn't it?"

Dionysus frowns. "No. I don't like it. It makes me think of Olympus. I like our building much better. I miss my loft."

I hadn't thought of that, but yeah, that makes sense. Traditional Greek architecture wouldn't hold the same appeal for him that it does for Nikon or even me. "We'll get you home soon, sweetie."

"Contessa McSparkles is probably missing me terribly."

I hear the loneliness in his voice, and my heart goes out to him. "She's looking forward to getting home to you too. She's been staying with Imari at the compound, but everyone is aware that the moment you're home, she's coming back to live with you at the penthouse."

Danika is watching us with a curious gaze. "His girlfriend is named Contessa McSparkles?"

"No, his unicorn pegasus."

Dani blinks, and the expression on her face is priceless. "Wow, you guys really do live a different life."

I shrug, smiling at the guys around me. "It works for us. We may be an unusual family, but we're a family all the same."

"I'm an honorary Cumhaill," Dionysus says. "There was a party and inauguration gifts and everything."

I nod. "True story."

"And Nikon is a part of all this?" She sends her ex a concerned gaze.

"He definitely is. He knew from what his grandfather told him of our past together that we'd be close and we'd meet for the first time in Toronto at a guild meeting. So, he bought a house in the city and waited for years, going to every guild meeting, waiting for our lives to finally collide."

"He could've told me about Hecate and the trouble she was causing him," Danika says.

I shrug. "He worried you'd dig in and get involved. He knew we'd handle it together somehow and has the patience of a saint. He also knew you loved him and would've fought for him. That would have gotten you killed. After the murder of his wife and baby, he never—"

Her gaze cranks around, and her mouth falls open. "Hecate killed his child?"

Shitshitshit. "Oh, no. I shouldn't have said that. He said he told you everything."

"He told me about Hecate killing his wife but not a child."

I glance around, and I feel sick. "He and his wife were expecting. It happened, but it nearly killed him. Please don't bring it up. I'm sure he'll tell you when he's ready, but this is neither the time nor the place."

"I won't say a thing. I'm glad he found a friend like you…even if it took over a thousand years of him waiting."

"Me too. He's one of us now. He'll never face anything like that alone again."

Danika's gaze softens as she watches him joke with Dionysus. "He really isn't an asshole, is he?"

"No. He really isn't. He's one of the most honorable, caring, loyal men I've ever met. Maybe I'm biased and too much of a romantic, but I think you should try really hard to forgive him."

She looks at me and shakes her head. "How about we work on getting the city back to its place in the human realm and learning the mystery of the mantle clock first. Love lives second."

"Okeydokey. That's fair."

The five of us from Team Trouble Toronto are escorted into the inner sanctum of the San Francisco office, and we split up to get the job done faster. Danika heads to Juniper's office to talk to her, and Trent strikes off to the vault to sign out the clock.

Sloan tags along with the big blue guy because well…because he's Sloan and he's dying to check out what treasures they keep behind locked doors.

That leaves Nikon, Diesel, Dionysus, and me to chat among ourselves.

"You and Dani seemed to have your heads together for quite a while." Nikon studies me as he speaks. "Anything I should know about?"

I smile. "Are you fishing, Greek? Do you want to know if we were talking about you?"

"No, no. I was checking in and making sure all is well."

I laugh. "You're such a liar."

He rolls his eyes. "Okay, fine. I'm a little curious about what was said. Two women I happen to love and adore were deep in conversation. Is it vain to hope that maybe some kind words were being said about yours truly?"

I reach up on my toes and kiss his cheek. "The kindest of words, Greek. S'all good."

He swallows, looking relieved. "I don't want her to hate me. She's an amazing woman, and I want things to be set right."

Yeah, he's still fishing. "She doesn't hate you."

Dionysus leans in and smiles. "You should do something flashy and daring to reestablish yourself as the man of her dreams."

Nikon blinks. "No, I think giving her time and space is the way to go."

Dionysus shakes his head. "No way. You want to stand out and be unforgettable."

Nikon chuckles. "This is coming from what experience? You're the god of good times. That's not the same as rekindling a second chance romance with an old flame."

He frowns. "I've dated. I know things."

"Suede, you mean?" Nikon says. "How many days did that last?"

Dionysus flashes him a droll stare. "It was weeks, and we're still together…sort of."

"After-dating sex doesn't count as together. Are you two still dating or just doing the horizontal?"

"Horizontal, vertical, some tricky maneuvers where I did this thing where—hey! Did you guys know it was me sending you cloud shapes?"

I bust up laughing, and two San Fran guys turn from their stations. "Yeah, we did. Nikon picked that up right away. Why didn't you write a message, though? Wouldn't it have been easier to get your point across?"

"Never take the easy route, Jane. It's pedestrian and boring. There was nothing about my cloud writing that was boring."

"That's true."

Diesel is chuckling along with us, and I'm glad he's settling in. I'm about to say so when Danika comes back looking confused, and Trent comes back with Sloan looking alarmed.

"Juniper isn't here and hasn't been for two days," Danika says.

"That's why nothing got logged into the vault," Trent adds.

I'm not sure what to think about that. She walked out before, but if she picked up the clock, she had to be heading back here, didn't she? "Do you think Brynali could've gotten to her and taken the clock? Maybe she's in trouble."

Danika rushes over to Juniper's console and starts calling up the projects she's been working on. "Trent, Nikon, and Sloan, can you come here, please."

I smile at Dionysus and Diesel. "I guess we didn't get picked."

Dionysus shrugs. "Doesn't matter. You'll always be my first pick, Jane. Besides, they're probably mathing or something equally distasteful."

"That can't be right," Trent says. "She was working on the phasing for three days. Where are the logs of what she was doing?"

"Here." Dani points at the screen. "Except she wasn't trying to *stop* the phasing. She was enhancing the phasing and locking it in place."

"What? Why?" I rush over to get a look. Yeah no, it's all code and gobbledygook to me. "To what end?"

"To keep the city locked in the fae realm." Sloan scowls. "If that's the case and we already know the clock was damaged and offline, it can only be her doing that the city is still here instead of in its rightful realm."

"So do we right the phasing or try to track down Juniper and the clock?" I ask.

"I think ye mean Juniper, Brynali, and the clock," Sloan says.

I scratch my forehead and scowl. "Stop. You're hurting my hamster. Now you think Juniper is working with Brynali?"

"It makes perfect sense, luv."

It does? Damn, the only drawback of loving a genius is getting left behind when he starts doing gray matter Olympics.

"Ye see, Juniper only arrived to run this office after the veil fell and one of the first things she did was take over all contact with the fae prison."

"You think she was part of Brynali's plans all along?"

Sloan nods. "I do. Assume for a moment he's able to tell her the mantle clock's importance and location. She could've set that information in Val Ryn's path to get him thinking about how to recover it."

Danika nods. "He did say he found the file with the information about the clock on Juniper's desk. Do you think she could've left it there on purpose?"

"Absolutely."

"Then her walking away when we got there wasn't about us pissing in her sandbox. It was about locking her console and leaving us to track down the information about lowering the prison warding."

"Which she needed help doing because she didn't have the spell or a Light Weaver."

"And we walked right into that one."

"We did."

I groan. "So, we dropped the warding, Val Ryn got his father free, and Juniper monitored the wardens' responses and kept an eye on things from downstairs."

"That's right."

"Then where did Brynali disappear to?" Nikon asks. "If he was there in the prison and he didn't go with Danika and Val Ryn, and he wasn't there while we were searching, where was he?"

"Hiding in plain sight," Sloan says. "Ye mentioned that Herman said sorcerers often use that tactic and find it entertaining to put one over on people. I think he glamoured himself as Alistair and we portaled him out of the prison ourselves."

I pull out a chair and plunk onto it before I fall. "So, from the time we left the prison and went to the fae realm, that was Brynali with us?"

Sloan nods. "I'd bet my life on it."

"So, Brynali killed his son?" Danika says, disgust thick in her tone. "Why? Val betrayed everything he loved to get him out of jail."

I straighten. "I know the answer to that one. After he killed Val Ryn, he was annoyed. He said Brynali never shared a thing after being tortured and Val Ryn was made of lesser mettle because he opened up to Dani and shared so much."

"Do you think Val realized it was his father who struck him down?" Danika looks sad. "That his father betrayed him?"

I shake my head. "I don't think so. It happened too fast. I don't think he saw it coming at all."

"I suppose that's some consolation."

"Then, where's the real Alistair?" Diesel asks.

Sloan frowns. "I expect Brynali killed him at the time of the explosion so he could assume his place. My guess is that he'd stashed his body in the common area or one of the cells at the time of the explosion."

"You think Joseph McWinn is dead then?"

"Aye, I can't see a man like Brynali allowing him to live when that could mean foiling his plans."

That's sad. "Joseph was a dolt and a jerk, but all he ever

wanted was to be a wizard and have great adventures like his grandfather."

"Be careful what you wish for," Nikon says.

Danika sighs and goes back to scanning the console in front of her. "My question now is, do we undo the programming Juniper set in place or try to find her or them first?"

"How long do you think it'll take to set things right with the city?" Sloan asks.

She shrugs. "By the look of things, without the mantle clock to support the magic, it's a matter of backing out of what she did. It shouldn't take me more than fifteen or twenty minutes."

Gazes meet across the room, and no one jumps with an immediate response so I take the lead. "The way I see it, if Juniper wanted the city locked in the fae realm to advance their plan in some way, we should do the opposite and put the city back where it belongs."

"I don't disagree," Sloan says, "but if I'm acting as the devil's advocate, I'd worry that we've made more than one hasty decision in this case that has resulted in us playing into their hands. Perhaps knowing their full plan is wiser."

"But they could be long gone. In which case, we're holding an entire city hostage indefinitely or maybe giving Juniper and Brynali more time to complete what they set in motion."

Sloan tilts his head from side to side. "Yer right. There's more logic behind breaking the hold Juniper placed on the city and returning things back to the natural order."

Danika glances around at the rest of us, and it seems unanimous.

"Put the city back in place."

CHAPTER TWENTY-TWO

Danika calls over two of her counterparts and the three pore over Juniper's console. While they're busy trying to remove the hold on our current position in the fae realm, Trent helps us come up with a few ideas on how to find Juniper and hopefully Brynali.

We have several options. Try to track the mantle clock's energy signature—but the explosion pretty much destroyed it.

Try to track down Juniper—but we're doubtful she broke Brynali Rilios out of prison just to have him back to her house for a visit.

"What about the idea that he has unfinished business?" Diesel asks. "Danika said Brynali needed to get something before he returned to the fae realm. What if the clock itself wasn't the goal but something hidden within the clock?"

Sloan considers that. "You might have something there. When we discussed Brynali's original crimes, Alistair said that to drain the blood of an entire coven of witches would create enough dark power to do something massive."

"But nothing was done," I add.

"Aye, but he did say that level of power could be used or

stored. What if he couldn't complete his task, but he had the potential power of the witches stored in a vessel of some sort?"

"Vessel?" Nikon says. "You mean like an amulet or a dagger or a box or something?"

Sloan nods. "Alistair said when they arrested Brynali, the only thing he had on him was that clock. They thought the clock held the power but what if it was something inside the clock?"

I both love and hate this idea. "Okay, so let's say that's true. Alistair said he could never figure out how to make the clock work. Maybe that's because he didn't know how to access the power vessel inside it."

Trent is nodding, and it seems he likes this theory. "So, we know they needed the clock, and we have a pretty good idea of the importance. What we still don't know is why. What is his unfinished business?"

"Something on the California coastline," Diesel says. "Alistair said the spatial event they interrupted nearly destroyed the California coastline."

"That's a lot of geography," Nikon says. "Can we narrow that down?"

"We can." I hold up my finger. "We need to track spatial anomalies and unexplained energy events along the coastline. Maybe we'll get lucky, and that will tell us where they are."

"It's worth a shot." Trent jogs to another console and taps the glass screen. "Dammit. I need us back in the human realm for our system to come online. I can't trace the California coastline from here."

"Do you think that's what the phasing is about?" I ask. "Were they trying to keep the Guild of the Empowered off their backs?"

"More likely the California Council of Sorcerers," Trent says. "Governing something like this is more their jurisdiction than—"

I grip the edge of the war table as the world blurs under a bombardment of magic. My ears ring, and Sloan wraps an arm around my hips, pulling me against his chest as my eyes pinch shut. My skin tingles with the searing pain of nettles, and I clench my jaw.

The world shifts around us and when it feels like my insides are slingshotted through a vat of thick pudding, I know Danika has done it.

Like the first time, the blink of the city stops as quickly as it started.

It takes a moment for the group to come back online, but when we've all straightened and are shaking off the phase between realms, I glance around the group, and it seems no one is about to assplant or puke.

We'll take that as a win.

"Tell me that was the last time," Manx says, shaking his head. "That's not natural."

Sloan looks as shaken as I feel. "No, *sham*, it's not, but I think that should be the end. By the look of things on the monitors there, we're home."

We all glance up at the images popping up on their high-tech monitor system. It's only beginning to reboot now, but one by one, familiar buildings, landscapes, and pictures start showing up.

"A big hells yeah." I sway to imaginary music as I do a happy dance.

Dionysus joins in without prompting, and the two of us enjoy the moment. "Maybe this might be over soon, and we can go home."

With San Francisco returned to the human realm, Trent's tracking systems come back online. Danika goes over to check on what he's doing, and the two of them are working their consoles and getting the job done with a rhythm of efficiency my team has when we're locked and loaded.

"Got it." Trent scowls. "Yeah, I can see why Alistair was worried about the coastline. If this is where Brynali took his stand the first time around, it's right on one of the main hinge points of the San Andreas Fault."

I frown. "Why would he want to disturb that?"

Nikon scoffs. "He's an asshole, murdering maniac, Fi. Why do you think you can figure out his motives?"

I suppose he has a point.

"Sloan, can you get us there?" Trent asks.

"Not me, I'm afraid. I've never been there, so I'm unable to access the coordinates. Nikon's our man."

Nikon's already tapping on his phone and calling for a Google Earth image of the area in question. "Give me two minutes."

I check my battle vest and call my armor. "What happens if he destroys the fault line?"

Danika sighs. "Earthquakes, fires, building collapse, transportation accidents, general mayhem, and panic."

"Oh, is that all?"

Trent finishes what he's doing and joins us. "Likely close to four thousand dead from the initial event and more in the fallout."

"What cities would that involve?" Diesel asks.

Danika pulls up an aerial map of the area involved. "Bodega Bay, Daly City, Desert Hot Springs, Frazier Park, Gorman, Moreno Valley, Palmdale, Point Reyes Station…maybe more."

"Let's avoid that," I say.

Everyone agrees on that.

"Got it." Nikon grins and tucks his phone back into his pocket. "All aboard the Tsambikos Express. Let's get ahead of this, guys. Rilios has done enough damage already."

I nod. "Remember, he's killed one or possibly two members of our group. No one else dies today."

The seven of us plus Bruin and Manx portal into a long, treeless plain and take in the surroundings. I breathe deep and am not going to complain that the ambient magic in the air is tingling over my skin.

"There's no place like home," I say.

Dionysus chuckles. "You're not home, Jane. You're only in your home realm."

I take out my phone, turn it on, and message the family WhatsApp group that we're alive and well. Then I message the SITFU group and tell Garnet, Maxwell, and Andy. "It's close enough to home to count. I truly wasn't looking forward to spending the rest of my life with gnomes and centaurs. Not that there's anything wrong with that...I just prefer to live in the world I was born into."

Dionysus grins. "I can't relate, but I get what you mean. I'm happy to get back too."

"Do ye feel that?" Sloan scans the gathered ground and the crack in the soil beneath.

I reach out to connect with the fault line but get nothing. "It looks like the puckered skin gathered to sew up a gash, doesn't it?"

"Aye, a bit."

"But no, I don't feel anything coming off the fault line."

Sloan shakes his head. "I didn't either, so I went beyond that. What do ye feel comin' off the animals in the area?"

I do as he suggests and reach out to sense the wildlife in the area. "Oh, yeah. I'm with you now."

"What is it?" Diesel asks. "What do you sense?"

I turn to stand with Sloan, and the two of us start hiking toward a ridge. "The animals are scared. There's something over here that's freaking out the locals."

When we get to the edge of the ridge, my stomach sinks. "Is that a mirage? Because unless I'm drunk or high, I don't think I should see that there."

In front of us, in the middle of a barren plain of dry, rocky ground lays a pocket of Jurassic green growth and a silver palace with iron gates and fortifications. It has a high wall encircling the small village on its outskirts and all matter of fae realm strangeness bustling around.

"I was not expecting that." Dionysus points as he picks up his pace. "Oh, look, griffons."

Nikon laughs. "Hey, Fi, maybe your old boyfriend is here, and he can stick his tongue down your throat and tell you how amazing he is. That was fun for all of us. What was his name again, Jacob?"

"No, that was her sexy valet," Sloan says.

"The chef then?"

"No, that was Jared," he answers. "Yer thinkin' of Jordan, her dreamy musician with the hair."

I flash them both a middle-fingered salute and roll my eyes. "The fact that you guys are so invested in my past relationships means you have too much time on your hands and need to get a life."

Sloan chuckles. "Or that we're so invested in yer life and happiness, we take note of things."

He's too cute.

Returning the group's attention to the issue at hand, I point at the discovery in front of us. "Danika and Trent would know best, but that shouldn't be here, right? It's not like a Disney thing where they've built a new amusement park on the unused plains of the California coastline?"

Danika shakes her head, looking baffled. "Nope. This is definitely new."

"Do you think it's the clock?" Diesel asks. "If the clock created a spatial irregularity that took San Francisco into the fae world, could this be a city from the fae world that got displaced here?"

"It makes as much sense as anything." My phone rings and I jump and *yip*. "Wow, it's amazing how quickly we forget."

The theme song of the Lion King is playing loud and clear, so I answer the call and tap the button for speaker. "Hello, bossman, you're on with everyone."

"It's good to have you back, Lady Druid."

"It's good to be back. I'll tell you about it once we wrap up the last loose ends we're dealing with."

"Would your loose ends have anything to do with a massive portal rift we're detecting on the coast of California?"

I make a face at Sloan. "Why yes, I think that's fair to assume. We're standing here looking at a fae kingdom that popped up out of nowhere."

"We had a massive rift show up ten minutes ago. When your text came in, I wondered if there was a correlation. Mayhem does tend to follow you."

I chuckle. "Rude. I can't help it that my shield is a magnet for trouble. Even so, I think this is beyond my power of chaos."

Sloan chuckles. "Aye, given what we've been up against the past three days, I'm sure it's the same. We're currently tracking the spatial device that displaced San Francisco. We believe a dark object within the device is enhancing its power to open portals and relocate cities."

"Find that device. Find it and destroy it before more fae cities take root."

"Have any other cities disappeared?" I ask. "Is it a one-for-one event or only an unexpected arrival?"

"It seems only one incoming city, but again, things change quickly. Whatever is causing it, stop it."

"Is Nikon there with you?" Maxwell joins the call.

"Yeah, Max, I'm here."

"I hate to do this to you, but that tear in the veil needs to be closed. I'm sending you the exact coordinates now."

"Oh, yay, lucky me." Nikon's voice is a bit pitchy.

"I'm sorry, my friend. Right now, you're the man with the gift."

I pat Nikon's shoulder and throw him a sympathetic smile. "All right. We'll try to stop this at our end and will close the rift. We'll keep you posted."

"You do that," Garnet says. "In case I forgot to say it, welcome home. We're glad you made it back."

I hold up a finger. "Before you sign off, can you guys do us a favor?"

"What's that, Fi?" Maxwell says.

"We believe the fae woman in charge of the San Francisco branch office named Juniper Ravello is involved with a man named Brynali Rilios and this all ties back to a case in the eighties. Can you look into her and help us figure out why she might help him break out of Alcatraz and import a palace?"

"We'll get right on it. Don't screw around with this, Fi. Our world is fucked enough without the immigration of entire fae kingdoms."

Garnet hangs up without awaiting an answer, and I smile at Trent and Danika. "He's a bit growly, but you learn to love him."

"We're part of his pride," Dionysus says.

I slide my phone into my pocket and frown at the silver palace. "You heard him, boys and girls. Find and destroy the mantle clock, stop the transferring of cities, close the rift, and bring Brynali and possibly Juniper to justice."

Danika chuckles. "I love the way you say that so matter-of-factly."

Nikon laughs. "Fi has a gift for understatement. I think we might need to reorder your list a little. As much as I hate it, that looks like our biggest problem."

I follow Nikon's pointed finger and grimace. "Holy crapamoly. Right you are, Greek. This is all you."

CHAPTER TWENTY-THREE

I'm not sure what the difference is between San Francisco being taken into the fae realm and the walled city of the fae realm being brought here, but the act of transplanting the silver palace has left the biggest spatial rift we've seen yet.

Nikon glares at the swirling vortex of energy. "This is going to suck."

It absolutely is.

"Hey, check this out." Diesel points at a—

"Wait a minute? Is that what I think it is?" I hustle over for a closer look and scratch my head. "It is. How the hell did Brynali's Port Gate Clock get here?"

"What do you make of it lying here, nestled atop a purple silk pillow?" Diesel bends to pick it up.

"I expect Juniper and Brynali needed it to bring this city here," Sloan says. "Perhaps when the job was over, it no longer held any use for them."

"So, they treated it to a comfy silk pillow so it could take a nap?" I say.

It seems crazy to me that the very item that people have been betraying, lying, and killing for was just left in the middle of an abandoned plain. "That's a mystery for another time. Right now, we need to close this rift."

I squeeze his arm and yank my hand away from his skin. The usual electrical barbs of energy from the portal are snapping off him like sharp-toothed piranha tearing the flesh off anything they contact. The anxiety in my chest doubles. "I'm sorry you have to do this, Greek, but I believe in you. You're the man."

"Give me two, Greek, and I'll be here with ye." Sloan *poofs* out.

I look around, scanning through empty air. "Where'd he go?"

Nikon shrugs. "Maybe he had to piss?"

I chuckle. "I highly doubt he'd risk the safety of both realms to take a pee break."

Before we get a chance to wonder more about that, he's back, and he's got Georgia and Herman in tow. "I was thinkin' that with a rift of this size and without Patty's magic to help, Nikon would be splittin' in two. We still don't know if there are any long-term effects we need to be worried about, but if we can prevent it, I'm sure that's better."

That's my guy, always thinking. "An excellent idea. Welcome, you two. Glad you could join us."

Georgia is scowling at the swirling vortex of energy behind me. "I've never seen anything like this. It's utterly terrifying."

True story. "Only for the moment. Nikon's got the goods to close it, but any amount of power or control you can offer to help with the task is greatly appreciated."

"Our magic stems from a different source, but we can try," Herman says.

Nikon frowns and looks at me. "That's what Patty said too. I feel another lava lamp night coming on."

"Maybe it won't be so bad. Maybe it was only Patty's powers your body didn't agree with."

"Yeah, maybe."

He doesn't sound hopeful, and I wish there was something I could do to help him when things get like this.

"You're Nikon-freaking-Tsambikos. Don't forget that for a moment."

Danika is taking it all in and frowning. "I take it this isn't pleasant?"

Nikon lets out a long sigh. "Not at all, but hey, duty calls, right?"

Sadly, it does.

Without dwelling further on the suckiness of the task, Nikon lifts his palms and begins to establish his connection with the energy.

Something unpleasant must meet his attempt because he pulls his hands back, then runs his palms down his pants and shakes them out.

After another deep breath, he takes another go at it.

I move out of the way as Sloan steps in behind him to help heal Nikon through the physical strain of the process. Herman and Georgia flank him on either side and raise their palms.

Nikon widens his stance and plants his feet. "Here goes nothing."

Dionysus, Diesel, Trent, Danika, Manx, and I step back to give them room to work.

"What does Nikon do to close the spatial tear?" Trent asks.

I turn a little and lower my voice so I don't disturb them. "A Man o' Green friend of ours described it like pinching shut a freezer bag. Nikon must find the beginning of the seam on both sides of the realms and zip it shut. With the strength of his gift compounded by him envisioning it happening, the seam should start to close."

I glance back to check their progress and turn away. I've seen this before, and it guts me every time.

"Fuck. It's so much power," Nikon groans. "Too much. I hate this."

"We're here with you, Greek." My heart hurts for him. "We heart you hard."

Manx groans and lays on the ground. "It hurts." Connected as he and Sloan are, he must be sensing Sloan's discomfort.

Now I'm worried about both of them. Sloan's never mentioned it being painful to him. Is that new or has he been bearing the burden and not letting on?

Knowing Sloan, it's likely the latter.

"This is awful." Danika scowls at the scene. "He's practically vibrating with uncontained energy, and nothing seems to be happening."

"Don't be so sure." The words come out more defensive than I meant, but there's no helping that. I will be Nikon's champion until the end of time. "He has to connect to the rift on this side in our realm and the other side in the fae realm. It takes a lot. Give him a chance."

"What about the power object in here?" Diesel asks, holding up the damaged clock. "If we were right about it being the contained power from the slain coven, there might still be some power left."

I look at Dionysus, Danika, and Trent. "Will that work? If there is a vessel and there is still magic left within it, can it be used for good instead of evil?"

Danika steps forward and scowls at the clock. "If an object was created, it wouldn't have any alignment—good or evil. It would simply be stored magic."

Magical energy explodes out of Nikon, and I duck and shield my eyes. Swirling chaos of colors radiates from Nikon and snakes its way around Sloan, Georgia, and Herman.

I wince as the prickling of shocks gets worse and bites my skin. Damn it. He's going to come apart again. I stare at the stupid clock that has caused all the trouble. "Yeah, it's worth a try. Diesel, do you think between you and Trent, you can break into the thing?"

The two giants look at each other and the clock. Without

answering, they each grab hold of the frame of the antique and pull.

It doesn't surrender to their might as quickly as one might think, but then…

A blast of energy explodes from it and knocks the five of us back behind a wall of power.

I ass-plant on the hard terrain and scramble to get back to my feet. "Wow, even battered and half burned up by the explosion in the prison, it still packs a wallop."

"I'm going to split apart," Nikon grunts. "It's happening again."

Danika and Dionysus are sifting through the graveled and sandy ground, and I hurry over to join the search. "What are we looking for, exactly?"

"I don't know," Danika says. "A gemstone or crystal, an empowered object… anything that doesn't fit in with the dirt."

Unfortunately, the power wave that detonated from the clock's destruction has scattered debris over ten square feet.

"Okay, maybe…" Dionysus bends to pick up a jet-black stone. "Ah, this could be it—"

"Don't pick it up!" Danika's warning comes too late, and Dionysus falls to the ground in a fit of convulsion.

"Tarzan!" I rush to get to him and make sure he doesn't hit his head on any of the rocks as he's seizing. "Diesel, hand me the pillow."

Diesel hurries to give me the purple pillow, and I slide it under Dionysus' head.

Danika squats, pries his fingers open, and takes the onyx stone. The moment it's out of Dionysus' hand, his body settles. "This obviously still contains potent witch magic. It's too much for a human mortal."

A human mortal?

Dionysus?

It's so strange to think of Dionysus as an ordinary human, but for now, I suppose he is.

"Hang on, Greek!" Sloan shouts. "Don't give up now. Yer close."

My attention snaps back to Nikon and his battle with the rift. Yep. The duplicate Nikon has appeared in the opening of the vortex on the fae side. The Nikon on this side is glowing with the kaleidoscope colors of the power fluctuations.

"Hang in there, Greek. Dani's coming. She's going to help." I shout the encouragement over the whistle and whine of the energy storm and tilt my head for her to get going. "Please help him."

Danika is staring wide-eyed at the two Nikons. "I don't know if I can. What's happening?"

"He'll worry about the split and his doppelgänger. He needs you to help boost his power to close the rift."

Dani closes her fist around the witch stone and stands. "Okay. I'll try."

Nikon's pain is too much, and I can't do anything about it. Instead, I focus on Dionysus' situation. "Tarzan? Are you all right? Open your eyes and look at me."

I hate this.

With my heart pounding in my chest, I squeeze his hand. "Please wake up, Tarzan. I need you to be okay."

Dionysus blinks awake and stares at me from where his head rests in my lap. "What happened?"

"You found the empowered vessel and touching it knocked you out. How do you feel? Are you all right?"

He lets his eyes drop closed and nods. "I think so. I've never gotten knocked out before. It's a bit disorienting, but I think I'm fine. How's Nikky doing?"

"Better, I think."

Danika has joined the front line and is channeling the power of the empowered vessel. She must understand the magic fairly well and be able to harness it because she seemed to hit the ground running.

I'm about to shout some encouragement about that when the screech and whine of the powerful storm ends, and the world goes silent.

The abrupt loss of noise after the cacophony is unsettling.

Trapped under Dionysus and holding his head, there's nothing I can do when Nikon crumples to the ground. Sloan half catches him and half falls himself.

Trent and Diesel rush over to check on everyone.

Other than his skin still glowing with color, he looks whole. "Nikon. Are you okay, sweetie? Were you able to pull yourself together?"

Danika is right there at his side helping him sit up.

He meets my gaze and gives me a shaky wave.

"Mischief Managed?" I ask.

He chuffs. "I'd like to retire from the position of official rift closer now. Please send everyone the memo."

"Ye did a bang-up job, Greek." Sloan pats his back a few minutes later. "I know ye hate it, but yer the hero of the hour fer sure. Even if people don't know it."

Diesel and Trent have scooped him up, and although he's still glowing through the colors of the rainbow, he seems to be doing much better.

I'm still as shaken as Nikon looks.

Between Nikon's pain, Dionysus having a seizure, and Sloan crumbling to the ground while trying to support Nikon, I've reached my limit for worrying about the men I love.

The only saving grace is that none of my brothers, father, or grandparents were involved. "I'm sorry it takes so much out of you, Greek, but he's right. You're a freaking inspiration."

Danika is sitting on a rock close by, looking a little weathered herself. "I admit it. I was completely wrong. You're much more than a glorified Uber. I'm sorry. I shouldn't have said that."

Nikon waves away her apology. "After what happened and the

way I left things, you had every right to be pissed. I'm sorry the mistakes of my past hurt you."

Now she's the one waving away an apology. "We've established that you were in an impossible spot and I deserved better—if not from you, then at least from the situation. It's over and done with now. We've both grown a lot since then."

Nikon turns a lovely teal as he shifts through a kaleidoscope of colors and I'm not sure if it's the color agreeing with him or the knowledge that she's forgiven him for something that weighed heavily on his soul, but he seems to glow a little brighter.

I shift my attention from them to Dionysus and give them the privacy to speak and heal old wounds. "How are you feeling, Tarzan? You took quite a jolt there."

He's sitting cross-legged on the ground while Sloan checks him out. "I'm tingly. I think the witch magic boosted me somehow or is lingering inside me. I don't feel quite so powerless as I have since the girls started my penance."

I feel horrible that he's suffering the loss of his powers in any way but will never regret his sacrifice...or forget what it means to my life that he made it.

The thought of sacrifice and dying while fighting the fight brings me back to Georgia and Herman.

The pair have dusted off and are speaking quietly to one another. Even though Georgia is currently in her granddaughter's body, and they look like a May-December romance, the two obviously shared great affection for one another in their past.

"I hate to ruin your quiet moment, but I think we need to talk about Alastair."

Georgia nods. "Yes, when your man brought us here to help, we noticed he wasn't with you and wondered where he'd gotten off to. He left soon after I explained about the fae woman taking the clock. There wasn't time to ask during that business with the rift but now that things seem to be sorted, where is he?"

I spend the next few minutes updating Georgia and Herman about what we learned and have hypothesized regarding Alistair, Joseph, and Brynali.

"The idea that Brynali killed Alistair and assumed his place to escape prison and seek out the clock was a lot to wrap our heads around at first, but the longer I think about it, the more I think Sloan is right."

"You think Joseph's been sacrificed in the process?" Herman asks.

"We haven't confirmed it yet, but we believe so."

Georgia presses a hand over her mouth and shakes her head. "I knew he shouldn't have taken that boy into the field. What a stubborn, selfish man."

I understand her stance on things, but I think Brynali was a foe Alistair considered his responsibility due to their past conflicts.

"You both have our deepest condolences. I hope we're wrong and someone finds him tied up somewhere and furious about missing all the action, but I have a feeling he's not."

"Uh, Fi? Sorry to interrupt, but we've got company coming." Diesel points at the silver palace with towering spires reaching to the sky. The tall iron gates at the front of the stone wall have opened, and two large magic-drawn coaches are coming to meet us.

"Fi, any alarm bells ringing we should know about?" Nikon scowls at the arrivals.

"No. Strangely enough, it's all good."

From the driver's seat perched high on the front of the first carriage, a gnome with a purple hat stands and strokes his long, silver beard. "Queen Wysteria would like to invite you all inside as her guests. Please, allow us to escort you into the palace."

I meet the gazes of the others. Sure, we're all apprehensive, but hey, we wanted to get into the city. Now we're being invited, and we didn't have to battle to get it done. "Thank you. We accept."

We divide into two groups and climb into the carriages to escort us inside the walled kingdom.

"What do you think this is about?" I ask Sloan as we zip along. Because we're moving by magic, no wheels are bumping over cobbled streets or anything, so the ride is smooth sailing.

"I'm at a loss," Sloan says. "Be ready for anythin'."

"Yeah, will do." I breathe deep into my lungs and try to connect with the magic of whatever is happening here. I get no sense of danger or deceit or anything untoward. How can that be?

We're going into a fae palace that shouldn't be here and just destroyed their spatial shifting device.

Aren't they angry about that?

The carriages bounce along in a soothing sway until they stop outside the palace's main entrance. We all unload and tilt our heads *waaay* back to look at the massively tall doors.

"This way, if you please," the gnome says. He stops at the doors, turns to assess our group, and strokes his beard again. As his stubby hand reaches the bottom tip of his beard, a blue and orange butterfly crawls out of the hair, flutters its wings as it looks around, and burrows back inside. "Lady Juniper is waiting."

My head turns, and my mouth falls open. "Lady Juniper? You can't be serious."

CHAPTER TWENTY-FOUR

I peg our Travelocity gnome tour guide with a look and let that one sink in. "Juniper? As in Juniper Ravello?"

He chuckles. "That is the name she took to fit better into your society, but here within the city walls she is known as Queen Juniper Raven Elloisa Wysteria of the Silver Spires."

I glance up at the city, but I don't have time to get a sense of its grandeur before the doors swing open and we're standing before Juniper in the grand entrance.

If the gnome hadn't told me we were meeting the leader of the branch office of the Guild of the Empowered, I wouldn't have recognized her. Gone are the clothes of our world and now, Juniper is wearing a long navy blue gown with a blue and silver train.

Behind her, several lemurs with purple collars are carrying her train and keeping the fabric from dragging on the polished cream floor.

"Danika. Trent. It's so good of you to come. Thank you for following up. I so hoped I would get the chance to explain."

"Explain?" Dani snaps, her tone hard and clipped. "Explain how you lied to us for five months? How you justify working with a murdering criminal like Brynali Rilios? How you came into the home of a man who's been working with us and stole the object of power we were trying to keep from that criminal at all cost?"

"I returned the device to you." She sounds surprised. "I left it for you to discover at the rift point. Did you not find it?"

"Oh, yeah, we found it. Propping it up on a silk pillow was a nice touch. As if presenting it with a flourish would lessen the damage you caused by stealing it."

She lifts a slim shoulder. "The device served its purpose. Beindeen Holm is now safely locked into the human world and free to thrive outside my grandfather's tyranny. I thought it best to return the thing to those who would no doubt need it to right the ship."

"Right the ship?" Danika looks like her brain is cramping up on that one. "That rift you caused by bringing your city here nearly killed Nikon and took five of us to close."

"I couldn't help it, I'm afraid. I needed to relocate Beindeen Holm at all costs."

"Because of your evil grandfather," she chides.

Juniper smiles. "Not so much evil as deadly, selfish, and misogynistic."

"So, you were in this with Brynali all along?"

She swings her braid forward. When we saw her over the past couple of days, her hair was shoulder-length and not something that stood out as unusual. Now, it's so long, it is plaited with flowers and hangs down to her thigh. "In a sense, but not the way you're thinking."

"You have no idea what I'm thinking," Danika retorts.

"You think I helped break him out of prison out of loyalty or support. I assure you, that isn't even close to what happened."

Trent frowns and moves in to join the conversation. "Then why don't you explain what you were involved in? Because from where we stand, it looks pretty bad and you're as culpable as he is."

"All right. Forty years ago, my grandmother entered into an agreement with a great sorcerer who assured her he could transport our palatial city into the human realm so we could live outside the reign of my grandfather."

"It seems like your grandmother went to a lot of trouble to get away from a bad husband."

"Not really. Under the laws of our land, if a woman of any status leaves her husband, not only is she hunted down and killed, but so too is her court, her servants, and everyone in her kingdom."

Harsh. "All right, that seems a little excessive, but that's what mutiny is all about," I say.

"Mutiny is overthrowing the captain of a ship, luv," Sloan says. "I think ye mean coup d'état."

I wave that away. "Yeah, sure."

Juniper nods. "My grandfather's cruelty ran well beyond our family troubles. The man believes a female is only of value when she is beautiful and lush. No woman in Beindeen Holm is permitted to live beyond her fiftieth birthday."

"What? How does he stop that?"

"He has them slain in the public square."

"That's barbaric," Danika says.

"Exactly. Not only does he have women killed, he genuinely expects us to be grateful for him ending our lives before the onset of age steals from us all that makes us valuable."

"All that makes you valuable. What about love, skill, and intelligence?"

"No traits beyond what he sees are considered of any worth to him."

Trent says, "That's messed up, but I fail to see how it justifies releasing a murdering asshole from prison."

Juniper shrugs. "If you've never witnessed a mass slaughter of your family and friends, perhaps you couldn't understand, but I have, you see. My mother made my grandmother a promise on the morning of her slaughter, and I made the same promise to her. I vowed that I would not rest until Beindeen Holm was free and our people safe."

"It's a compelling story." I imagine the horror of what her people have gone through. "I'm not sure it justifies the actions you've taken. You engineered the escape of a murderer who turned around and killed not only Val Ryn but likely a young sorcerer working with us."

She has the decency to look remorseful. "I do sympathize and apologize, but I swore an oath to my mother and in turn, my people. When a fae takes an oath, there is no justification needed. If I failed to fulfill my obligation at the first chance I got, I would die the same way Brynali Rilios would have had he not come straight to me to fulfill his oath."

"So, all this time in prison, he's still been bound by an oath he took forty years ago?" I ask.

"Of course. An oath is forever sworn in the fae realm. There was no other outcome acceptable."

Danika shakes her head and sighs. "I take it that when the sorcerers arrested Brynali Rilios forty years ago, he was in the process of transferring this palace out of your grandfather's control and into an unused section of the California coastline?"

"He was."

"By using the harnessed power of the dead coven of witches," I say.

She looks at me and nods. "My grandmother, the queen, had no idea he would go to such lengths to gather the power needed for the city's relocation. To commit one mass slaughter to prevent another wasn't supposed to happen. Unfortunately, she found out after the foul deed had happened and though appalled, there was nothing to be gained by letting the sacrifice of those witches be for naught."

Seriously? "Oh, right. He might as well use the powers of murdered witches since he'd gone to all the trouble of killing them. That makes perfect sense."

She pegs me with a scowl and continues, speaking directly to Trent and Danika. "They had struck a bargain. Unlike here in the human realm, in the fae realm, a bargain is irrevocable."

"Did you know Val Ryn was Brynali's son?" Danika asks.

"I did. It was one of the reasons I infiltrated the San Francisco office. I knew how important Val Ryn's quest was to help his father complete his oath and I knew if I watched him and gave him a little nudge here and there, he would help me get things done."

"Instead, you got him killed."

Juniper waves that away. "I did no such thing. To take on the personal responsibility for the actions of others is ridiculous. I am responsible for my actions and cannot be held responsible for the actions of others. Everyone makes their own choices, and that includes Val Ryn and his father."

Trent frowns. "We know Brynali posed as Alistair and came to you the moment he learned you had the Port Gate Clock. Since the clock is here and your kingdom is—"

"Queendom," Juniper corrects, holding up a finger. "Beindeen Holm is now and forevermore a queendom."

Trent rolls his eyes and shakes his head. "Fine. So, you had the clock, Brynali came to you, he brought your queendom here, and what? How do we find him now? How much of a head start does he have? Did he mention where he was going?"

Juniper chuckles and waves away Trent's questions like he's silly to ask her such irrelevant things.

"We need to track him down, Juniper," Danika says. "Just because he finally fulfilled his oath to your grandmother doesn't mean he gets a free pass for the things he's done."

"I understand that." She lifts her gaze and signals to a guard by the entrance. "Despite what you think about what happened here and why, the facts remain. I am still the woman you worked with for the past five months."

"Except for the lying and you being a queen," Danika says.

Juniper's smile is sad but unconcerned. "Perhaps in time, you'll grow to understand. Here, I give you a parting gift I hope will help restore your opinion of me."

The guard returns with Brynali Rilios sitting in a wheelchair of sorts. His hands are tied and bound in a magic suppression bag, and though he appears to be sleeping, I would guess he's sedated.

"Please return him to the prison. I spoke to the warden a short time ago, and he is expecting you."

Danika frowns. "Capturing the man you helped escape is good, but it doesn't wipe the slate clean. You'll still have to come with us and answer for your actions."

Juniper seems genuinely amused. "You intend to arrest me and bring me into your headquarters like a common criminal?"

"Why yes, yes I do. You can spin the optics of things any way you like, but you still committed crimes and will be held accountable."

Juniper lifts her hand and makes a slight gesture to the room. From out of the two entrances into the castle, a dozen well-armed warrior men step in and stand on guard, ready to defend their queen.

My shield wakes up in warning but for now, it isn't predicting imminent danger.

Juniper smiles. "You are new to the laws of the fae, so I'll not take offense to you threatening to treat me as you would a common, human realm empowered. The people of Beindeen Holm are now safe. They will live peacefully within the walls of our city and will be governed and policed in accordance with fae laws. You needn't concern yourselves with my people or me from this moment onward."

Well, all righty then.

I suppose that's the end of that.

Our stop at Alcatraz is short and bittersweet. We meet the warden, transfer Brynali Rilios back into their custody, and they confirm the body of Joseph McWinn was found in the rubble of the common area as we suspected.

Trent takes possession of the body of Alistair's grandson, and Nikon takes us next to Humphrey House.

The next night, a small but reverent group stands around the pyre erected on the vast back lawn of Humphrey House. Our hands are linked as we say goodbye to a guy we barely knew and didn't like but who didn't deserve to die.

Diesel stands as the sentinel at the beginning of our mourners' line. Then Sloan holds my hand to one side while Dionysus holds the other. The chain of linked souls continues with Nikon, Danika, and Trent standing as our tower on the other end.

Herman and Georgia are officiating and standing on the platform raised to give them access to the torches.

Manx and Bruin round out our group.

I've been to a couple of druid funerals, and they are full of the power of the elements and the idea of returning to the earth in nature's endless cycle. A sorcerer funeral doesn't have that. I'm not sure what they're connected with, but then again, this isn't about me.

Blessed be, Joseph McWinn. I hope you find the acceptance in the next life you always sought in this one.

When Herman and Georgia finish saying their piece, they light the pyre, and we all stand witness to the end of the McWinn family line.

"What will happen now?" I ask Herman when we're back inside and sharing a meal. "All the magical knowledge in that house? The treasures, the spellbooks? What do people in your community do with things like that to ensure they don't fall into the wrong hands?

"We've been discussing that very thing, Red," Herman says. "Georgia and I decided everything of power and strength should go home with you and your team."

"Really?" I stop chewing, remembering all the amazing items in the McWinn Spellitorium. "Are you sure? Wouldn't you like to keep things within your local sorcerer community?"

He shakes his head. "When Alistair passed the first time, he left me and a few others what he wanted to share. The rest, he left hoping for future heirs."

The idea that a great and powerful empowered family has died out is sad. I can't imagine the loss to the druid community if Clan Cumhaill died out.

Then again, the six of us all love and want kids. I can't imagine us not all having big families of our own.

"You mentioned Sloan safeguards enchanted objects and categorizes them in case a situation comes up, and they can be of benefit. Is that right?"

"It is. He's built a secured shrine in Toronto, and we have a secondary shrine deep in the underground of the Irish hills for anything truly dangerous."

"Good, then I think that's the right decision. Alistair sometimes took things a little too far. I don't believe his belongings are for general consumption."

I hug Herman. "I assure you, we'll take every precaution to keep them safe and use them for the best purpose."

Herman winks. "I have no doubt."

Movement in the doorway brings the medium, Grace Astoria, into view. "I'm ready, Mr. Humphrey. Whenever you are."

He forces a smile and draws a labored breath. "Now, if you'll excuse me, I must say goodbye to a dear friend and would like to be alone. Please feel free to access the McWinn home and sort through what's there. Thank you, Fiona, for everything."

"Yes, dearest." Georgia joins us and hugs me. "Thank you for everything you've given us this week. It's been wonderful. Best of luck going forward. Remember, chin up and never forget the power of a strong woman."

I chuckle. "I'll do my best. Good luck in your next adventure."

CHAPTER TWENTY-FIVE

"Home sweet home." Dionysus turns in a slow runway circle and smiles at his loft. "Oh, I've missed this place."

"It's missed ye right back, Greek." Sloan chuckles as Dionysus jogs around the space hugging his throw pillows and patting the heads of his blow-up animals. "Yer Chia Pets seemed to miss ye most. Either that or they didn't like us."

True story. Those things are harder to keep alive than you'd think.

He waves that away and flops on his couch. "Thank you for bringing me home. I never realized that not having a door or entrance to the rest of the building would be such an imposition."

I chuckle. "Funny how things change when you find yourself mortal, right?"

"Exactly. At least I have the patio landing pad and barn door entrance for Contessa. We'll be able to come and go that way, I suppose."

"Yeah, about Contessa McSparkles. I wanted to talk to you about—"

Dionysus' face falls. "Wait, Jane. Don't tell me she doesn't want to come home. Did she only love me for my powers and not my excellentness? Have I been dumped for being a Muggle?"

"Oh, nonono, nothing like that, sweetie. I just wanted to make sure you're not going to go out and do trick riding in the skies while you're mortal. I'm worried you'll get hurt or fall off and splat on the ground or something."

The rich laughter when Dionysus is truly tickled by something is infectious. "Oh, Jane, you're hilarious. I've been riding horses since the beginning of time, and Contessa McSparkles is a magical unicorn. She's not going to let anything happen to her rider."

"Still, I'll worry. Promise me you'll be careful."

"For you, I'll promise, but there's nothing to worry about. If having no powers is going to kill me it's going to be from being bored or unable to travel or from a hangover. Do you remember how awful it was when I had a hangover?"

"I do."

"I vomited."

"I remember."

He thinks about that for a moment longer, then shivers and makes a face. "I don't even want to think about that. Oh! I haven't shown you…"

He jumps off the couch and runs to open the barn door that he slides open for Contessa McSparkles. "I think touching the witch stone zapped me with powers. Watch, I can do something amazing."

"Amazing? Are you sure it's not your powers coming back online?"

"Oh, no. This is new."

I meet Sloan's gaze and shrug. "I have no idea."

Sloan chuckles. "I'm afraid to guess."

Dionysus races back to stand before us and grins. "Well, as a god, I've always had the ability to command nature, but check this out." He tips his head back, closes his eyes, and raises his arms to the side.

I wait a long moment, glancing around, but nothing seems to be happening.

Sloan tilts his head like a curious dog, and I can't look at him anymore because I know I'll crack up.

"Exposure to the witch stone gave him the power to play the part of a scarecrow?" Sloan whispers. "How is that an advantage? Well, to anyone other than a farmer."

Dionysus goes red in the face, his focus intense.

I lift my hand to stop him before he starts bursting blood vessels. "Cool, dude. That's really—"

I stop talking when a robin swoops in and lands on his arm. Then a blackbird perches on his wrist. The flutter and flap of dozens of wings close in on us, and I raise a hand over my head and take a step back.

The avian arrivals continue until Dionysus is surrounded by birds, is holding a flock on each of his arms, and has a very fat pigeon roosting on his head.

I rub a hand over my mouth. "Okay, well…I'm not sure how your new power works in a practical setting, but it sure does draw a happy crowd."

Sloan glances at me. "Is it wrong that I have an incredible urge to throw stale bread at him?"

"Yes, it is." I bite my bottom lip and meet his playful gaze. "Let him have his bird moment."

I glance at where Dionysus is grinning at the birds and am unsure how to end this. "That's super great. How about you release them to go back to their regularly scheduled program and we'll order a pizza before we're all covered in bird poop? Don't forget, any mess you make has to be cleaned up by hand now."

Dionysus frowns. "Oh, I didn't think of that. I don't want to clean poop."

"Does that mean you've changed your mind about getting a kitten?"

He frowns. "Do they poop too?"

"Yes, all the cute and furry friends do. But hey, you can teach cats to use the toilet."

His expression brightens as he brushes off the fluffs and feathers. "Excellent, then I want one of those."

I laugh. "All right. We'll work on finding you a good match once you get settled and are used to being an ordinary guy."

Dionysus arches a brow. "Jane, you overstep. I may have lost my power privileges for the moment, but I will never be ordinary."

I laugh. "No, of course not. My mistake."

A knock on the glass door brings our attention to Garnet Grant standing between the two sets of security doors awaiting entry into STOA—the Shrine of Toronto's Objects and Antiquities.

Sloan's happy place is on the seventh floor of the Acropolis building Nikon bought for us to use as a home base and he's poured his passion for enchanted objects and magical history into it. It's convenient because everything we do together from working to fight the conflict in the city, to working out, to an art studio, to this shrine, to Dionysus' loft, are all in one place.

Sloan releases the doors and Garnet strides in to join us. "Welcome back to you all. I'm sorry I missed you when you came in to give your report."

I finish emptying another box and hand it to Diesel to break down and add to the pile for the recycling bin. "Not a problem. I think everything should be straightforward. We figured out the city blinking and the forced containment were two different issues, and we corrected both."

He nods. "San Francisco is in place once again, the man

responsible is behind bars, and the device is destroyed. The rest is white noise."

"It still bugs me that Juniper gets off without having to take any responsibility for what happened or the lives lost in the process."

"I understand that, but the laws of how to govern fae communities are still evolving. You did the right thing by stepping back."

"Shouldn't there be something we can charge her with? What about moving your queendom into the human realm without permission?"

He flashes me a lopsided grin. "I'm not sure that will hold water."

I point at the full box on the floor, and he lifts it to the table for me to get into next. "There is sometimes a gap between the laws we enforce and the justice we want to achieve, but we do our best."

"Yeah, I get that. After all the years of listening to Da and my brothers talk shop, I understand that. I just wish I felt better about how things ended up."

"Well, maybe I can cheer you up."

Sloan comes out of the vault and extends a hand. "Garnet. Welcome. I'm sorry the place is such a mess."

Garnet waves that away. "I read in Fi's report that the sorcerers entrusted the McWinn family's magical collection to you. Congratulations. It looks like you're going to be busy cataloging and reading through texts and spellbooks for weeks."

Sloan beams at the thought. "Aye, there are some truly rare and interesting pieces. I'm lookin' forward to gettin' lost in the process of discovery."

"How did you enjoy your first mission with the team, Diesel?" Garnet asks.

Diesel chuckles and winks at me. "It was fun."

"Right?" I laugh. "I told you."

Garnet chuckles. "You think everything is fun."

I shrug. "Most things, yes. My family raised me to believe we should enjoy life. You never know how long you've got, so live each day to the max."

Garnet nods. "I'll never argue with that, Lady Druid. It's wisdom of the ages."

"So, until the next calamity strikes, let's all laugh and count our blessings Cumhaill-style."

"Yes, let's."

ENDNOTE

Thank you for reading *Sorcery in San Francisco*, book 2 in the Case Files of the Urban Druid. While the story is fresh in your mind, and as a favor to Michael and me, please click HERE and tell other readers what you thought.

A quick star rating and/or even one sentence can mean so much to readers deciding whether to try a book, series, or a new-to-them author.

Thank you.

If you want more of Clan Cumhaill, continue with book three of the Case Files of an Urban Druid and claim your copy of *Necromancy in New Orleans*.

AUTHOR NOTES - AUBURN TEMPEST

JUNE 5, 2022

As I'm writing the last words of Sorcery in San Francisco, I'm sitting in a hotel room in Madrid. Neither hubby nor I have ever been to Europe but when Michael (and his incredible support team) announced a conference here, we jumped at the chance.

Yes, we'll be able to write off some of it, not all (Canadian tax law is funny about destination conferences), and hey, why did we need three weeks in Europe for a two-day conference...lol.

But the most important point is that we got here, we enjoyed the conference—which ended yesterday—and I finished the final touches on the book today.

I love my life as a writer and thank each of you for supporting my stories and spending your hours with me and my characters.

I'll be submitting this in for Michael's LMBPN team to work their magic, then I'm planning book 3 of Chronicles of an Urban Elemental, and then on to Necromancy in New Orleans.

AUTHOR NOTES - AUBURN TEMPEST

Thank you for hanging out with Fi and the Cumhaill Fam Jam. Stay tuned for tons more fun.

If you want to say hi and talk about the books, you can join us on the Chronicles of an Urban Druid Facebook page: https://www.facebook.com/groups/167165864237006

Or, feel free to drop us a line: UrbanDruid@lmbpn.com

Slainte Mhath,
Auburn Tempest

AUTHOR NOTES - MICHAEL ANDERLE

JULY 19, 2022

Thank you for reading this book and these author notes as well!
So, this will be a fun set of author notes to write.
One thing that many people don't know about Auburn Tempest is that *she is Fi.*
I think I had mentioned in one of our earlier author notes the story behind Auburn and I creating this series. In short, my effort is to pull out of the author who they are, what they like, and some of the things that make them tick that are interesting to me.
In short, what lights up my eyes with wonder and curiosity?
Our first effort/series idea was something that simply did not resonate with Auburn. It took her maybe a day or two to return and give me that feeling that she was so-so about the whole story, and I am totally fine with that.
So, we went back to the drawing board, so to speak, and I tried to understand what made Auburn tick. What caused her eyes to light up and caused me to enjoy talking with her so much?
From there, I asked her what she thought about a druid but with a twist of putting it inside Canada and a city area instead of a forest.

From there, it was off to the races, and she took it and ran... and ran...and...you get the idea!

Now, when Auburn talks about thanking you for playing with clan Cumhail, in essence, she is thanking you for joining her family. She and her brother (whom I met a little bit at 20Books Vegas last year) are a riot, and I understand the rest of her family is the same way.

Or so she claims.

I did enjoy the few moments that Auburn and I got to talk during Madrid, and I look forward to reading this next book which I have in my grubby little hands right now!

It's good to be the publisher, right?

Ad Aeternitatem,

Michael Anderle

MORE STORIES with Michael newsletter HERE:
https://michael.beehiiv.com/

BOOKS BY AUBURN TEMPEST

Auburn Tempest - Urban Fantasy Action/Adventure

Chronicles of an Urban Druid

Book 1 – A Gilded Cage

Book 2 – A Sacred Grove

Book 3 – A Family Oath

Book 4 – A Witch's Revenge

Book 5 – A Broken Vow

Book 6 – A Druid Hexed

Book 7 – An Immortal's Pain

Book 8 – A Shaman's Power

Book 9 – A Fated Bond

Book 10 – A Dragon's Dare

Book 11 – A God's Mistake

Book 12 – A Destiny Unlocked

Book 13 – A United Front

Book 14 – A Culling Tide

Book 15 – A Danger Destroyed

Case Files of an Urban Druid

Book 1 – Mayhem in Montréal

Book 2 – Sorcery in San Francisco

Book 3 - Necromancy in New Orleans

Chronicles of an Urban Elemental

Coming soon…

If you enjoy my writing and read sexy/steamy romance, my pen name for the books I write in Paranormal and Fantasy Romance is JL Madore. You can find me on Amazon.

BOOKS BY MICHAEL ANDERLE

Sign up for the LMBPN email list to be notified of new releases and special deals!

https://lmbpn.com/email/

For a complete list of books by Michael Anderle, please visit:

www.lmbpn.com/ma-books/

CONNECT WITH THE AUTHORS

Connect with Auburn

Amazon, Facebook, Newsletter

Web page – www.jlmadore.com

Email – AuburnTempestWrites@gmail.com

Connect with Michael Anderle and sign up for his email list here:

Website: http://lmbpn.com

Email List: http://lmbpn.com/email/

https://www.facebook.com/LMBPNPublishing

https://twitter.com/lmbpn

https://www.instagram.com/lmbpn_publishing/

https://www.bookbub.com/authors/michael-anderle

www.ingramcontent.com/pod-product-compliance
Lightning Source LLC
LaVergne TN
LVHW041755060526
838201LV00046B/1017